Praise for Jennifer Weiner's *New York Times* bestseller

THE LITTLEST BIGFOOT

∽

"Young readers who have ever felt too big or been made to feel small will feel just right in the cheerful glow of Weiner's contemporary fairy tale."
—*New York Times Book Review*

"A charming story about finding a safe place to let your freak flag fly." —*People*

"Enchanting right up to the sequel-beckoning end."
—*Kirkus Reviews*

"A heartwarming tale about friendship and belonging that will resonate with those young readers who have ever struggled to fit in or find their place in the world."
—*SLJ*

"Weiner makes a winning children's book debut with this witty story of outcasts coming together."
—*Publishers Weekly*

Jennifer Weiner

THE BIGFOOT QUEEN

A **LITTLEST BIGFOOT** Novel

ALADDIN

New York   London   Toronto   Sydney   New Delhi

ALADDIN
An imprint of Simon & Schuster Children's Publishing Division
1230 Avenue of the Americas, New York, New York 10020
First Aladdin hardcover edition October 2023
Text copyright © 2023 by Jennifer Weiner, Inc.
Jacket illustration copyright © 2023 by Ji-Hyuk Kim
Endpaper and interior illustrations by Sara Mulvanny
copyright © 2023 by Simon & Schuster, Inc.
All rights reserved, including the right of reproduction in whole or in part in any form.
ALADDIN and related logo are registered trademarks of Simon & Schuster, Inc.
For information about special discounts for bulk purchases, please contact Simon & Schuster Special Sales at 1-866-506-1949 or business@simonandschuster.com.
The Simon & Schuster Speakers Bureau can bring authors to your live event. For more information or to book an event contact the Simon & Schuster Speakers Bureau at 1-866-248-3049 or visit our website at www.simonspeakers.com.
Book designed by Laura Lyn DiSiena and Irene Vandervoort
The illustrations for this book were rendered in ink, pencil, and Photoshop.
The text of this book was set in Calluna.
Manufactured in the United States of America 0923 BVG
10 9 8 7 6 5 4 3 2 1
Library of Congress Cataloging-in-Publication Data
Names: Weiner, Jennifer, author.
Title: The Bigfoot queen / Jennifer Weiner.
Description: First Aladdin hardcover edition. | New York : Aladdin, 2023. | Series: The littlest bigfoot ; book 3 | Summary: In alternating points of view, Alice, Millie, Jessica, and Jeremy must work together when the secret world of the Bigfoot is threatened by someone with a personal vendetta against them.
Identifiers: LCCN 2022055222 (print) | LCCN 2022055223 (ebook) | ISBN 9781481470803 (hardcover) | ISBN 9781481470827 (ebook)
Subjects: CYAC: Sasquatch—Fiction. | Friendship—Fiction. | Body image—Fiction. | Boarding schools—Fiction. | Schools—Fiction. | LCGFT: Novels.
Classification: LCC PZ7.1.W433 Bi 2023 (print) | LCC PZ7.1.W433 (ebook) | DDC [E]—dc23
LC record available at https://lccn.loc.gov/2022055222
LC ebook record available at https://lccn.loc.gov/2022055223

For Lucy and Phoebe

THE
BIGFOOT
QUEEN

PART ONE

CHAPTER 1

Charlotte

CHARLOTTE HUGHES HAD BEEN BORN IN A dying town, to parents who didn't survive to see her second birthday. They'd perished in a car accident after their minivan had hit a patch of black ice and skidded off the road. Charlotte's father had been pronounced dead on the scene. Her mother had died in the hospital later that night. Baby Charlotte, strapped into her car seat, had survived without a scratch, and had been sent to live with her father's mother, her only surviving relative, who, clearly, had no interest in raising another child. Grandma managed Upland's only bed-and-breakfast, and it was an exhausting, thankless job—but one Grandma always said she was lucky to have, given how many in town couldn't find any work at all.

In the winter, when the skiers who weren't able to locate lodging closer to the mountain resorts booked rooms, Grandma worked from sunrise to late at night, doing laundry, cleaning, and cooking, and as soon as Charlotte was tall enough to push a broom or carry a load of dirty towels to the basement, she had to help her. There were floors to be swept and mopped, beds to be stripped and made, trash cans to be emptied, carpets to be vacuumed, and toilets to be scrubbed. Even when they didn't have guests, there was always cleaning. The big, old house seemed to generate its own dust and grow its own cobwebs. Little Charlotte would wake up at five in the morning to iron napkins and to bake scones and clear snow off the porch. She made beds and cleaned bathrooms. She learned to be invisible, to slip in and out of the rooms when the guests were gone, so quickly that they hardly noticed she was there. Her hands would chap and her skin would crack and she'd yawn her way through her school days.

And, all around her, Upland was dying.

When Grandma Hughes was a girl, Upland had been a thriving town, with a ski resort and two different fabric

mills that stained the river with whatever dyes they were using that week: indigo, crimson, goldenrod yellow, or pine-tree green.

Then one of the mills had caught fire, and the other mill had closed, and the Great Depression and the two World Wars had come.

Young men had gone off to fight and hadn't returned; families packed up and moved to more prosperous communities. In 1965, the interstate highway, which went nowhere near Upland, was completed. Skiers used it to travel to the mountains that were close to the highway, and Upland was not. Two years after the interstate opened, Mount Upland was closed.

For as long as Charlotte could remember, her hometown had been full of run-down houses and rusty trailers, roads with more potholes than asphalt, where the schools were ancient and the bridges were elderly and every third storefront had a faded "GOING OUT OF BUSINESS" or "EVERYTHING MUST GO" sign hung over its soap-covered windows. Every year, more and more people moved away, to bigger towns with better opportunities.

Then, when Charlotte was twelve, Christopher Jarvis had come to town.

Famous Scientist to Establish New Labs in Upland, read

the headline in the newspaper Charlotte saw on her grandmother's desk. *Famed scientist Christopher Jarvis, owner of Jarvis Industries, which holds patents on everything from dental tools to heartburn medications, is opening a new research and development facility in Upland. A spokesman for Dr. Jarvis said the renowned scientist and inventor has purchased the eighty acres of land that were formerly Ellenloe Farms, and plans to break ground on the labs next month, with an eye toward opening next year. "We'll need everything from support staff, such as custodians and cooks, to researchers and security personnel," a spokeswoman for Jarvis Industries said.*

"Maybe we'll get some more guests," Grandma had said, not looking especially hopeful. She spooned a clump of macaroni and cheese onto Charlotte's plate, where it landed with a dispirited plop. Charlotte tried not to sigh. She couldn't remember her parents, not even a little bit, but somehow she thought that if her mother had survived, she'd buy name-brand mac and cheese, not the generic kind, and she'd make the sauce with milk instead of water.

The next day, the school was buzzing with the news. Courtney Miller said her mom had already applied for a job as an administrative assistant, and Lisa Farley said her mom had gotten a call about working in the cafeteria. Ross Richardson said his dad had heard there was going to be a job fair at the community center, and Mrs. McTeague, who taught English literature, said she'd heard that the lab would bring more than five hundred new jobs to Upland.

Charlotte took the long way home after school, wondering whether her grandmother would ever go to work for Jarvis Industries. Maybe they could sell the inn and move to a regular house, where they didn't have to sleep in cramped bedrooms in the attic and worry about being quiet so the sound of their feet or their voices wouldn't disturb their guests. Charlotte would be able to get a job babysitting, or she could be a lifeguard in the summertime, instead of making beds and scrubbing toilets for no money, not even an allowance. She could get an iPhone, instead of the crummy knockoff with limited data that was all her grandmother could afford, and a pair of the clogs that all the girls were wearing that year. She could get new clothes and concert tickets and a car when she was old enough to drive. Maybe her grandmother wouldn't have to work so hard, and maybe she'd stop being so grumpy with Charlotte when she wasn't so exhausted, with her back and her knees hurting her all the time. Maybe everything would change.

When Charlotte arrived at the inn that afternoon, she saw a shiny black car in the driveway, and a man in a suit and shoes as shiny and black as the car standing on the front porch. "I hope you'll give our offer some serious thought," he said to Grandma Hughes, who didn't answer. The man shrugged, climbing into the car and giving Charlotte a quick, two-fingered salute before driving away.

Charlotte could tell from her grandmother's tight-lipped expression that asking questions would only cause trouble, but she couldn't keep quiet. "Who was that man?" Charlotte asked, taking her place in front of the kitchen sink to start on the afternoon's dishes. "What'd he want?"

"He's from the Jarvis company. They want to buy the place," her grandmother said. She'd pulled a bunch of celery out of the refrigerator and was going at it with a cleaver as if she were imagining it was the Jarvis representative's head.

"And you won't sell?" Charlotte asked. Her heart was sinking.

"This place belonged to my parents. And my father's parents before them," said her grandmother. "It should have gone to my son. It'll be yours someday, I imagine."

I don't want it, thought Charlotte. "Wouldn't it be easier just to sell it? You could probably retire!"

"*Easier* doesn't always mean *better.*" Her grandmother kept chopping, dicing the celery into tinier and tinier pieces. After a minute she muttered, "And it's dirty money."

"What do you mean?"

"I've learned a few things about Jarvis Industries." Chop, chop, chop, went the heavy silver blade. "All those pharmaceutical companies are bad news. Profiting off people's illnesses. Making their pills so expensive that regular people can't afford them. Getting rich, while sick people suffer and go without to afford their medication. Dirty money."

Charlotte decided she didn't care if Jarvis Industries' money was dirty or clean. If they'd offered it to her, she'd have taken it, and if Charlotte inherited the inn and the Jarvis people still wanted it, she would sell it to them and never look back.

Her grandmother pressed her lips together even more tightly. "I've heard other things too," she said.

"What kind of things?" asked Charlotte.

Her grandmother set her cleaver down with a thump. She stomped across the kitchen, jerked open a drawer of the desk built into the wall, and pulled out a tabloid magazine printed on thin paper that felt flimsy, almost greasy. *SECRETS OF JARVIS INDUSTRIES REVEALED!* the headline screamed.

Charlotte's heart sank even further. "Grandma," she said. "That's not a real newspaper."

Her grandmother rattled the pages in Charlotte's direction. "It's paper. And it's got news. That's real enough for me." She pulled her reading glasses out of her brassiere, pushed them into place, and read out loud. "'Hobie Beukes, sixty-seven, worked as a janitor at the Jarvis facility in Florida. One afternoon, he was lifting a dumpster, and the lid slipped off. Mr. Beukes was horrified to see dozens of dead animals, mice and rats and even rabbits, inside.'"

Charlotte tried to keep from grimacing. "Grandma, they've got to test those drugs on something. Wouldn't you rather have a lab rat suffering than a kid?"

Her grandmother glared at Charlotte, then held up one knobby finger and continued to read. "'"But that wasn't the worst," Mr. Beukes told the *National Examiner*. "Some of those animals had extra legs, or extra eyes. A few of the rats had extra paws, right in the middle of their chests and their bellies. Not sewn on. Like they'd been born with them there."'"

Charlotte shook her head. "If that's really what's going on, why hasn't the regular media reported it? The big newspapers, or one of those TV shows that do investigations?"

Her grandmother scoffed. "Who do you think buys ads during those TV shows? And in the papers? Jarvis Industries! Of course those places won't say a word against Christopher Jarvis!" She shook the tabloid in one of her big hands, which were permanently reddened and chapped by hot water and cleansers. "That's why I only trust the *Examiner*. They can't be bought." With a sniff, she set down the paper, swept the celery to one side of the cutting board, and started in on an onion.

Charlotte looked at the tabloid. There was a story about vampire babies on the front cover, a headline promising a *Miracle Cure for Arthritis the Doctors WON'T Tell You*, and a photograph of a woman in a bikini beneath the headline *Saggy Stars in Swimsuits!*

"I heard that every single person who works there has to sign a contract swearing they won't tell what goes on in the labs, and that, if they do, they'll owe Christopher Jarvis millions and millions of dollars." Thwack, thwack, thwack, went Grandma's knife. "If I went to work for that man, or if I let him buy the inn, I'd be taking dirty money. And some things aren't worth the cost."

That night Charlotte dreamed of bloody rabbits and mice that were missing their eyes. She dreamed of iPads and diamond earrings, and a pile of money that turned into mud when she touched it, and when she woke up she knew that her grandmother wasn't going to change her mind. Her classmates' families would all get rich, and she, Charlotte, would be stuck sweeping and scouring, ironing and folding, smiling for guests when they could see her, whispering when they couldn't, setting the table and scrubbing the toilets until her grandmother died and the inn was her own.

Jarvis Industries had its job fair. Charlotte's classmates' parents got jobs, and her classmates got new clothes, new shoes, new everything. Her best friend, Tessa, got a brand-new iPhone and a gold necklace with a pendant shaped like a heart. Logan Sinclair, who sat behind her in math class, took a trip to New York City with his family, where they saw two Broadway shows and got courtside seats for a basketball game. And Mrs. McTeague, who'd been Charlotte's favorite teacher, left the school and went to work at the lab's public relations department. "I'll miss you, scholars," she'd said on her last day, when she'd pulled into the parking lot in a new Prius, "but this was too good of an offer to pass up."

One winter morning, Charlotte was trudging to school, thinking about one of her grandmother's sayings: *A rising tide lifts all boats.* Charlotte could picture it: the tide coming in, and all kinds of boats—ferryboats and tugboats and giant cruise ships, the tiniest, crummiest rowboat with peeling paint and the biggest, sleekest yacht—rising up with the water. Jarvis Industries had been the tide, and the people of Upland were the boats, and all of them had been lifted. All of them but her grandmother and her newspaper and its stupid prejudice against pharmaceutical companies, and now Charlotte probably wouldn't even be able to get her ears pierced for her birthday, like she'd planned, because what was the point of having pierced ears if you couldn't afford to buy earrings?

She'd been so angry she'd given the nearest rock a good, hard kick, which only made her toes ache, and left her even angrier. She was looking for something more satisfying, or at least more yielding, to attack when a big black car glided up to the curb beside her, and the window slid down.

"Charlotte Hughes?" The man who spoke from the back seat had a blandly forgettable face and could have been anywhere from thirty to fifty. His eyes were pale, his hair was cut short, his white skin was lightly tanned.

13

It took Charlotte a minute to realize that she'd seen him before, leaving the inn. He'd been the one with the shiny briefcase, the one who'd made the offer to buy the place.

"Yes. That's me."

"I represent Dr. Christopher Wayne Jarvis, of Jarvis Industries." The man nodded in the direction of the new construction where the Jarvis Industries complex had risen above the town over the past six months. His smile showed small, even white teeth. "I'd like to offer you a job."

"I have one already," Charlotte muttered. Sweeping floors and scrubbing toilets, gathering the wet towels that strangers left on the bathroom floor and picking their hair out of the drains.

"I know," said the man. "You help your grandmother at the inn." His voice was sympathetic. "You must work very hard."

Charlotte looked at him curiously. "You know I'm just twelve, right?"

"And perfectly situated for this task," said the man. "Really, it's barely a job at all. Hardly any work. Easy-peasy. I just want you to keep your eyes open."

"What am I looking for?" she asked.

"Not what, but who," the man said. "You're looking for anyone unusual or out of the ordinary. People who

don't look like the normal run of visitors you get here in beautiful, bucolic Upland." His expression didn't change, but Charlotte thought she heard a hint of scorn when he said *beautiful, bucolic Upland*. Like maybe he didn't think Upland was beautiful or bucolic at all. "For this small task, my employer is willing to pay you a hundred dollars a week."

Charlotte stumbled and almost fell. "A hundred dollars a week? Just for watching?"

The man gave her a smile that showed his teeth and extended his hand out the window, toward Charlotte. In his palm was a box containing the newest iPhone; the same one Tessa had been showing off. "Keep it charged," said the man. "There is one number stored in the contacts. That's the number you'll call if you see any unusual people."

Charlotte's tongue felt thick. "Unusual how?" she managed to ask.

"Oh, just folks that look different," said the man, with a nonchalant wave of his hand. "People with too much hair, or people missing limbs. Or with extra ones. You'll know them when you see them," he said, and gave a tittering laugh that made Charlotte want to clap her hands over her ears.

She swallowed hard, thinking of the story from her grandmother's newspaper, the lab rats with extra limbs and eyes. "You're kidding, right?"

Instead of answering, the man held his hand out through the window again. When he spread his fingers, Charlotte saw five twenty-dollar bills.

Charlotte felt her own hand creep out of her pocket, reaching toward the car's window, and the money. She drew it back and folded her fingers into a fist. "If I do what you're asking—if I see these people, and I call the number—then what happens to them?"

The man didn't respond. His face was an absolute blank.

Charlotte looked at the money and felt a prickle of unease work its way from the nape of her neck down her spine. Then she turned her head and looked toward the inn, and all the work that was waiting for her. *Dirty money,* she heard her grandmother say . . . but money was just money, and this money, clean or dirty, would let her buy the things she wanted. And what were the chances that she'd ever see unusual-looking people, that she'd need to call the number? It sounded like something that would happen in a movie or a comic book, not real life.

Charlotte walked to the car and took the cash and the phone.

"Don't forget, now," said the man. His voice was calm, with not even the hint of a threat.

"What do I tell my grandmother?" she asked.

The man smiled again. "Tell her you won the lottery," he said. "In a way, it's kind of true." He gave her a wink, and the car pulled away.

That had been three years ago, and in that time, Charlotte had seen her town come back to life. There was an organic supermarket and a French café on Main Street. The elementary school's bricks had been power-washed and repointed, and ground had been broken for the construction of a new high school that would have a natatorium and a technology lab with a pair of 3-D printers.

On the south side of town, about five miles away from the town center, Jarvis Industries occupied a sprawling campus of modern-looking buildings, all of them enclosed by a handsome brick fence topped with unlovely razor wire and guarded by men and women who wore fatigues and carried rifles. Everyone agreed that Jarvis Industries was a great place to work, even though none of them could, or would, talk in specifics about what was being done there.

Research and development, they'd say when they were asked. Charlotte knew that the lab was full of scientists who'd come from other places—other cities, even other countries—and that the locals who made up the support staff had been subtly discouraged from asking too many questions. The pay was well above what they could earn anyplace else nearby, and the benefits and vacation policies were generous.

Every Fourth of July the company hosted a picnic at Lake Upland for employees and their families where there was face painting and games and carnival rides and chefs in tall white hats grilling steaks and burgers and hot dogs. Every Thanksgiving each employee was sent home with an organic turkey from a local farm; on the first day of December they each received a five-hundred-dollar gift certificate. Jarvis Industries, everyone agreed, was a wonderful place to work . . . and if the employees were troubled by the frequent shipments of lab rats and mice and rabbits that arrived, or the incinerator that sent ribbons of smoke into the sky all night long; if they'd heard strange noises that sounded like screams late at night, or saw barrels by the dozen labeled "MEDICAL WASTE" being loaded onto garbage trucks by men in hazmat suits, they'd learned it was best not to ask too many questions. People who asked questions were people who lost their jobs.

For three years, Charlotte had followed their example. She kept her special phone charged and at the ready. She kept her eyes open, looking for what she'd been told to watch out for. She collected the crisp twenty-dollar bills that showed up in her locker every Monday morning, in a plain white envelope, and deposited them in her savings account, dreaming of the life she would have someday, far away from Upland, Vermont. She bought herself an iPhone for her personal use, and got her ears pierced, and had almost convinced herself that she'd never have to make good on her promise; that the creatures that man in the shiny car had told her about didn't exist outside of fairy tales.

She was wrong.

CHAPTER 2

Jeremy

WHEN HE WAS TEN YEARS OLD, JEREMY Bigelow saw a Bigfoot in the forest near his house in Standish, New York, and his life was changed forever. Jeremy spent every free moment of the next two years with his phone in his hand, walking in the woods, desperate for a glimpse of the creature he knew, without a doubt, that he'd spotted. When he wasn't in the woods, Jeremy was online, alone or, eventually, with his friend Jo. They'd visit all the Bigfoot blogs and websites; they'd message other Bigfoot hunters; they'd sort through the conspiracy theories and scrutinize blurry photographs and photocopies of old newspapers, looking for any and all mentions of Bigfoots in upstate New York.

When he was twelve years old, Jeremy had his second sighting: a smaller, gray-furred creature on the shores of Lake Standish. He'd rallied the residents of Standish to join him in the woods one afternoon, where he'd seen, and run after, what he thought was a Bigfoot. But the chase had led to the gates of a private school called the Experimental Center for Love and Learning. The creature they'd been chasing that day turned out not to be a Bigfoot. It was, instead, just a girl named Alice, a student at the school, whose fur vest and bristling red hair gave her the appearance of something other than human. One by one, all the students and teachers stepped forward, proclaiming that they, too, were freaks—that Alice was bigger than other girls her age, that her cousin, Millie, the gray-furred person Jeremy had seen, had a glandular condition that made her face look furry, and that being different didn't mean they had to be ashamed.

Jeremy had never been so humiliated in his life. In spite of his shame, he was still convinced that there were Bigfoots living in the woods. When he'd found a strand of reddish-blond hair mixed in with Millie's fur, stuck to a branch in the forest, he and Jo had sent it to a scientist they'd met online. Jeremy hadn't hoped for much, but then the scientist had confirmed that there were two different strands of DNA, neither of which was human.

Freshly vindicated, bursting with pride—he might have been wrong about which girl was the Bigfoot, but he hadn't been wrong about their existence—Jeremy had tracked down Alice at the school and given her the news. Alice had been, understandably, extremely freaked-out. Jeremy could still remember the look on her face, the ache in her voice when she'd asked him, *What am I?*

Jeremy hadn't had an answer . . . but, over the next few months, he and Alice had become friends. Alice was desperate to know who she really was, and how she'd come to be. Jeremy was happy to help her. What Alice didn't know was that Jeremy was also helping a man named Milford "Skip" Carruthers. Mr. Carruthers worked for the government, for an agency called the Department of Official Inquiry, whose logo was a single, all-seeing eye. He'd chased Jeremy down when Jeremy had been on his bike one morning, and he'd explained to Jeremy that his agency could mess up his life, and his parents' lives, if Jeremy and Jo didn't cooperate. Mr. Carruthers had done it, too. Jeremy's mother's credit cards stopped working. Jeremy's dad found out he was being audited by the IRS. His parents were stunned and terrified. Jeremy was sick with guilt, because he knew what had happened was his fault. Mr. Carruthers seemed like he understood and sympathized with Jeremy's quest. He might have been frightening, and mysterious, and kind of a jerk, but he, like Jeremy, believed that Bigfoots were real.

Jeremy never completely trusted Mr. Carruthers. Still, he'd agreed to help him. He'd told him pieces of the truth, mixed in with lies, because grown-ups, in his experience, would use whatever information the kids had discovered, then take all the credit for themselves. And he never told the government agent anything that could put Alice in jeopardy.

Meanwhile, he and Jo kept searching, looking for clues about Bigfoots in Standish. They found an elderly woman named Priscilla Carruthers Landsman, whose father, long ago, had captured a Bigfoot, a creature that spoke like a human but had claws instead of hands and feet and was covered in fur. He'd kept her in a cage and named her Lucille. He'd been ready to sell her to a circus when Priscilla had freed her, sending her back to the woods and to her family. Priscilla told Jeremy and Jo that they'd have to find the biggest heart if they wanted to learn more, and it was Alice who'd solved that riddle, because she remembered that there was a giant model of a human heart in the Standish Children's Museum. They'd gone there, and walked into the heart, where they'd found a hidden door leading to the labs of Marcus Johansson. Dr. Johansson had once worked for the government—the Department of Official Inquiry, in fact. Then he'd gone rogue. Dr. Johansson promised to help Alice learn the truth of who, and what, she was. He'd given Alice the phone number for a place called the Wayne Clinic, and Alice had made an appointment and had gone off to New York City to keep it. With Dr. Johansson's encouragement, Jeremy had gone to the city to follow her, to watch her and make sure that she was safe. He'd told his parents he was going on a field trip and was glad, for once, that they barely noticed him, because all of their attention was reserved for his superstar brothers, who were fifteen and sixteen years old, tall and smart and handsome, where Jeremy was small and shrimpy with grades that were nothing special. Jeremy wasn't a musical prodigy or an exceptional athlete. Jeremy was just a regular, normal, twelve-year-old boy, with dark-brown hair and normal brown eyes and an interest in the supernatural.

Jeremy had followed Alice and her classmate Jessica all the way to New York City, and to Carnegie Hall, where her "cousin" (not that Jeremy believed for a minute that

Millie was actually Alice's cousin) was going to audition for a television talent show called *The Next Stage*. He'd been in the audience, watching, as Millie started singing, and was interrupted by the sounds of a fight. Millie had gone running offstage, screaming Alice's name. Jeremy had run off after them. He'd gone outside in time to see two men in suits trying to wrestle Alice into a white van, with Mr. Carruthers at the wheel. The goons had almost gotten her inside when a red-haired woman had come racing down the street. She'd thrown herself at the man holding Alice, wrestled Alice free, then pushed Alice into a Prius driven by a tiny, white-haired woman. Millie had gotten into the car, and they'd gone driving off. The goons, who'd seemed intent on having something to show for their efforts, had grabbed Jessica Jarvis and bundled her into the van. Jeremy had watched, feeling stunned and stupid, as he'd realized that Mr. Carruthers must have known about Alice all along. He hadn't moved as the van had driven away and Benjamin Burton, the famous judge of the television show, had come outside and collected him. Benjamin had taken Jeremy down to his office and talked to him for a long time before driving him back to Standish where, just as he'd predicted, Jeremy's parents hadn't even noticed he was gone. Attention and love were in short supply in the Bigelow household. Jeremy had always assumed that his two talented brothers had taken every drop of it and that, by the time he'd arrived, his parents had been as empty and depleted as those bags chefs used to decorate cakes, after every bit of frosting had been squeezed out. But if this worked the way Jeremy hoped it would, his parents would finally see him. The whole world would see him. His brothers would beg him to hang out with them and their friends; the kids at school would invite him to their parties and want him to sit with them at lunch. His parents would see him as a boy who was smart, capable, brave, inventive, and worthy of their attention and love.

Jeremy had showered quickly to wash all the city smells off him, as Benjamin had instructed. Then he'd gone to the woods and restarted his hunt, walking and calling and calling and walking. For hours, Jeremy paced through the snowy woods, shouting, "I am your friend!" and "I come in peace!" and other conciliatory phrases that he'd learned from reading science fiction or watching old episodes of *Star Trek*. In spite of everything he'd learned and everything he'd seen, part of him still doubted that anyone would answer.

But then, someone had.

"Please, sir," the Bigfoot had said, her body trembling all over, her big eyes in her furry face filled with tears. "Please help me find my lost Millietta." This was Millie's mother—a Bigfoot—and she'd talked to Jeremy, speaking to him like he was an adult, someone important and powerful and not a twelve-year-old kid who was regarded as a weirdo and a loser by almost all of his classmates. Jeremy had told her not to call him sir. He'd said he was just a kid, thinking that would make her comfortable enough to talk to him more, but, so far, though, she hadn't. As soon as he'd agreed to help her, she'd beckoned him toward her, turned around, and led him deeper and deeper into the woods.

Jeremy shot quick glances over his shoulder as he hurried after Millie's mother, but he saw nothing but trees and unbroken snow. "What is your name?" Jeremy asked her. His question emerged in a frosty cloud of breath. It was always cold in Standish in the wintertime, and even colder in the heart of the woods with the sun going down.

The Bigfoot didn't answer. No, not Bigfoot—Yare. *That's what they call themselves,* Benjamin Burton had told him. The nameless Yare kept walking over the snow. *Real,* thought Jeremy. He could see the shape of her body, could feel its warmth in the air. He could hear the whisper of her feet—her *bare* feet, her *bare fur-covered* feet—as they seemed to glide over the snow, along with the drip-drip-drip of icicles as they sent water pattering down onto the icy crust. Jeremy could smell his own anxious sweat, along with her scent, a faint odor that reminded him of the way his dog's paws sometimes smelled, like corn chips mixed with cinnamon. He hurried on behind her, trying not to look back too many times, as he cataloged what he'd already learned.

The Yare spoke English. Or, at least, when this one had spoken to him, it had been in perfectly understandable English. She wasn't unusually tall or large. Her proportions were those of a regular human woman, and her dark-blue dress was the kind of thing Jeremy's mother might have worn. Except Jeremy's mom had left the house that morning bundled into a puffy, down-filled coat, with a hat and mittens and fur-lined boots on her feet; this woman wore only the dress. She had no need of a coat, or a hat, or a scarf, or boots or mittens. All the exposed parts of her—her hands, her feet, her face—were covered with glossy black fur. Not shaggy fur, Jeremy noted, but smooth, soft-looking fur; well-groomed-looking fur. He wondered, a little wildly, if

Bigfoots took baths and showers, if they used shampoo and conditioner and blow-dryers and brushes like people did.

"Is it much farther?" he asked.

The woman gave no answer. Jeremy tried again.

"Can you tell me where we're going?"

Silence. Jeremy was starting to feel a little uneasy, even though he knew he could still turn around and find his way home. He was also comforted by the knowledge that Benjamin Burton was back there, somewhere, keeping track of his progress. At least, that's where Benjamin had told him he would be. Jeremy snuck another look over his shoulder, hoping to catch a glimpse of the man, but he couldn't see anything but the trees.

She's scared, Jeremy realized. When she'd spoken to him, she'd been trembling all over, her eyes wide, like she wanted to run. But she hadn't. *Please, sir,* she'd said, and when Jeremy had said, *I'm just a kid,* she'd said, *Please, sir kid. Please help me find my lost Millietta.* Mixed in with the excitement of knowing that she was real, that Bigfoots were real, and that he'd been right all along, Jeremy had felt almost sick with guilt. Millie was this Bigfoot's daughter, and Jeremy had chased Millie, he'd threatened to expose her; he'd stalked her through the woods, first, all the way to the Experimental Center for Love and Learning, and then all the way to New York City. He'd led the bad guys right to her, and now he didn't know where she was, or if the grown-ups who'd taken Millie and Alice were good guys or not. At least Millie and Alice were together, he thought. At least Millie wasn't alone.

Jeremy and the Yare continued to tromp along, Jeremy moving as noisily as he could, his boots cracking the snow and his breath huffing out of his mouth, hoping Benjamin would hear him and be able to follow. The woman went gliding along without a sound. Just as Jeremy was about to try another question, the woman reached the top of a ridge and pushed aside a heavy pine bough. Jeremy looked down into the valley at the bottom of a gentle slope and saw a bonfire, blazing high and hot.

"Where are we—" That was as far as he'd gotten when he felt strong hands gripping his shoulders and lifting him off the ground. Jeremy gave an undignified yelp, kicking his legs frantically, arms flailing, legs kicking at nothing.

"Help!" he yelled.

"We aren't going to hurt you," a deep voice rumbled in his ear. Then something fell down over his head, and everything went dark as the world disappeared.

CHAPTER 3

Jessica

JESSICA JARVIS STOOD ON THE SIDEWALK, staring blankly at the back of the departing van from which she had just been summarily ejected. One minute, the goons in suits had been wrestling her into the back seat and driving away. Then Goon One had gotten on the phone and said things like "Yes," and "No," and "Sorry," and "We're not completely empty-handed. We got one of the girls." Evidently, though, Jessica wasn't the right one of the girls, because they'd asked what her name was. She'd thought about not telling them, except then she realized that the name tag they'd given her for *The Next Stage* was still hanging around her neck.

"Jessica Jarvis," the goon had said into the phone. The voice on the other end had squawked. The van had pulled over. And they'd shoved Jessica out onto the sidewalk and driven away.

She took a deep breath, trying to short through everything that had happened prior to her being snatched and dumped.

Millie had been on *The Next Stage* stage, explaining to the judges of the reality show that she'd been too shy to sing on camera, so Jessica had lip-synced for her on the audition tape she'd sent. As Millie trembled and stammered through her explanation, Jessica stood still, bathed in the spotlight, basking in the attention of *The Next Stage*'s audience. She was right where she wanted to be, right where she was *meant* to be. She could imagine it unfolding—the judges ignoring Millie to look at the beautiful girl standing behind her; Benjamin Burton, the head judge, saying that the auditions were over, that everyone else could go home, that Jessica was the star they'd been looking for. Benjamin would come onstage and declare her the winner, and he would hand her a gigantic million-dollar check as the sky rained down glitter and everyone cheered. *You're perfect,* Benjamin Burton would tell her, and Jessica would know that it was true.

Millie had been singing, and Jessica had just reached the part of the fantasy where her hands closed around the edges of the million-dollar check, when she'd looked to the wings just in time to see men in suits, with mirrored sunglasses and earpieces, grabbing Alice and dragging her away. Jessica and Millie had run out of the theater after them, and the men had almost succeeded in tossing Alice into a van that was waiting at the curb. Then some woman with red hair had come streaking down the sidewalk, charging right into the man who'd been holding Alice, knocking him off his feet. The woman grabbed Alice and threw her into a car. Millie had climbed in with them, and the car had sped away.

The man who hadn't been knocked over had stretched out his hand and pulled his colleague off the sidewalk, shaking his head and looking disgusted. Then the two of them had looked at her . . . and, before Jessica could scream, or run, they'd grabbed her and pushed her into the van that had been waiting for Alice, a white vehicle with tinted windows. They'd sped away, leaving a crowd of confused onlookers snapping pictures with their phones and trying to figure out what had happened.

"Who are you?" Jessica had demanded. "Where are you taking me?" *And why was Alice your first choice,* she thought. The driver ignored her. The goon in the passenger's seat pulled out a cell phone and started talking in a low, apologetic voice. "Yes," Jessica heard, and, "No," and, "We did get a girl." The man turned around, staring at Jessica.

"What's your name?"

Jessica didn't reply. She also, unfortunately, didn't remember that the producers at *The Next Stage* had given all the contestants name tags, with their names and ages and hometowns written on them. "Her name is Jessica Jarvis," the man said. His face darkened at whatever he heard on the other end of the line. He said something, low-voiced, to the driver, who pulled over.

"Our apologies, miss," he said, and helped her out of the van and onto the sidewalk. The van then sped away, leaving Jessica standing there, trembling, shaking all over.

Part of her terror was adrenaline, the natural reaction to being so close to an attempted crime. But some of it—most of it—had to do with the monogram she'd seen on the van. It was a tiny thing, a small golden decal over the driver's door handle reading "JARVIS INDUSTRIES." Which was run, Jessica knew, by Christopher Wayne Jarvis, the scientist and researcher. Dr. Jarvis had done groundbreaking work in neural and genetic engineering. He'd become fantastically wealthy thanks to the invention of a procedure that allowed people to see what diseases they were genetically at risk for. With headquarters in New York City, and a big campus in Vermont, Jarvis Industries employed hundreds of scientists, all of them working to cure diseases and help the environment—or, if you believed the conspiracy theorists, all of them working to create bioweapons, genetically-engineered viruses, and cyborg supersoldiers. Christopher Wayne Jarvis was unimaginably rich, notoriously reclusive, adored and despised in equal measure.

Christopher Wayne Jarvis was also Jessica's grandfather.

Jessica could remember the only time she'd met him, when she was quite little, maybe four or five years old. He'd been really short for a grown-up, his back bent and stooped. He'd worn dark glasses and a dark suit, and he'd been leaning heavily on a cane, and Jessica could clearly recall how frightened and unsettled she'd felt. There was something wrong with her grandfather, something off about him, the same way that a painting hanging crookedly was off, only you could straighten out a painting, and Jessica suspected that whatever was wrong with her father's father couldn't be fixed. She hadn't known exactly what was wrong. The only thing she'd known for sure was not to ask her parents.

That was her grandfather's company. Which meant that those had been his men who'd tried to kidnap her classmate. But why?

Jessica made herself take the deep, calming breaths that the entire school had learned during the last daylong yoga retreat. *Breathe in for a count of four,* she could hear Lori, one of the Center's founders, chanting in her soothing voice. *Hold for a count of four. Exhale for a count of four.* Jessica usually declined to participate in the collective breathing. She thought yoga was stupid. She thought Lori was stupid. She thought the Experimental Center for Love and Learning was stupid, and she'd been furious at her parents for sending her there. Now, as she stood on the sidewalk, alone, with nobody even bothering to ask if she was all right, Jessica repeated the calming breath four times, with her eyes closed. *In, two, three, four; hold, two, three, four; out, two, three, four.* When she finished, she found, annoyingly, that it actually had worked, and that she could think a little more clearly.

Fact: There had been some kind of kidnapping situation involving Alice, her ECLL classmate, and Millie, who was Alice's homeschooled friend. Only the kidnappers hadn't gotten either girl, and thank goodness they hadn't been interested in grabbing her.

Fact: Alice and Millie were in a car with two women, and Jessica had no idea who the women were or where they were going.

Fact: Jessica was supposed to be staying at Alice's apartment for the weekend. It was only Saturday, not even noon. Nobody at school would be expecting her back until tomorrow, which gave Jessica time to try to solve the mystery.

Jessica walked until she found a coffee shop. At the counter, she ordered a blueberry muffin and a green tea. She carried her snack to a table for two and sat down to think.

Fact: Millie had some kind of skin condition that made her face furry. That's what Alice had said. Jessica believed it, mostly because of her own situation. Strange things happened in the world. Sometimes they even happened to beautiful girls like her, she thought, and winced, the way she always did when something reminded her of the thing she most desperately wished she could forget: namely, her tail.

Jessica stirred honey into her tea. She knew that girls got kidnapped; she'd heard about stranger danger all her life. But why would her grandfather's men want to kidnap Alice? What made her so special?

Jessica nibbled her muffin. She could call her parents to come get her. She could tell them what she'd seen and ask them what it meant. But would they tell her the truth? Probably not.

Fact: Parents tried to protect kids, long past the point that kids actually required protection. It was their way of keeping them not safe, but young, in Jessica's opinion. It let them pretend that kids didn't live in the real world. All parents, in Jessica's experience, were like that, and her own parents took it to extremes. As recently as last year, when she was twelve and she'd had to have her wisdom teeth out, they'd told her that the tooth fairy would come to collect them.

Her parents wouldn't tell her the truth. So who would?

She thought and thought, remembering a long-ago fight, the weekend she'd finally stopped telling herself that the tail wasn't real, or that it would just fall off, like a scab. Her tail was small, and it curled up neatly against her back, which made it easy to hide. Leggings or tight pants might have been an issue, but Jessica had always preferred skirts and dresses, things that were fitted at the waist and looser around her hips, so keeping the tail concealed wasn't a problem. She could have just kept it hidden, and kept it a secret, but she was so completely freaked-out by the tail's appearance that, finally, she'd told her mom.

A tail? her mom had said. *Come on, Jess. Stop teasing.* When Jessica had shown her, her mom's face had gone very pale, and her body had gone very still. *Go to your room, honey,* this statue-mom had instructed, and Jessica had gone, but even through her closed door, she'd still been able to hear her mom in the kitchen, hissing at her dad. *This is all your fault. Your family's fault. Your father's fault.*

In the coffee shop, Jessica got to her feet and tossed her empty plate and cup into the trash. She opened up her mapping app, planning on using her phone to figure out how to get where she needed to go. Then she realized that it was possible there were people who had access to her data, including her parents. She didn't want them to be able to track her. Instead, Jessica turned off her Wi-Fi and got back in line. "Can you tell me if there's a library around here?" she asked the girl behind the counter. Ten minutes later, three blocks away, Jessica sat down in front of a terminal at a branch of the New York Public Library, ready to learn everything she could about her grand-father, and then figure out how to contact the woman she thought would be able to tell her what Google couldn't.

CHAPTER 4

Alice

MISS MERRIWEATHER KEPT THE LITTLE white car humming along at just five miles over the speed limit—fast enough to keep up with cars in the left-hand lane, but not so fast that they'd be noticed, or pulled over and stopped.

Alice looked out the window, but all she could see was the glaring afternoon sunshine rushing past the glass. She turned around and saw an SUV behind them, but whether it was the same car that had been pursuing them in the city, she couldn't say. Her head ached, and it was hard to breathe. She felt a little dizzy, strange in her own skin, like she'd gulped down a big bottle of seltzer

40

and her insides were fizzing and bubbling uncomfortably. In the past twenty minutes, she'd learned that her mother wasn't the woman she'd believed her to be and that the man she'd always known as her father wasn't her real father. And she'd had it confirmed, from her own mother's lips, that she wasn't entirely human. She was half-human, half-Yare.

Learning even one of those things might have left her confused and unsettled, with her insides tied in knots. Learning all of it made her feel like she barely knew her own name.

And there was Millie, her first real friend, sitting beside her, looking (if it was possible) even more freaked-out than Alice felt.

Which made sense. Even though Alice had just learned that pretty much nothing she'd grown up believing was true, even though she was in a strange car, driven by a woman she didn't completely trust, speeding down a strange highway toward an unknown destination, at least this world of cars and highways was familiar to her. Millie had only ever been in moving vehicles a handful of times in her life—normally, just once a year, on Halloween, when the Yare children would pile onto a repurposed school bus and then head into the world to go trick-or-treating with human kids, because everyone assumed they, too, were human. Millie's trip to New York City in the Center's van had been her first time on a highway, and she'd looked terrified and sick the entire time. Now she was in a strange new car, with No-Fur strangers, the people she'd been taught, all her life, to fear.

"It's going to be all right. We're going someplace safe," said Alice's mother. She wrapped her arm around Alice, giving her a squeeze. Even in her fear and her confusion, Alice felt her body yearning, wanting to sink into the comfort of her mother's embrace, to close her eyes and shut off her brain and let the grown-ups take care of everything.

"What about Jessica?" Alice asked.

Alice's mother met Miss Merriweather's gaze in the rearview mirror. "Jessica isn't who they're looking for," Miss Merriweather said. "She won't be hurt." Alice wasn't sure, but she thought she could hear doubt in Miss Merriweather's voice. Nor was *She won't be hurt* the same as *She'll be safe*. Millie must have heard the difference too, because Alice heard her friend give a tiny whimper.

Be brave, she told herself, pushing away the million questions she wanted to ask. Be brave for Millie. "Are you okay?" she asked her friend.

Millie peered at her with wide, frightened eyes. "Home," she said. "I would please like to go home now." Millie was shivering all over, her skin pale and unhealthy-looking without her familiar fur. "I am not liking it here in the Big Apple at all! Not one bit!"

"Okay," said Alice's mother, patting Millie's shoulder gently. "Don't worry. We'll keep you safe. We won't let anything bad happen to you."

Millie appeared not to hear as she started to cry. "I . . . miss . . . my . . . mother!" she managed to gasp between sobs. "I miss her! I should never have gone!" She gulped and swiped at her eyes, and said, "My parents don't know that I am here. I told them I was doing an over-sleep at Alice's school. When I don't come home, they will look for me there, and they won't find me, and then . . ." Her shoulders shook as she cried. "I am sorry for all of my lying! Please take me home!"

"Don't be scared." Miss Merriweather's voice was calm. "You'll be safe. I promise. We're all going to get to exactly where we're meant to be."

"What does that mean?" asked Alice.

"It means no more lying." Alice's mother's voice was firm, almost steely. It was so different from the way she normally spoke, from her usual high, airy voice, twittering about inconsequential, frivolous things, that Alice had to keep looking at her, sneaking glances to remind herself that this woman was really the same woman she'd known all her life. *Hiding in plain sight,* her mother had said, to explain why she'd always been so thin and so stylish, so different from her daughter, and why she'd kept sending Alice away. Alice's mother had been playing the part of a fancy New York City society matron so that the government wouldn't find her. And she'd sent Alice away, moving her from one private boarding school to another, and to different summer camps every summer—not because she didn't love Alice, but because she was desperately trying to keep her daughter safe, out of view of the government agents who'd want to hunt her. Her mother's name was not Felicia Mayfair but Faith Nolan. And, once upon a time, she'd been married to a Yare.

"No more lying," Faith repeated. "No more hiding. No more being afraid."

Millie had stopped crying and was staring at Alice's mother, with her silvery eyes wide. "You cannot mean . . ."

"It wasn't always like this." In a gentle voice, Faith said, "Your parents will have told you that there was a time when the Yare didn't hide. When they lived with humans."

Millie gave a small, frightened nod. "But that was in

the long-ago! My parents say that if the No-Furs learn about the Yare they will put us in cages! Or to hospitals, for studying! They will hunt us and hurt us. They will steal our littlies and make our homes into amusing parks!"

Faith reached across the seat and stroked Millie's hair. "I promise that nobody is going to make your home an amusing park." Millie whimpered, and Alice took her friend's hand. "People do hunt the Yare," her mother said. "They have tried to hurt them, and use them. The way I see it, we have two choices. Keep running and hiding, or go public, and expose the hunters and the thieves for what they are."

Millie started to cry again. "What will become of us?" she whispered. "What will become of me?"

"I know it feels scary right now, but I promise that this is a good thing," Faith said. "You and your parents won't have to hide, and you won't have to sneak off and lie to everyone if you want to be part of the human world. You'll be able to go wherever you want to go. Do whatever you want to do."

Millie shook her head, looking miserable and unconvinced. Alice could guess what she was thinking, before Millie even whispered, "I am done with the human world. I just want to go home."

Alice could sympathize. Except Millie had a wonderful home, snug and cozy, with parents who loved her, even if they didn't understand her, who'd tried to keep her safe and hadn't lied about who they were, or what they were, or made Millie feel bad about who she was. Alice, meanwhile, had a father who wasn't really her father and a mother who'd lied about everything, who'd made Alice feel awful, almost every day of her life. Even if she'd had good reasons; even if she'd never meant to make Alice feel bad, she had. Alice couldn't forget it, and she wasn't sure she'd ever be able to forgive her mother.

Alice did her best to ignore her own confusion and resentment so that she could comfort her friend. "You know, before everything happened"—"everything" being Alice getting snatched from her spot backstage, the two of them getting thrown into a car, being separated from Jessica—"your singing was so beautiful. I bet, if the judges had been able to tell you, you would have won."

Millie brushed tears off her cheeks, which were already starting to regrow their coating of silvery fur. "You are not just saying that?"

"I'm not," Alice said. "I promise." She turned to her mother again. "So . . . where are we going?"

Her mother met Miss Merriweather's gaze in the

rearview mirror again, and Alice felt some wordless understanding pass between them. Faith leaned forward, speaking quietly to Miss Merriweather, who nodded and slowed the car, signaling as she drove to the off-ramp. Alice saw her mother's hands tighten on Millie's shoulders, and she knew, with a sinking feeling, that the plan of taking them "somewhere safe" might be more of a wish than a promise.

Beside her, very softly, Millie began to sing. It was her competition song, the one she'd planned on performing for the judges that morning, the one that began "Something has changed within me / Something is not the same."

"North," her mother finally said. She put her hand on top of Alice's head and stroked her hair gently. "Alice and I need to go back to where all of this began. But there's someone we need to see first."

CHAPTER 5

Jeremy

THEY PUT A HOOD OVER HIS HEAD AND dropped Jeremy down into a hole in the ground. At least, that's what he assumed had happened, since he'd ended up somewhere that felt and smelled like it was underground, and he could see, through the rough weave of his hood, the faint, flickering light of the bonfire he'd glimpsed coming from a point far above his head.

Not knowing exactly where he'd been put was bad. Not knowing who'd put him there—the Yare? The government agents? That was worse. His knees felt watery, and his stomach felt like it had come unmoored from his insides and was now rolling around his body. He pictured

the men in suits and dark glasses who'd tried to kidnap Alice, and wondered if those men had tracked him down and captured him, and if they had the female Yare too. Or maybe it was the Yare that had taken him prisoner. Maybe the woman he'd been following had led him right into a trap.

"Hello?!" he shouted again. "Help! Somebody help me!"

No one answered. Jeremy tried to look around. He could tell that the sun had set. It was dark, and it should have been cold, but it wasn't. The air was warm, and when Jeremy touched the dirt wall, that was warm too. *Hot springs?* he wondered. He'd never heard anyone talking about Standish having any hot springs. Then again, he'd never heard much talk about Standish having Bigfoots, and he knew for a fact that it did.

"Help!" he yelled. His voice was hoarse from shouting. He'd spent what felt like an hour calling for help, yelling to whoever was listening that there were people who knew where he was; people who'd be looking for him, very soon; people who'd be able to find him by tracking his phone. Except whoever had captured him had taken his phone, plucking it right out of his coat pocket when he'd been kicking and screaming, before shoving the bag over his head. For all he knew, they'd put the phone into a moving car, or they'd mailed it to Los Angeles, and whoever was trying to track him down would end up following a post office van across the country. He doubted his parents would be looking for him. It might be hours, or an entire day, before they even noticed he was gone. He hoped that Benjamin Burton had told him the truth; that he'd been in the woods, watching, and that he'd seen what had happened.

Jeremy's throat hurt, and his voice was raspy. He sighed and slumped to the ground, his back against the warm dirt, his legs stretched out in front of him. He went through his pockets again, hoping he'd overlooked something helpful the three previous times he'd emptied them out. There was a house key. An energy-bar wrapper. His student ID. A tiny scrap of lint. A blue pen cap. Nothing that could be turned into a weapon, or a way to communicate, or a tool he could use to tunnel his way to freedom.

The Yare won't hurt me, he told himself. He remembered the first one he'd seen, the gigantic, hairy figure in overalls and incongruous gold-rimmed glasses. Jeremy had been a little kid, and the giant had run away from him like Jeremy was the terrifying one. But if it wasn't the Yare who'd captured him . . .

Jeremy thought he heard a sound from overhead. He jumped to his feet. "Hello?" he called.

No one answered. But the silence had a different quality now, as if someone was standing above him, listening. Jeremy wondered, again, where the woman who'd led him here had gone, if she'd been captured or part of a plan. "Please!" he shouted in his hoarse voice. "I didn't come to hurt anyone, or tell anyone about you! I came to help!" He pulled in another breath and pictured the woman who'd asked him to help find her daughter. "My parents will be looking for me!" Nothing. No answer came. Not even a sound.

Jeremy could understand why they were afraid of him, why the Yare might think that he—that any human—was an enemy. Yare, he had learned, were practically immortal. They lived long, long lives; they hardly ever got sick. They were immune to diseases like cancer. And their blood could cure human ailments, which made them desirable, and made some humans hunt them. Even before people had understood what Bigfoots could do, what their bodies might offer, humans had hunted them, to put them in cages, to display them in circuses, to use them in any way they could. He remembered what Priscilla Landsman had told him, how her father had captured a Bigfoot and put it in a cage and tried to sell it to a circus. If that was what the Yare had seen, if that was how they knew humans behaved, it was no wonder they'd taken Jeremy prisoner.

Then there was his own history, the things he'd done to put the Bigfoots of Standish in danger. He'd sent out press releases claiming that he'd seen a Bigfoot in the forest. He'd led the citizens of Standish on a chase through their woods, in pursuit of Millie—a hunt the news stations had covered with cameras and helicopters. He'd brought scrutiny and attention to a Tribe that wanted only to stay hidden and invisible. Even worse, Jeremy remembered, feeling sick with regret, was how the locals had been noisy and rowdy. Some of them had been drunk and all of them had been disrespectful. They'd yelled about Yetis and Teen Wolf; they'd called the Bigfoots monsters. Then, when it turned out that they hadn't been chasing a Bigfoot at all, just a regular girl with a lot of bushy red hair, wearing a fur vest, the pursuers, pumped up on adrenaline and the hopes of fame, had started calling her a freak.

Donnetta Dale, the beautiful Channel 6 News anchor (and Jeremy's secret crush) had been there. In the bright light from her team's cameras, Alice and Millie had looked not just human but adorably human—and small, and

scared. They all looked normal. Jeremy had looked like the villain. In that moment, he'd certainly felt like the bad guy.

Jeremy felt his face get hot. He squeezed his eyes shut, pressing his lips together, digging his fingernails into his palms as his hands curled into fists. He wasn't surprised that the Bigfoots had thrown him down in a hole in the dirt. If the situations had been reversed, if he'd been the one whose daughter or sister or friend had been chased and hunted, whose Tribe had been exposed, he'd have done exactly the same thing, if not something even worse.

He groaned softly to himself . . . and then he almost screamed as he heard someone, or something, jump down into the pit and land lightly behind him. Strong hands gripped him just underneath his armpits, and pulled his back against a chest that felt like a warm stone wall. "Hold on," said the voice, and with one great leap, they were up and out of the pit. Jeremy felt the cold ground under his feet, the warmth of a fire on his face. The hands moved him, urging him forward, pushing him down, until he was sitting on something hard and damp—a log, he guessed. When the hands pulled the hood off his head, Jeremy squeezed his eyes shut.

"Open your eyes," said the voice. Jeremy opened his eyes. For a minute, he blinked, seeing nothing, his gaze dazzled by the firelight. When he managed to focus, he saw that the bonfire was surrounded by other Bigfoots, maybe a dozen of them. They all appeared to be male, and they were all broad-shouldered and covered in fur, bulging with muscles, and well over six feet tall. Jeremy's oldest brother, Ben, played football, and was big and strong. At least, Jeremy had always thought so. But each one of these creatures looked like they could have lifted Ben up and snapped him in half over their knee.

They wore human clothes, pants and shirts or overalls. Their feet were bare and seemed impervious to the cold. None of them had jackets or hats. Their hands seemed to be covered in thick, callused skin, with fur on the backs, and their short, curving black nails looked more like claws than fingernails. One of them held a smooth stick in his hands, and wore bib-style overalls. Perched on his furry face was a pair of gold-rimmed glasses. Jeremy's heart leaped to his throat.

"You," he whispered, lifting one finger to point. "I saw you!"

Instead of replying, the man stepped forward, so close that the straps of his overalls brushed Jeremy's jacket as he looked deeply into Jeremy's eyes.

"We are the Yare," he said.

"We are the Yare," the others repeated. Their deep voices seemed to make the very ground shake. Jeremy's mouth went dry as his hands and face went cold. If the Bigfoot, or Yare, or whatever the man was, recognized him, Jeremy couldn't tell. His face was impassive as he spoke.

"We live in shadow. We walk in silence. We guard the secret places of the world."

The chant came back in a low, pulsing rumble, like a gust of wind before a storm. It was some kind of ritual, Jeremy realized. His fingers itched for his phone, for a pen and paper, so that he could record what he was hearing or at least take notes. Then he realized it was unlikely that anyone would ever hear any recording he made, or read any notes he managed to write. If these creatures decided he wasn't leaving, he'd be staying here. And if they decided to kill him . . . Jeremy gulped as the chant continued.

"We are the forgotten. We are the unseen. We are the protectors and the guides. We are the Yare and we survive."

Jeremy felt like he could barely breathe as the other Yare repeated the words, bowing their heads as they said, "We survive." When they looked up, the man—the Yare—holding the stick began to speak.

"I am Maximus of the Yare," he said. "I am Leader to this clan. I am husband of Septima. Father of Millie." He paused, then added, "Uncle to Alice Mayfair."

Alice! thought Jeremy. If this guy was her uncle, that meant that she was at least part Yare. *I've got to tell her,* he thought in a burst of excitement, just before he realized that he couldn't tell her, because he had no phone and also no idea where Alice might be or if he'd ever see her again.

Maximus, meanwhile, took up the chant again.

"We live under the earth," he said, in his deep, rumbling voice. "Hidden in the darkness. Hidden from the eyes of those who would do us harm."

"Hidden away," the rest of the Yare chanted.

Maximus was looking at Jeremy, staring at him hard. "Humans have despoiled the gifts of creation. You have hunted us. You have stolen our land. You have polluted the water we drink. You have poisoned the skies that shelter us."

Jeremy bowed his head. He didn't know what to say to that, but by sixth grade he'd taken enough American history, and read enough news stories, to know that it was true. Or at least, it was more true than false. Humans had stolen land; they did pollute. They'd dumped toxic waste in the oceans, and filled the air with chemical fumes. They'd paved paradise and put up a parking lot, as the song his mother used to play put it.

"What is your name, No-Fur?" Maximus asked. His voice was very low and his face was solemn as he held the smooth stick out, inviting Jeremy to take it.

Jeremy gulped, trying to remember everything he could about the rules of first contact from *Star Trek*. Slowly, he got to his feet on legs that felt like they were made of water. His voice, at first, was a choked squeak. He gripped the stick hard, cleared his throat, and tried again.

"Greetings, Maximus of the Yare. I am Jeremy of the Humans. Son of Martin and Suzanne. Brother of Ben and Noah." Ben, who was a superstar three-sport athlete, and Noah, a STEM genius, Jeremy couldn't help thinking, a little bitterly. He wished that the two of them could see him now!

Maximus, meanwhile, looked like he was trying very hard not to laugh. He took the stick back and asked, "Will you eat with us, Jeremy of the Humans?"

Jeremy nodded, feeling almost faint with relief. If they found him amusing, if they were going to feed him, it probably meant that they weren't going to kill him. Unless, of course, they were fattening him up, like the witch fattened up Hansel and Gretel. Jeremy tried to push that thought away as a small, elderly-looking female Yare stepped out of the shadows. She wore a dark-green dress with a pattern of red birds, and had curly white hair on her head and face and feet.

"Bring forth the Snickers," Maximus instructed.

"The Snickers," all the Yare in the circle repeated.

The Snickers? Jeremy thought. The older Yare walked away. She'd taken maybe twenty steps when she seemed to disappear, vanishing as completely if she'd fallen down a hole. Jeremy stared. Maximus noticed.

"Humans have hunted us. Hated us. Despised us for our differences," Maximus said. "Once, we lived and worked alongside you. Now, we hide in the dark."

The older Yare popped back into view. Walking slowly, with her head lowered and hands held out flat before her, with a platter balanced on top of them, she approached Maximus and bowed before him. The rest of the Yare bent their heads. Hastily, Jeremy did too, but not before seeing that the older Yare did, indeed, have a Snickers bar on her platter.

Maximus picked it up. Slowly, he walked around the circle, his breath frosty in the cold air, his feet soundless

on the snow. Up close, Jeremy saw how much taller he was than the adults Jeremy knew, closer to seven feet than to six, his body big and solid as a house.

"Human boy. Do you pledge with your truest heart to keep our secret?"

Jeremy nodded. In a dry, husky whisper, he said, "Yes. I do. I will."

"Do you swear that you will not reveal us, no matter how you might suffer?"

At the word "suffer," all Jeremy could manage was another jerky nod.

"And do you vow . . ."

"Oh, for all goodness, Maximus, let the boy have a snackle and a sip. Then you can scare him with all of this blood vow nonsense." The older female Yare was regarding Maximus with a kind of fond exasperation that Jeremy recognized from the way his grandmother regarded his own father, like she was thinking, *You might be a big-deal grown-up, but you're still my kid.*

Looking a little sheepish, Maximus unwrapped the Snickers bar. He took a bite and handed it to Jeremy. But before Jeremy could accept it, a bigger hand came from behind him and snatched the candy away.

Jeremy saw Maximus's eyes widen. "You," the big Yare

breathed. Jeremy turned his head, peering over his shoulder, feeling almost faint with relief.

"Me," said Benjamin Burton, in a voice just short of a growl. "It's been a long time . . . brother."

CHAPTER 6

Jessica

AFTER A FEW HOURS IN THE LIBRARY, JESSICA walked to the Port Authority Bus Terminal, where she used cash to pay for a bus ticket. Once she was aboard the bus, she found a window seat, settled her backpack on her lap, and began reviewing everything she'd learned about her grandfather and her parents, about her school and the reason she'd been sent there. Namely, her tail.

It had happened all at once. One night, she'd gone to sleep, a girl with the usual number of limbs and toes and fingers. The next morning, she'd woken up, thrown back the covers, and gotten out of bed, wriggling her feet on her pink-and-white bedroom carpet, getting ready for another day of being at the top of the social pyramid at her school, the prettiest and most popular of a pack of pretty, popular girls. She'd raised her arms over her head, stretching, and, as she'd lowered them, her hand had brushed against an unfamiliar lump at the base of her spine. She'd prodded it with her fingertips, first gingerly, then harder, learning its shape, which was corkscrewed, exactly like a pig's tail. She'd pulled at it, at first gently, and then hard enough to hurt. She'd run to the bathroom, where she'd pulled off her pajama bottoms and stood in front of the full-length mirror, twisting around to look, with her mouth dry as cotton and her heart thundering in her chest. Finally, she'd used a hand mirror to show her what she was feeling—a small, neatly curled tail, the same color as her skin. She'd looked it over, inspecting it inch by inch, for signs of glue or staples or stitches, but she hadn't found any. Just the tail, which she discovered she could wiggle a bit when she flexed her muscles.

"Jess?" her mother called from the kitchen. Jessica could hear the gurgle of the coffee machine, the squeak of her father's shoes on the kitchen floor. She could smell coffee and English muffins, all the scents she associated with a normal morning on a normal day. She swallowed the scream she'd come very close to screaming, ignored the outfit she'd chosen and laid out the night before, in close consultation with her three best friends, and pulled on her loosest pair of sweatpants, turning in every direction to make sure that the baggy cotton hid the new development before running to the kitchen.

"Sweatpants?" her best friend, Amelia, had asked, crinkling her nose when Jessica got to school that morning. Jessica had shrugged, trying to look like it didn't matter. "Spilled something on my skirt," she said, and kept her voice light. "My mom was rushing me out the door."

Amelia rolled her eyes at the mention of mothers, then asked Jessica if she thought that Roman liked Madison.

"Roman S. or Roman R.?" asked Jessica. "And which Madison?"

While Amelia talked, Jessica nodded. She said, "Mm-hm," or "You think?" or "Oh, really!" and tried to look like she cared. Meanwhile, her mind was churning. Would the tail fall off on its own, like a scab or a bit of gel nail polish? Could she cut it off? How had it gotten there? Did other girls have them too? Somehow, she didn't think so. If this was normal, the textbooks, or the book called *Your Changing Body* that her mom had given her for her tenth birthday, surely would have mentioned it. There might have even been an illustration or two.

"Hey, Amelia," she'd said, interrupting her friend when Amelia had paused to take a breath. Jessica cleared her throat. "Do you . . . I mean, have you noticed . . ." Jessica couldn't figure out how to ask what she wanted to ask. Meanwhile, Amelia was staring, her expression a little suspicious.

"What?"

Jessica squeezed her hands together, to prevent herself from moving toward her backside. "Just . . . anything weird. Any, like, changes that you weren't expecting."

"Changes? Like . . ." Indicating her flat chest, Amelia said, "As you can see, I'm still waiting for the big one. Why?" Amelia's eyes seemed to sparkle with interest, and Jessica knew that confiding in her friend would be the equivalent of hiring an airplane to fly a banner back and forth above the school, a banner reading "JESSICA JARVIS HAS A TAIL."

"No reason," Jessica said. When the bell rang, she was the first one into the classroom.

Telling her friends was out, but Jessica knew that she had to tell someone. It took her days to settle on the person and the words; days where she would wake up feeling a few

seconds of peace before remembering what had happened. Then she'd reach down, and the tail would still be there, and the knowledge would come slamming back into her body with the force of a punch, leaving her breathless and occasionally weepy. She couldn't eat. Whatever she swallowed sat like a rock in her belly, and she could sleep for only a few hours at a time. Finally, on a Wednesday night after dinner, a few weeks after she'd made her unpleasant discovery, she'd grabbed her mom in the kitchen and blurted out the news. Her mother had sent her to her room, but Jessica had still been able to hear the things she'd said to Jessica's dad. *Your family,* and *Your father. All your fault!* and *How are you going to make this right?*

There was no dinner that night. "Order a pizza," Jessica's mother said tersely when Jessica finally came out of her bedroom. At ten o'clock that night, when Jessica was getting ready for bed, her mother appeared at the door of her bedroom. "Don't worry," she'd said, her voice thick with tears. "Everything's going to be okay. We are going to figure this out." She'd turned out the light without giving Jessica a hug, or a kiss good night, without even touching her. *Like it's catching,* Jessica thought bitterly, and wondered if it was.

She'd thought she could keep her tail a secret. In the absence of either parent telling her what to do, she'd thought that was the plan. And she'd managed, for almost six weeks . . . until one afternoon in the cafeteria, when Amelia had been describing the dress she wanted to buy for the Fall Ball. "It's got a sash that wraps around here," she'd said, touching Jessica's hips to show her. Then her hand had brushed Jessica's tail, and her eyes had gotten wide.

"What is that?" she'd whispered, and Jessica had stammered out, "It's nothing!" She'd gone running to the bathroom, and Amelia had followed her, her eyes full of sympathy, her voice low as she'd asked, "What is it? Do you have, like, a tumor? Are you sick?"

"It's not that," Jessica had said, her voice low. Then she'd told Amelia what it was.

Big mistake.

By the next morning, the entire school was buzzing with the news that Jessica Jarvis had a tail!

That afternoon, she'd come home from school to find a stranger waiting in the hallway.

"Jessica, this is Miss Merriweather," her mother said. Her voice was bright and chipper, but there were circles under her eyes. "She's an educational consultant. She's going to help us find the very best school for you!"

Frowning, Jessica said, "Don't I already go to a good school?"

"An even better school!" Her mom was trying hard to sound cheerful, but Jessica saw how she was twisting her hands together, and how she hadn't put her makeup on that morning. There were deep grooves running from the corners of her lips to her nose, and her skin was colorless, unusually pale.

Jessica followed her mother and Miss Whoever into the living room. She watched as her mother perched on the edge of the couch, then stood up, straightened a pillow that didn't need straightening, and crossed the room to give the drapes a twitch. "Your dad and I were talking about boarding schools! So you'll be resilient and have grit!" While Jessica's mother paced and fussed and blurted random buzzwords, Miss Merriweather gave Jessica a warm handshake and a kind smile. She had curly white hair, a soft, sweet-looking face, and sharp, watchful eyes behind her glasses. "Don't worry, dear," she'd told Jessica. "There's a place for girls like you."

Girls like you. The words had tolled in Jessica's brain, like funeral bells. What did that mean? Other girls with tails, or extra parts that didn't belong? Girls with three eyes, or just one eye, or tentacles, or worse?

Never mind. Jessica tilted her chin, tightened her lips, and made herself smile. When she went upstairs, she found suitcases lying open on her bed. Mindlessly, Jessica emptied her drawers and her desk and her closet. A black car was waiting in the driveway when she got back downstairs. She'd hugged her mother goodbye and climbed into the car, which had delivered her to upstate New York, to Lori and Phil at the Experimental Center for Love and Learning. The place called itself a school, but Jessica knew what it really was. It was exile. She'd been the most popular girl in her school, with lots of friends and even a few ninth-grade boys who liked her. Then she'd grown a tail, through no fault or intention of her own, and her parents, who had always loved her, who'd always told her she was beautiful, smart, talented, capable of being anything she wanted to be, had sent her here, to some weirdo school in the woods with a bunch of other freaks. They hadn't even given her time to say goodbye to her friends!

For the first four nights at the Center, Jessica had cried herself to sleep. She'd fantasized about taking a razor and slicing her tail off, even though she knew she'd never be able to go through with it. The tail was a part of her. It hurt when she tugged it too hard. Cutting it off would be like removing one of her own fingers. Jessica knew better than to try.

After the fifth night, she realized that her tears were

getting her nowhere. No one was coming to rescue her. No one would bring her home. She decided that she was done hoping. She decided, instead, to make her parents pay for what they'd done. Her first move would be to establish herself in this new place at the top of the social pyramid, just as she'd been at her last school.

Her plan had been working. After just a few months, she'd been the queen bee, the best dressed, the most popular. And then her stupid, sullen, frizzy-haired roommate Alice had befriended Millie. And Millie, somehow, had recognized Jessica for what she was. The day of the hunt, the day that every other kid and teacher at the school had come forward to declare their own particular weirdness, Jessica had kept quiet, until Millie had bared her teeth at her and bristled, until, finally, Jessica had stepped forward and confessed, in front of an entire crowd of people, and television cameras (just from local stations; thank goodness).

Millie was dangerous, Jessica realized. So when Millie decided that she wanted to audition for *The Next Stage*, Jessica had agreed to help her out of the goodness of her heart, but also so that Millie would be grateful. Millie would owe her. And Millie would, therefore, be unlikely to ever tell anyone else the truth about Jessica's tail situation. *Keep your friends close, but your enemies closer,* people said, and if Jessica kept Millie close, Millie would be unlikely to go blabbing. But now Alice and Millie were gone, and her grandfather had tried to kidnap them.

So what was the connection?

Jessica shifted in her seat and closed her eyes. Years ago, in second grade, she'd done a family tree, and she'd asked her parents questions about their own parents: What were their names and their jobs? Where were they born, and how many kids did they have?

She remembered that her parents had been perfectly forthcoming about her mom's side of the family. It wasn't until she'd started asking about her dad's father that things had gotten strange. Instead of just naming a regular job—a doctor or a lawyer or an accountant or a teacher—her father had said, "Your grandfather is an entrepreneur. A businessman." When Jessica had asked for details, like what kind of business her grandfather did, her dad had said, "Your grandfather is a man with his thumb in many different pies." Jessica had pictured an old man in a bakery, literally stabbing his thumb through piecrusts, before her dad had gotten to his feet and gone into the kitchen. They kept over-the-counter medication in a cupboard next to the sink—aspirin for headaches, Pepto-Bismol for upset stomachs, Band-Aids and antiseptic cream. Her dad opened this cupboard and pulled out a bottle of heartburn pills. "See this?" He pointed to the logo on the bottom of the label— the words "Jarvis Industries" on a tiny blue shield, like the kind a knight would carry into battle. "That's your grandfather's company. He invented this medicine."

"So he's a scientist?"

Her father and her mother had exchanged a look over Jessica's head. Then her dad had nodded. "He's invented some very important medications—one that helps people who have high blood pressure, one that helps men who've lost their hair. He's done a lot of good for the world. But now . . ." Her dad's voice had trailed off.

"Now what?" Jessica prompted.

"Now we don't really talk much," her father finally said, and nodded at Jessica's family tree. "Just put 'entrepreneur.' That should cover it."

Jessica had written it down, after asking her dad how to spell it. Then she'd asked her dad about his mom. Her father had gotten quiet, and a flush had crawled up the back of his neck.

"Tell her," Jessica's mother had called from the kitchen, her voice gentle and sympathetic.

"I was only a few weeks old when she died," her father told Jessica.

Jessica had been so busy filling in the blanks that she hadn't even thought about what her father had just told her—that his own mother had died when he was just a baby. "Okay, but what was her name?" Jessica said. "And her job? I have to put that."

The flush had crept past her father's jawline, suffusing his entire face. "Ellie," he'd said. "Her name was Eleanor Gold."

Later her mother had given Jessica the rest of the story—how her father had been raised by nannies, then sent to boarding school as soon as he was old enough to go. How her grandfather had thrown himself into work, becoming vastly wealthy. How he had never remarried, or even dated. How, in Jessica's mother's opinion, he blamed himself for his wife's death. "Here he was, this brilliant scientist, and he couldn't save her," Jessica's mom had said. "I can't imagine how he must have felt." Now her father's father lived as a recluse up in Vermont, seeing no one, not even his own son. "I've only met him once. The day he met you," her mother said. "We invited him to our wedding, but he didn't come."

Jessica had been left with the mental picture of a

brokenhearted recluse, a man who lived in his lab and invented medications that brought health and healing to the masses. Sure, it was weird to ship your only child off to boarding school, and not even come to his wedding, but maybe he was just anxious, or socially inept, or paralyzed with grief and sadness, and not necessarily a villain.

Except now . . .

Jessica opened her eyes. She could feel anxiety sitting like a knot in her chest. She did more calming breathing, then began to think, reviewing what she'd learned about Christopher Wayne Jarvis. The Internet had been full of information, from the name of the hospital where he'd been born, the schools he'd attended, to the year he'd graduated from high school and from college, and the year he'd gotten his PhD. She knew that his wife's name had been Eleanor Sarah Gold, and that his only son, her father, had been just six weeks old when she'd died. She knew that her grandfather owned many, many things, ranging from part of a casino in Connecticut to part of a professional football team in Indianapolis to a research laboratory in Upland, Vermont.

It was this last one that interested Jessica the most. But no matter how many different ways she had tried to ask her questions, the Internet just kept spitting out the same nonanswers, a bunch of vague euphemisms and the kind of slogans you'd see on brochures. "Building a Better Tomorrow." "Biotechnology for a Healthy Future." "Pharmaceutical research." "Improving health and health care for the new millennium."

Not very specific, Jessica thought. *What are you trying to hide, Grandpa?* She scrolled down to the end of a non-story about the ribbon-cutting at a new facility, where scientists would research ways to "maximize human potential," when she felt her heart leap in her chest.

There, in a white lab coat, with a pleasant smile on his broad face, was one of the men in suits who'd grabbed Alice. Jessica clicked on the photo, enlarging the man's face and the caption beneath it. The man's name was John Witherspoon, and according to his biography, he wasn't a bodyguard, but an endocrinologist who'd previously worked at the Centers for Disease Control and Prevention in Atlanta.

Interesting, Jessica thought. She closed out of her search screen, googled the one last bit of information she'd need, printed out a map, and went on her way, out the door, downtown to the bus station, and then off to New Jersey, and another family member—one she hoped would be able to help.

CHAPTER 7

Alice

After Miss Merriweather had pulled off the highway, she took back roads south, driving slowly, until the familiar New York City skyline came into view.

"We are back," Millie said softly. "Why are we back?"

Alice thought she knew, but she wasn't certain until Miss Merriweather stopped the car at the curb in front of her parents' apartment and put the blinkers on. "We'll wait here," she said.

Alice's mother nodded, then led Alice through the doors, past the doorman, into the elevator that would carry them up to their apartment. Barely twelve hours had passed since Alice and Millie and Jessica had left the apartment that morning, on their way to Millie's audition at Carnegie Hall, never imagining what would happen there. It only added to Alice's sense of dislocation and unreality, seeing this familiar place, again, on this strangest of days. She wondered what other revelations might be in store, if Jerry the doorman might pull off his mask to reveal that he was the president, or if the retinue of pugs who lived with Mrs. Stott on the nineteenth floor might turn out to actually be aliens from outer space.

Alice felt the familiar swooping sensation in the pit of her stomach as the elevator rose, up and up and up. She followed her mother down the hallway, watching, as she turned her key, and the door swung open.

"Hello, ladies."

And here was Alice's father—or, Alice thought, the man she'd always believed was her father—standing by the door.

"I'll give you two a minute," said Alice's mom, who had a sad, resigned expression on her face. She turned, hair swishing, and disappeared down the hall. Then it was just Alice and her dad, and for once, he wasn't wearing a suit. He wasn't on a business call or poking at his phone or an iPad. He didn't look busy or distracted, on his way to somewhere else. He wore a pair of dark nylon track

pants, a University of Pennsylvania T-shirt, and reading glasses. His eyes, behind them, were gentle as they fixed on Alice, and his face looked sad.

"So now you know," he said.

Alice nodded. Her mother had explained it, on the wild ride away from Carnegie Hall, with Millie beside her and the bad men from the government chasing them. She'd told Alice how she'd met a man when she was a college student in Vermont, and fallen in love and gotten pregnant, only to learn that the man wasn't a man at all, but a Yare—a Bigfoot. The government had captured him, and hunted her, but she'd gotten away. Alice's mother had given birth, all alone, then snuck baby Alice out of the hospital and walked all the way into the woods of New York, to deliver her baby to his Tribe. Alice had been left with the Yare for the first nine months of her infancy. Alice's mother had gone to New York City, to transform herself into a fancy society lady, the type of person the government agents would never suspect had once been the farm girl and college student who'd given birth to a daughter back in Vermont. As part of the transformation, she had married Mark Mayfair. *Mark was an old family friend,* she'd told Alice. *He'd always had a crush on me, and I'd never been interested.* Mark and Faith had gotten married, Faith had reclaimed her daughter, and, together, they'd raised Alice as their own.

And now Mark Mayfair was looking at Alice, with his expression kind and regretful. *How much of the truth does he know?* Alice wondered. *Did my mom love him, even a little?* She could tell that her father loved her mother. She knew it, from the way his eyes would follow her when she got up from the table or sat down on the couch, the way he'd stand up a little straighter when she entered a room, and leaned toward her as she talked, and from the way his voice sounded when he said her name. Which, Alice realized, was not really her name at all. Her mother was not Felicia Mayfair, she was Faith, and her given last name was Nolan. *Faith Nolan* sounded more like the woman in sweatpants and a ponytail who'd tackled a security guard and wrestled her daughter away from him. *Felicia Mayfair* sounded like a society lady, a woman who would swan about in cocktail dresses and evening gowns, her hair done and her lips glossy and fake lashes fluttering against her cheeks. That was who her mother had been the entire time Alice had known her. But that had been a disguise; one that her mother had discarded.

Her father—she couldn't stop herself from thinking of him that way—patted the couch. Alice sat down beside him. Her eyes felt prickly, and her throat felt tight.

"Do you know?" she asked her dad. Her voice sounded husky. "About me? About where I came from?"

He put his arms around her shoulders and pulled her close. Alice thought, a little wildly, that she'd never been touched by her parents as much in a year as she'd been just in the last few hours.

"Most of it," he said. "Faith swore me to secrecy, though. So where are you two headed?" He looked at Alice, eyebrows raised.

"I don't know," Alice said. "I don't know where we're going, or what happens next. I think . . ." Alice cleared her throat, swallowed, and tried again. "I think the plan is to find the people who've been hunting the Yare—the Bigfoots—and, um, expose them somehow. To go public. I guess." *No more hiding,* her mother had said, looking brave and fierce and more beautiful than Alice had ever seen her. *No more hiding, no more being afraid.*

"I'm glad," her father said. "I'm glad you'll get to be who you really are. And your mom . . ." Alice saw his throat working as he swallowed. *He loves her,* she thought. *This must be breaking his heart.* He had married Faith Nolan knowing she loved someone else, knowing she'd had a baby with that man, and he'd married her anyhow, and given the baby his name, and followed his wife's instructions, doing whatever she told him to do to keep her and her daughter safe.

Oh, Dad, Alice thought. "I'm so sorry!" she blurted.

Mark shook his head. "Don't be," he said. "I knew what I was signing up for. And I felt lucky, truly. To get as much of the two of you as I did." There were tears in his eyes, and as Alice watched, they rolled down his cheeks. "I will always be lucky to have been your father."

"Oh, Dad." She didn't know what to tell him, how to say what she was feeling. Instead, she put her arms around him and hugged him as hard as she could, with all the strength that she normally tried to hide. He patted the wild, wiry mass of her hair and kissed her cheek.

"Alice." She turned and saw her mother in the hallway, with two zippered duffel bags slung over her shoulder. Faith had put on a jacket, in a light olive-green shade. That, plus her brown sweatpants and sneakers, would let her move through the woods undetected. With her hair pulled back and her face scrubbed clean, without her lipstick and her false eyelashes, she looked, to Alice, like a different person, like a stranger. She looked older, and sadder; like she'd seen things that had hurt.

Both of them got to their feet. Alice's father held out

his arms, and with a tiny, pained cry, Alice's mother ran to him and stepped into his embrace. She put her head on his chest, leaning against him, as he wrapped his arms around her, rocking her gently and saying things that Alice couldn't hear.

Alice knew that Mark Mayfair was not her mother's great love. That man, or whatever he was, was still out there, somewhere. Or maybe he wasn't. Maybe the government had killed him. Either way, soon she and her mother would know for sure. But now, as she watched Mark holding her mother, pressing her against him and talking softly into her ear, she thought that, even if Mark Mayfair was not the love of her mother's life, he still loved her. And she loved him. And both of them had loved Alice, as best they could.

She watched them embrace, still feeling sad, but also, a little angry. *Why couldn't you have told me the truth?* she imagined asking her mother. *How could you have used him this way?*

She had questions for her father, too. *Why did you agree to this? Why did you let her treat me the way she treated me? Why did you let her keep sending me away?*

She could have asked them, but Alice suspected they'd have had the same answer to all of her questions: *We had to keep you safe*. That justified the lying, the sham of their marriage, the way they'd shipped her off to boarding school after boarding school and summer camp after summer camp where she'd never had friends or been happy. True, she'd been safe enough—she'd survived, at least—but if she'd been miserable for all those years, what was even the point?

She stared at her feet until her mother whispered something to Mark, then turned to Alice. "We need to get going," she said. Faith's eyes were wet, her lips trembling, but she was trying to smile as she held out her hand.

"Wait!" said her father. He hurried out of the room, into the kitchen. When he came back, he had a packed grocery bag in his arms. "I got you some snacks. For the road."

Alice's mother took the bag. They were almost at the door when Alice turned, crossed the room, and flung herself at her father's chest, not even trying to stop the tears from falling as he pulled her close.

"Honey," he whispered. "Don't worry. Everything is going to be fine, and I promise, I'll be here for you. Always. No matter what."

Alice gave him one last, long hug, feeling his hands warm on her hair as he held her. "No matter what," he said again. Gently, he took her hands off him, first the

left one, then the right. He gave her shoulders a final squeeze, then urged her in her mother's direction.

"Go on, now," he said. "You'll be fine."

"I love you," Alice said. Then, without looking back at him or looking up at her mother, she walked through the door, down the hallway, into the elevator, and off to whatever was waiting for them.

CHAPTER 8

Jeremy

FOR A FEW MINUTES, JEREMY THOUGHT THAT his discovery of the Bigfoots was going to be an extremely short-lived triumph, insofar as Maximus and Benjamin Burton seemed intent on killing each other and, with his luck, him too.

At first, Benjamin and Maximus hadn't even spoken. They'd just kind of . . . bristled, exchanging murderous glares and making growling noises in their throats as the Yare who'd been standing around the fire scrambled out of their way. Maximus's fur seemed to stand up around his head. Benjamin bared his teeth. As man and Yare circled each other, Jeremy scrambled toward the edge of the circle. *I need to get out of here,* he thought . . . but as soon as he started moving, Maximus turned and put one hand on his shoulder. Benjamin Burton grabbed the other, and together, they hauled him forward and pushed him back down onto the log, where he half-sat, half-fell onto his bottom.

"You led him here." Maximus's voice was a rumble so low it was more of a feeling than a sound as he glared at Jeremy.

"You think I couldn't find this place, brother?" Benjamin's last word, delivered in a rumbling sneer, sounded flippant and mocking. Even though one of them had fur and the other didn't, Jeremy could see the resemblance in their features, the set of their shoulders, the shape of their faces. They undoubtedly were brothers, maybe even twins. And Maximus had called Alice his niece. Which meant that Benjamin Burton was Alice's father, the one responsible for her nonhuman blood, even though Benjamin was—or at least, appeared to be—completely human. How had he done it? Jeremy wondered. How had he gotten rid of his fur, and the claws that Maximus and the others all seemed to have? How had he managed to live in the human world? Why had he decided to do it? And were there more like him, more

Yare and half-Yare, out in the world, living human lives, looking like regular people?

All these questions raced through Jeremy's mind as Maximus stepped to Benjamin, so close that they were chest to chest. "Where is my daughter?" Maximus asked, in a whisper that was somehow more menacing than a shout.

"Have you misplaced her?" Benjamin asked, his own voice light and mocking. "Your daughter and mine, too?"

"You abandoned your daughter," Maximus snarled in response. "And your wife. And your Tribe."

Benjamin Burton raised his chin. "At least I never sent a littlie out, alone, to wander some dirty city . . ."

"You dare!" Maximus growled. "You think I let her go? You think that I'd expose her to such dangers?"

"Why not?" asked Benjamin. His tone was flippant, but Jeremy could hear the hurt and anger underneath it. "You couldn't keep my daughter safe. Why should I think you'd do any better for yours?"

"I never lost your daughter. Your wife came back and took her!" Maximus snarled. "We tried to keep her, we begged her to let us, we told her we could keep the baby safe, but she said no, she was the mother. What could we say to that?"

The two men sprang at each other. Jeremy got himself

as far away as he could, convinced that they were going to start tearing each other apart, until the small, elderly female Yare, the one in the green dress, stepped forward. Her voice was like the crack of a whip.

"Enough!"

Both Benjamin and Maximus froze. Standing on her tiptoes, the old woman grabbed one of the men's ears in each of her hands and twisted. Not gently. "We will not be finding any daughters if you two keep this up!" With one final wrench, she let go.

Maximus rubbed his ear. Benjamin smoothed his beard. Both kept glaring at the other, but at least they'd stopped making those rumbling snarls, and Maximus's fur no longer looked quite as bristly.

"Now." She turned to Jeremy. "I am Old Aunt Yetta. Healer of this Tribe." She tilted her head. "Both girls were in New York City, yes? At this singing contest?"

Jeremy nodded, even as Maximus stepped toward Benjamin again.

"You enticed my Millie!" he growled.

"I," said Benjamin, "did no such thing. She sent in an application where some other girl pretended to be singing. I had no idea who she was, or what she was, until she stepped onstage."

Maximus shook his head. "You didn't smell her?" he asked. Under other circumstances, the question might have been gross or weird or even a little bit funny, but neither man looked like this was a joke. Maximus's expression was furious. Benjamin Burton looked a little sad, even ashamed, as his brother asked, "Are all of our ways forgotten? Did you shed them with your fur? Are you No-Fur, through and through?"

"My fur will grow back," Benjamin said, through clenched teeth. "Maybe it's time I came back as Leader. It doesn't seem like you've done very well at it."

Maximus looked shocked, but, before he could respond, another Yare spoke up.

"We don't want you! Not you, not your No-Fur wife, not your half-breed daughter!"

Benjamin turned and gave the speaker a hard look. His hands were still clenched into fists, but his voice was mild when he spoke. "Ricardan. Still here, I see."

"Still here," Ricardan replied. "Why would I not be? Not all of us wished to go see the world. The old ways were good enough for my parents, and their parents before them. They are good enough for me, too."

"Oh, the old ways. Of course," Benjamin said, his voice cool and polite. "I only thought you'd be a Leader by now.

With your own Tribe. But I see that hasn't happened."

"Stop making trouble," Maximus growled at his brother, as Ricardan looked bewildered, then enraged.

"So wait," said Jeremy. The words were out of his mouth before he realized he'd said them. He gulped as all of the Yare's gazes swung toward him.

"Never mind," he muttered. Benjamin Burton raised his eyebrows. Maximus made a beckoning motion with his hands. "Speak," he said.

"Okay." Jeremy gathered his courage and nodded at Benjamin. "You're Alice's father. And his brother," he said, pointing at Maximus. Benjamin nodded tightly.

"You're one of them," Jeremy said, just making sure. "A Yare."

"He left." Ricardan said angrily. "He, who should have been our Leader! He left, to go see the No-Fur world. He found some way to change himself, some magic, so that he looked like one of them. And he found some No-Fur woman and had a baby with her, a stunted little half-breed thing. And he abandoned them."

"I *never*," Benjamin Burton snarled. "I was trapped! And when I got free, they were gone. I searched the world to find them! I would have given anything . . ." He stopped, gathering himself, and glared furiously at his brother. "And when I came back, you told me that they were gone. My wife and my daughter. You let me think they were dead!"

Maximus's face was stony. "It was better that way. Safer."

"They were my family," Benjamin snarled. "My wife! My child! You had no right!"

"That is in the past," said Old Aunt Yetta. She clapped her tiny, gnarled hands three times in a row. At the sound, the rest of the Tribe appeared. Jeremy felt his mouth drop open. It was almost like seeing a magic trick. The Yare had just materialized, out of nowhere, like one instant they weren't there, and the next they were. There were maybe thirty of them in all, in human clothes, overalls or pants and shirts or dresses. Septima, the Yare who'd found Jeremy in the forest, the one who'd asked for his help, crept toward the circle to stand close to Maximus.

The young ones, he saw, were giving him curious looks. One boy in particular, in blue jeans and a green-and-black plaid shirt who seemed to be about Jeremy's age, was full-on staring. Jeremy raised his hand in a wave. The boy gave a shy smile and waved back, before his mother gave his ear a tug. The boy dropped his gaze and shrank back behind her.

Old Aunt Yetta took the smooth stick that Maximus

was holding. "This is Jeremy Bigelow of the Humans. Son of Martin and Suzanne. Friend of Millie."

Jeremy gave the group a tentative wave.

Old Aunt Yetta turned to Jeremy. "Now," she said. "What happened in New York?"

Jeremy tried to explain it all, as succinctly as he could—how he'd followed Millie and Alice to New York. ("New York!" he heard some of the Yare murmur, and "Auditions!" Some of the younger Yare were whispering among themselves, and he heard one of the adult women say, her voice piercing and shrill, "I knew no good would come of that place across the lake!")

"Hush," said Old Aunt Yetta, giving the woman a stern look. "Jeremy, continue."

Jeremy continued. He explained that they'd been at Carnegie Hall, and Millie had been singing for the judges of *The Next Stage*.

"Singing in front of No-Furs!" the female who'd found the school so objectionable marveled, in the same tone Jeremy's mother might have used to say something like *Tearing the wings off butterflies!* Or *Going to church naked!*

"It's that school!" said Ricardan, waving in the direction of the Experimental Center for Love and Learning. "That school, and those No-Fur littlies, with their top-laps and their Wi-Fi! Beguiling our young ones! Tempting them with worldly things! Leading them astray!"

"Enough," said Old Aunt Yetta again. She nodded at Jeremy. "Tell the rest of it. Tell it all."

Jeremy did. He told them how Millie had been singing onstage with Jessica. He told them how men in suits and sunglasses, including one Jeremy recognized, had grabbed Alice and carried her outside. How a red-haired woman had come charging at the man holding Alice, getting her free. (He thought he saw Benjamin give a quick smile at that part of the story, but he couldn't be sure.) How Alice and Millie had gotten into a small white car with Alice's rescuer, and how the men had grabbed Jessica and put her in the van. How there'd been another woman behind the wheel, small, with white hair, who'd driven them all away.

"And then Benjamin grabbed me and brought me back inside, so that's all I saw," Jeremy said.

Jeremy could hear low murmurings from the Tribe. He noticed that the young man who'd been staring at him was now hiding behind his mother, looking miserably at his feet, like he was trying very hard to vanish from the face of the earth. Maximus noticed too. The

Tribe's Leader took the young Yare by the shoulders and marched him into the center of the circle.

"Frederee," Maximus rumbled. "What are you knowing about this?"

Frederee was trembling all over, so hard that his fur was shivering. All the other Yare, adults and children alike, were staring at him. Maximus's look was especially poisonous. "I—I told her it was a bad idea!" Frederee said shrilly. "I did say!" As the Tribe stared at him, he hung his head. "She had me hold the top-lap while she sang," he muttered. His mother gasped. Ricardan shook his head, looking disgusted.

"You knew that Millie was going to New York?" Maximus asked.

"I told her!" Frederee spluttered. "I said bad! I said dangerous! But she wouldn't listen! She said that nothing bad would happen. She said it was her dream. She said she had to go; that she'd die if she didn't."

"You terrible scoundrel!" Frederee's mother hissed, reaching forward to give the back of his neck a smack. "You have shamed us!" Frederee yelped, then rubbed his neck, looking affronted. Old Aunt Yetta, meanwhile, looked unsurprised. She nodded at Millie's mother, who seemed to gather herself before she stepped up, toward the fire. Her fur was trembling, but her voice was steady when she spoke.

"I also knew where Millie had gone."

The Tribe gasped. All of them did it quietly, but all of them did it together. Millie's mother raised her head.

"It was her dream." Her voice was low and carrying as she gave her husband, then the rest of the Yare, a pleading look, with her hands clasped in front of her. "It was all she wanted. To go, and to sing, and to try . . ." Her voice cracked. Benjamin Burton's expression had become a little smug. Maximus looked angry and sad and confused.

Old Aunt Yetta turned to Benjamin Burton. "Where would she go?" he asked. "Your wife. Faith."

"I don't know." His voice was flat and lifeless. "Don't you think I've been looking? For her, and for my daughter?" His face was anguished as he said, "I've never stopped. I've searched the world for them."

Old Aunt Yetta tugged thoughtfully at the fur on her right cheek. "What's the last place where the two of you were together?" she asked him.

He bent his head low, murmuring something in that low growl that Jeremy couldn't hear. But Old Aunt Yetta heard. She gave a single short nod.

"We'll start there, then." Lifting her head and raising

her voice, she said, "We must make to leave this place."

A sigh moved through the assembled Yare. Jeremy saw shoulders droop and heads hang. The littlest of the littlies started to cry, and a young male who seemed to be about Jeremy's age put his arm around her shoulder and pulled her close. The rest of the adult Yare seemed sad but resigned, mournful but not entirely surprised. Jeremy wondered if they'd been expecting this. He wondered how long the Yare had lived in the forests of Standish, and how many places they'd been forced to leave in their long history.

Old Aunt Yetta looked up. The sun had just set. The moon hung in the clear, starless sky, and the forest was quiet, without the sound of a single bird chirping or an icicle melting, dripping cold water onto the snow. "One hour," she decreed. "We'll travel in the dark, and rest in the day."

Jeremy raised his hand hesitantly. "I should go home," he said.

Old Aunt Yetta tilted her head, and smiled when she said, "You're with us now, Jeremy of the Humans."

Jeremy felt a thrill go through him. If singing onstage had been Millie's dream, hearing the Yare say *you're with us* had been one of his.

"Call your parents," Benjamin said. He held out his hand. Maximus reluctantly pulled Jeremy's phone out of his pocket and handed it to Benjamin, who passed it to Jeremy. "Make up some story. Tell them you'll be gone for a week."

"Now?" Jeremy asked.

Preening a little, Old Aunt Yetta said, "We have the Wi-Fi here. Come sit," she said, ushering him toward one of the stumps, where a plaid wool blanket had been spread. One of the women came forward with a steaming cup of what turned out to be cocoa. Jeremy sipped it slowly, trying to think of a story his parents would buy. At the sound of whispers, Jeremy turned and saw three smallish Yare peering at him from behind a pine tree's boughs. When they noticed him looking, one of them giggled, then they all ran off over the snow on their silent, bare feet.

Old Aunt Yetta sat down beside him with a grunt. She held out one tiny, gnarled, fur-covered paw, then looked at Jeremy. "Shake hands!" Gingerly, Jeremy took her hand in his own, and let it rest there, as light as a palmful of feathers. He gave it a gentle shake, feeling her shrewd gaze moving over him, from the cowlick at his crown to his ordinary brown eyes, his face and his shoulders and his hands, all the way down to his big (for a human boy) feet.

"I know humans," Aunt Yetta said softly. "I was captured, once. I lived among you, for a time, until a human child freed me. I owe your kind a debt."

Jeremy felt his eyes get wide as he realized that this was the Yare Priscilla Landsman had seen all those years ago.

"Long and long ago," said Yetta, and gave a long, sad sigh. "Your people have hunted mine, for years on years." She took her hand back, and got to her feet. "Time to stop it, I think." Her gaze was intent, her bright eyes unblinking. "Will you help?"

"I'll do whatever I can," he promised, and meant it.

"Fair enough, Jeremy of the No-Furs," she said, and reached out with her tiny, gnarled hand and pinched his cheek.

CHAPTER 9

Jessica

WHEN JESSICA WAS LITTLE, HER NANA, HER mother's mother, had lived in an apartment in a high-rise building in New Jersey. Jessica had vague memories of sunny, high-ceilinged rooms that had plants on every ledge and windowsill, and paintings on every wall. Nana's bedroom had an enormous bed with a pink satin coverlet where she and Nana would have sleepovers, and where Nana taught Jessica to play card games like Hearts and Crazy Eights and War. They'd eat milk-chocolate-covered cherries and dark-chocolate-covered orange rinds, and stay up past midnight, with the television playing softly in the background.

Then, when Jessica was eight, Nana had slipped on an icy walkway and broken her hip. She had moved out of her apartment and into an assisted-living facility, which Jessica had misheard, at the time, as Sister Living. Four times a year, on Christmas and the Fourth of July, the day after Thanksgiving, and Nana's birthday in April, Jessica's family would visit Nana in her new residence. Every visit, Jessica expected that she'd finally meet the sisters that had given the place its name, and she was disappointed every time. Nana had her own bedroom, about half the size of the one Jessica remembered, but she'd somehow managed to cram in every piece of furniture from her old place—the big bed with its satin quilt, a love seat and a matching chair, an antique desk covered with framed family photographs. Nana usually received her visitors in the facility's sunroom, where other old people sat at tables, working on puzzles or reading the paper or just staring at nothing. Jessica would eat graham crackers and play Scrabble with Nana for an hour, at which point Nana would give Jessica's parents a wry smile and say, "You've done your duty. You're dismissed."

The afternoon after she'd witnessed a kidnapping, the bus dropped Jessica off three blocks away from Greenwood Acres. As she walked through the glass doors,

Jessica started to worry that the nurses, or whoever was in charge, would want to know why she was alone, and why she wasn't in school. But the woman behind the desk smiled when Jessica gave her name. "Oh, your grandma will be so glad to see you!" she said. "She's been a little down."

Jessica felt a stab of guilt. The woman handed her a visitor's badge and pointed her toward the sunroom, where a dozen elderly people sat at tables or on couches against the wall. Some were playing cards. A few more were staring at *Judge Judy* on TV.

Jessica found her grandmother at a table in the center of the room, with three other residents.

"Hi, Nana."

"Jessica?" Nana said, getting to her feet, looking pleased and slightly puzzled to see her granddaughter. "What a nice surprise!" She seemed to have shrunk since Jessica had last seen her, but her hair was in its familiar silvery pixie cut, and her eyes were the same pale blue, watery and faded but still sharp. She wore a light-blue tracksuit with a zippered jacket. Her nails were painted coral, and her gold wedding band hung loosely on the third finger of her left hand.

Jessica let herself be hugged and petted and introduced to Nana's friends, who all agreed that it was lovely

that Jessica had come for a visit. Jessica held her breath, hoping that none of them would ask if her parents were there, too, but none of them did.

"Jessica and I are going to have a nice chat," Nana finally announced. She grabbed her walker and led Jessica to a quiet table in the corner of the sunroom.

"It's lovely to see you, dear," she said, looking at Jessica closely. "But what brings you to Greenwood? And how did you get here?"

"I took the bus. I was in New York for the day. I wanted to see you." Nana raised a skeptical eyebrow. Jessica swallowed hard, her face warm with guilt. "And I want to ask you some things about my grandfather," she said. "Dad's father. Christopher Wayne Jarvis."

Nana didn't speak. She tilted her head, pressing her lips together, looking thoughtful.

"I don't know how well you know him . . ." Jessica's voice trailed off.

"Well enough," Nana said. Her face was still expressionless, but her voice sounded a little cool.

Jessica braced herself. This was going to be the hard part. "Do you know why I went to boarding school?" she began.

Nana shook her head.

Jessica plowed on. "Something happened to me." She wanted to point toward the affected area, but couldn't bring herself to do it in public.

Nana looked at her shrewdly. "Teeth?" she asked.

"What?" Jessica was certain she'd misheard her grandmother.

"Did you grow extra teeth?" Nana repeated patiently. "Or extra fingers? Or . . ."

"No, no." Jessica said, feeling stunned. She wanted to say *It was nothing like that*, except it was something like that . . . and, somehow, her nana knew it.

"Can you see in the dark?" asked her grandmother.

"No!" Jessica blurted, and wondered if that was a possibility, if maybe she could have ended up with some superpower or special ability instead of what she'd ended up with. She lowered her voice. "I. Um. I have a very small tail."

"Oh." Nana looked relieved—but not, Jessica noticed, shocked, or even especially surprised. "Does it hurt?" Nana asked.

"Does what hurt?"

"Your tail." Her grandmother's voice was very matter-of-fact. "Does it hurt?"

Jessica shook her head. Nana sighed, her look of relief deepening. "I did wonder," she said, almost to herself.

"I wondered if something had happened. I tried to ask your mother a hundred times, after she told me you were going to boarding school. I dropped hints. I hoped that she would talk to me. But she never said a word."

Jessica spread her hands flat on the table, bracing herself. "I think that my grandfather—Dad's father—that he might have something to do with what happened to me," she said. "I heard my parents fighting about it, and I think—I think that maybe they think so, too." She felt her heart give a great leap in her chest when Nana nodded.

"I've been waiting a long time to see if anyone would ever figure it out," said her grandmother. "What he's done. What he is."

Jessica leaned across the table, lowering her voice. "What's he done? What is he?"

Nana bent her head. "What he's done is hurt children. And as for what he is . . ." Her voice trailed off, and when she raised her eyes, Jessica saw that they were brimming with tears. "He's a monster. He isn't human. Not anymore."

Get us a snack, her nana had said. Jessica made a cup of tea and a cup of hot chocolate, and gathered a bunch of graham cracker packets wrapped in crinkly plastic. Her grandmother took a sip of tea, patted her lips with her napkin. She pulled in a deep breath, let it out in a sigh, and then began.

"You remember I used to be a reporter, right? Back when there were newspapers," Nana said. "When your mother started dating your father, I wanted to find out everything I could about him and his family." Nana rearranged her folded hands on top of the table. "So. Christopher Wayne Jarvis. He was—he is—a very wealthy man. He was brilliant, and a loner, and a little bit odd. I don't think he dated much, until he met your grandmother."

Jessica nodded, breaking a graham cracker in half and nibbling its edges as her grandmother kept talking.

"When they were married, your grandfather was almost forty, and his wife was just twenty-six. She came to his company for a job interview. The story I heard was that, after she left, your grandfather called his human-resource director and told him to offer your grandmother whatever salary she asked for, and any perk she requested, and to throw a car and a driver in with the deal, to give her anything she wanted, as long as she agreed to come work with him."

"Was she that good of a scientist?" Jessica asked.

Nana gave a rueful kind of smile. "She was a brilliant scientist. But I don't think that's why your grandfather wanted her to come work with him. I think he fell in love with her. Love at first sight."

"So what happened?"

"Well, your grandmother took the job," Nana said. "Six months later they were married. They lived in a penthouse in New York City, and they built a summer place, way up in the woods in Vermont, and your grandfather bought a bunch of land there, too. That's where the Jarvis labs are now." Nana sipped her tea and patted her lips. "Your grandparents were working on a cure for cancer, and for Alzheimer's. They were studying cell replication and DNA mutations. They were very rich, and happy. For a while."

Jessica held her breath. Nana folded and refolded her hands, with their painted nails and swollen knuckles, in her lap. "Then your grandmother got pregnant. Midway through the pregnancy, she was diagnosed with breast cancer. She refused treatment, because she didn't want to risk harming the baby. Your father. It was a gamble, and in the end—" Nana's voice broke off. She patted her lips with a paper napkin, and continued. "In the end, the baby survived. His mother didn't."

Jessica gulped. The sunroom, with its white-and-yellow

floral wallpaper and cream-colored carpet, with its smells of warm chicken soup and cough drops and the hum of conversations and the television's drone, felt very far away.

"Your grandfather closed up the apartment in New York City. He took a leave of absence from his company. He sent your father to boarding school as soon as he was old enough to go—or, really, I think he found a place and gave them so much money that they'd have agreed to enroll his puppy, if he'd wanted that. He sent your father off to school, and he went to his place in Vermont and locked himself away. He wouldn't see anyone, and no one saw him." Nana unwrapped a graham cracker, broke it in half, then set it down without tasting it. "I know that there were rumors, about the mad scientist in the mansion who was trying to become immortal, to find a cure for death itself. People said he was doing experiments. Creating things that were never meant to be."

Teeth, thought Jessica. *Tails. Extra fingers.*

Nana raised her teacup to her mouth and took a sip. "And then children began to disappear."

Jessica's hands felt icy, and she was shivering, her skin bristling with goose bumps, her teeth trying to chatter. She clamped her jaws together tightly, and made herself keep listening.

"A boy would leave school at the end of the day, and never make it home. A girl would head off to the lake to meet her friends, but she'd never arrive."

Jessica could hardly breathe. "Were they . . . was he . . ."

"The children would be found in a day or two. Sometimes a week. They wouldn't remember anything between the moment they'd said goodbye to their teacher, or their parent, and the moment they'd been found, at a picnic table in a park five miles away from where they lived, or in the stands at a Little League game two towns down the highway. They wouldn't remember being taken, or where they'd gone or what had happened to them. They wouldn't look any different, and when doctors examined them, they couldn't find anything wrong, or missing, except the gaps in their memory. But something had happened to those children." Nana's eyes were far away. "They came back different. Changed."

"What do you mean?" Jessica whispered.

Nana shook her head. "I only heard stories. Whispers. Rumors. People said that one of the boys who had vanished and came back grew a third eye, right in the middle of his forehead." With one coral fingernail, Nana solemnly tapped the spot on her own forehead. "They said that one of the girls who'd been taken grew extra fingers.

One girl grew another set of teeth, behind the ones she already had."

Jessica felt a shudder ripple through her. She remembered what her mother had said to her dad: *Your fault. Your family.* "Did my grandfather do something to my father?" she whispered. "Did he do something to me?"

"I don't know," said her nana. "Not for sure."

Jessica's mouth was so dry she could barely speak. The hairs at the nape of her neck stood up. *Finally,* she thought, as her heart thundered in her chest. *Finally, we're getting close to what I am.*

"I also heard," said Nana, "that your grandfather and grandmother had found some other kind of people. Not human. Different. Creatures who lived hidden, deep in the woods."

Jessica's skin went prickly as she thought about the fur on Millie's face, and Alice's strength and speed and head of wild, wiry hair. When Jessica had made that mean poster, with Alice's picture side by side with an illustration of a Bigfoot, it seemed that, entirely by accident, Jessica had landed on the truth. She felt her tail give a tiny twitch, and her eyes filled with tears.

"Jessica?" Nana was peering at her, frowning and concerned. "Are you all right?"

"I think," Jessica said, "I think that maybe he's still doing experiments with children. This morning, in New York, his men tried to kidnap two of my friends. I saw his logo on the van they were using, and I know one of the men works at his lab in Vermont."

Nana nodded, looking unhappy—and, Jessica noted, again, unsurprised.

"But why?" Jessica asked. "All these experiments . . . and kidnapping. What was the point? Is he really trying to become immortal?"

Nana gave her a level look over the rim of her teacup. "All I know for sure is that your grandfather lost his wife tragically. He's brilliant, and stubborn, and he doesn't like losing."

Jessica's mind was whirling, gathering whispers she'd overheard, snippets from scary movies and scraps from horror stories and bad dreams, trying to spin them into an explanation. "So he's trying to . . . what? Resurrect her?"

"No, I don't think so," Nana said, her tone as conversational as if Jessica had inquired whether her grandfather was planning to buy a new car or host a Labor Day picnic. "I think he's trying to cheat death. To spit in its eye, to tell it, *You took my wife, but you can't take me.* I think he wants to live forever, and he's willing to use other people—even children—to figure out how." She gave Jessica another level look. "At least, that's what I think. I've been watching him. Watching for a long, long time."

"Does he know?" Jessica asked, keeping her voice low.

Nana gave her a wry, resigned sort of smile. "Maybe he does. But I don't think he's too worried." She sighed, and pulled down the cuffs of her warm-up jacket. "I'm just a little old lady in a nursing home."

"We have to stop him," Jessica said, her voice ringing through the room. At least, in her head it was ringing through the room. In reality, *Judge Judy* was probably louder. But the nursing home had faded into mist, becoming less real than the world she saw in her mind, a world of strange creatures and mad scientists and boys with three eyes and girls with teeth behind their teeth. Jessica felt alight with courage, glowing with bravery, like a warrior, or a knight riding into battle, knowing that her cause was just. "Will you help?"

Nana looked at Jessica. Slowly, a smile spread over her face. Her cheeks flushed, her eyes gleamed. "Hot dog!" she said, and practically jumped to her feet. Jessica was reminded of Grandpa Joe in *Charlie and the Chocolate Factory*, leaping out of bed after Charlie comes home with the Golden Ticket. "I've been waiting for this day.

You have no idea. Come on! Quick! Not a minute to waste! Hand me my walker," she ordered, pointing at the device in question. Jessica did as she'd been instructed, and followed her nana, who moved briskly down the wide, carpeted hallway and into her bedroom. There, Nana moved swiftly through the furniture-crammed room to stand on her tiptoes in front of her closet. She reached up, grunting softly, and pulled down a suitcase, which she set on top of her bed. She unzipped it, opened up her dresser, and started grabbing handfuls of clothing—nightgowns, more tracksuits, rolled-up balls of socks—and tossing them into the suitcase. Next, she opened her purse, unzipped her wallet, and peered at the driver's license behind a square of plastic. "Doesn't expire until next year," she said with a satisfied nod.

Jessica cleared her throat. "Nana, do you think you should be driving?" She knew, from overhearing her mom and dad talking, that getting her grandmother to agree to give up her car keys and sell her car had long been one of their goals, even before moving her into what both of them called The Place.

Nana gave Jessica a look of fond exasperation. "I've been driving for almost seventy years, dear. I'm a very safe driver." This wasn't what Jessica's parents had said, but

Jessica didn't argue. "Come on!" Nana said, and nudged Jessica playfully. "We've got to get on the good foot! There's adventures to have! Fair maidens to save! Evil to conquer! It's going to be glorious!"

Jessica had her doubts. "Where are we going?" she asked.

"Vermont." Her grandmother had unfolded a tote bag from somewhere and was sweeping the numerous bottles of pills on top of her dresser directly into the bag.

"But that's far, right? Can't we fly? Or take a train? Or get an Uber? Or . . ."

"We have to get to Vermont," her grandmother said patiently, "without anyone knowing that we're going there. All of those things you mentioned—plane tickets, train tickets—they leave records. Paper trails. And if we take an Uber, our route would show up online. Right?"

Jessica nodded. She knew that every time she used Uber, her parents could see where she'd been picked up and where she'd gotten dropped off. They could even trace her progress in real time.

Nana's eyes were shining as she bustled around the room, and she was moving easily. After days spent with nothing to do but watch TV and play board games and finish puzzles and wait for death or your grandkids,

whichever came first, a mission, a job, a cause, must feel wonderful. It certainly seemed to have improved Nana's mood. Jessica watched as Nana maneuvered through the crammed obstacle course of her bedroom, collecting her purse and her cardigan and her reading glasses, a nightgown and an e-reader and a pair of fur-lined boots, and tossing them all into her suitcase. "See if you can find a new toothbrush in the top drawer in the bathroom," Nana said.

Once the suitcase was zipped and the tote bag filled to overflowing, Nana exhaled, and sat on the edge of her bed. "I should tell you," Nana said.

"What?" Jessica asked. Her heart was beating hard, her fingers were twitching. Also, her tail wanted to wag, which was annoying. Jessica struggled to keep it still.

Nana cleared her throat. "Well," she said. "I'm, ah, technically not supposed to be off the grounds unsupervised." She fiddled with her wedding band. "Also, we might have to commit a small, nonviolent crime."

Jessica's chest felt tight. She was suffused with some emotion she couldn't name—fear, or excitement, or a combination of the two—that left her exhilarated and a little queasy as Nana beckoned her close. "One of the night nurses has one of those magnetic boxes for a spare key underneath her front wheel," Nana whispered. "She was showing it off in the parking lot, and I happened to overhear."

"Are we going to steal her car?" This day, Jessica thought, just found ways to keep getting weirder.

Nana stood. She slung the rattling, pill-stuffed tote bag over her shoulder and clipped a fanny pack around her waist. "Borrow," she said. "We'll bring it back, of course."

Jessica stopped and stared at her grandmother, suddenly terrified at the thought of what would happen to both of them if they got caught. She'd had friends who'd stolen makeup and perfume from the local Sephora, and they'd gotten in trouble when they'd been caught . . . and a car was much bigger than a tube of lip gloss. "We could buy a car," she proposed. "A used one. We could pay cash."

"I like the way you're thinking," Nana said. "But we'd have to trust that whoever sold us the car wouldn't blab." She shook her head decisively. "No. The best way for us to do this is to get in a car and go."

Jessica gulped, and followed her grandmother out into the hallway, out of the facility's front doors, and into the wintry sunshine. They crossed the parking lot and walked, casually, to a small blue car parked at the edge of the lot.

"Act normal," said Nana. Jessica immediately glanced over her left shoulder, then her right, noting the positions of security cameras and the presence of a guard in a booth. She was positive that they were being followed, that the man in the booth was staring at them, that the lady behind the front desk was already calling the police. "Normal!" Nana hissed as she bent down and fumbled with the magnetic box. A moment later, the key fob tumbled into her hand. She looked at it smugly.

"Yep. Still got it," she said. She unlocked the car and settled herself behind the wheel, adjusting the seat and the mirrors. Jessica stowed the luggage in the trunk and climbed into the passenger seat. Her whole body was shaking, and her heart was perched in her throat as Nana got the car started, put it in reverse, and pulled up to the gate. *Now is when the cops will come speeding down the street with their sirens blaring,* Jessica thought. *Now is when the van comes back, only this time the men in suits and sunglasses drag me away.* But none of that happened. The guard didn't even look at them. The arm of the gate swung up obligingly, and Nana drove through, and out onto the street. "Whoo hoo!" Nana exulted, and pumped her fist, nearly veering into the car beside them. The driver honked, gesticulating furiously. Nana waved, mouthed an apology, and straightened out the car. "Grab my phone and pull up Google Maps, dear. And use an anonymous browser."

"What's your password?"

"One two three four."

Jessica rolled her eyes. So not exactly a criminal mastermind, she thought. Then she unlocked her grandmother's phone, plugged in Vermont as their destination, and waited until the satellites told them which way to go.

CHAPTER 10

Jeremy

FROM HIS SEAT BY THE FIRE, JEREMY CAUGHT Frederee staring at him. Jeremy gave a friendly smile. Frederee and the girl-sized Yare with him both quickly looked away, but he could hear them whispering, their furred heads bent together. Finally, the Yare who was wearing a dress and a ribbon in her head-fur walked over to Jeremy. "Excusing me," she said. "Do you eat Yare?"

Jeremy blinked. "Do I what?"

"Eat. Yare." She was standing on her tiptoes, poised to run if Jeremy made any sudden moves. "My best friend's brother told her that No-Furs eat Yare."

"Well, we don't." He gave what he hoped was a

friendly smile. "We eat pizza. And sandwiches. Stuff like that. And we don't call ourselves No-Furs, either. We call ourselves humans."

She wrinkled her nose. "My mama and papa are saying No-Furs, but Millie is saying we're s'posed to be saying who-man. But No-Fur means no fur, and who-man means nothing!" That argument advanced, the girl nodded, looking pleased with herself.

"What's your name?" Jeremy asked.

"Tulip," she said.

"Do you live here?"

Tulip rolled her eyes in a very human (or who-man) fashion. "Where else would I be living?" She told him that she lived with her parents and that her favorite foods were dried plums and strawberry-rhubarb hand pies, and that she had a kitten named Mitten and that her favorite game was Hide.

"Hide-and-seek?" Jeremy asked.

"Just Hide." Her playful expression became sober and strangely adult. "It is the first game that all littlie Yare learn. For when the hellercopters and the hunters come." She reached for his hand. "Want to see my house?" she asked.

Jeremy did. He wanted to see everything, to know

everything, to speak to every member of the Bigfoot Tribe, to find out how they lived and how they'd kept themselves hidden for so many years. He still couldn't quite believe that he was here, that they were real.

Tulip held his hand and led him away from the fire, deeper into the woods. A snow-edged stream burbled along, the water flowing over ice-covered rocks. Jeremy followed her, looking around to see if any of the Yare would stop them, but the other adults had slipped away, leaving just Benjamin Burton and Maximus and Old Aunt Yetta standing by the fire. He waited to see if Benjamin would stop him, or if Maximus would tell him to stay close, but none of them seemed to be paying him any attention. The brothers were talking, their voices too low for Jeremy to hear, and Old Aunt Yetta seemed to be watching them . . . probably to make sure they wouldn't start fighting again. Jeremy was reminded of his own brothers, of his own mom standing guard, making sure their disagreement didn't become physical.

He followed Tulip until the stream widened and the banks grew higher and steeper. Just as he was beginning to wonder whether she'd lured him away from Benjamin Burton to trap him, or get him lost, she led him up to a wall of banked dirt where she brushed aside a tangle of weeds and trailing vines, exposing a wooden door that only came up to Jeremy's waist.

"Come in! Come in!" Tulip knocked twice. Jeremy bent down, ducked through the door, and looked around at a small, cozy, low-ceilinged room with white walls and a hardwood floor with a red-and-gold woven rug. A rocking chair stood in one corner, with a basket full of yarn and knitting needles on the ground beside it. Against the wall was another basket, this one filled with wooden blocks and cars and carved wooden soldiers. A woodstove was lit in the corner. Jeremy saw a pipe running from its top and disappearing into the ceiling. He wondered where they vented the smoke, how they'd disguised it so it wouldn't reveal their presence.

Along one wall there was a small kitchen with a sink and a stove and even a microwave. So they had running water and electricity, Jeremy thought. A round wooden table with four chairs was set beside the woodstove. A female Yare stood at the table, folding quilts and clothing into an old-fashioned-looking needlepoint bag. Her expression was somber.

"Honey, get your—" The woman stopped talking and went very still when she saw Jeremy. "Oh."

"This! Is! Jeremy!" Tulip said, dancing around the room.

"Hello," Jeremy said, feeling shy. The woman gave him a hard look. Without introducing herself, or responding to Jeremy's greeting, she went back to her task. "Tulip, choose out your things," she said. "Two dresses, two books, and your brush."

"What about my toys?" asked Tulip. "What about my collectionables? What about my hair decors? What about my—"

Her mother put her hand on Tulip's shoulder. "We can't carry all of those things," she said. "You know better."

Tulip's lower lip began to quiver. "What about Mitten?" she whispered.

"We did talking about this." Her mother looked sad, but kept her voice steady. "We have told you for long-and-long that a day would come when we might have to leave. We can't take more than what we can carry."

Tulip put her hands on her hips. "I can carry Mitten! Mitten is tiny!"

"But we don't know where we're going, or how long it will be until we make a new home. Mitten will be fine here. There are lots of good things for cats to eat in the forest, and Mitten is a good hunter."

"But . . ."

"No more," said Tulip's mother. Her voice was gentle,

but Jeremy was familiar enough with his own mother to recognize absolute refusal when he heard it. "No more now. Go pack."

Tulip heaved a sigh. Her shoulders slumped as she walked slowly into the dim recesses of the dugout. In the kitchen, her mother pulled a basket off a hook on the wall and began filling it with food from a humming refrigerator, the same make and model as the one in Jeremy's house.

"You have electricity?" he asked.

"We have a generator. We aren't stealing," she said, looking defensive. Her voice was anxious, as if Jeremy had accused her of theft.

"I'm sorry," he said. "I didn't think you were." He still couldn't get over how familiar this was. If you'd shifted the refrigerator and the rocking chair and the rug to his own house, they wouldn't have been out of place, and if you'd added a few windows to the dugout, it could have been any human house he'd ever visited.

The woman saw him looking. "We're people," she said in a quiet voice. "Mothers and fathers and littlies. Just like you."

Jeremy jumped as he felt something warm and furry brush against his ankle. He looked down into the green

eyes of a kitten, a fluffy little bundle of gray fur, with a white bib and a bit of white at the tip of its tail. "Mreow?" the kitten purred interrogatively as Jeremy bent to scratch behind its ears. A moment later, Tulip emerged with a bulging brown sack slung over her shoulder. "Two dresses. Three books. My brush," she said rapidly, and turned sideways, trying to sneak out the door. Her mother stepped in front of her, hand extended. Sighing, Tulip slid the knapsack off her back and handed it over. Her mother unzipped it and pulled out the two dresses and the brush, but Jeremy counted five books, not three, plus a set of jacks and a rubber ball in a soft cloth bag, a sketch pad and a palette of watercolors, a blue clay vase, and a small wooden box, no bigger than a deck of cards, with a fancy letter *T* carved on the lid.

"My collectionables!" Tulip cried as her mother opened the box. Jeremy saw five bright pennies. A binder clip and a paper clip. A single AirPod. A miniature box of dental floss, the kind you got in the dentist's office after a checkup. A tube of ChapStick, a butterscotch candy wrapped in crinkly plastic, a dented double-A battery.

"I found these items in the forest," Tulip said. "They are No-Fur belongings that are being dropped. I like No-Fur things. I'm not stealing," she said, echoing what her mother had just said. "I found. I didn't take."

Jeremy discovered that there was a very large lump in his throat. He swallowed hard, thinking that what Tulip called her collectionables was basically trash. And yet, to her, these things were precious.

"Can I bring them?" Tulip asked.

Her mother sighed.

"Please, Mama, they're my treasures," Tulip pleaded.

"Fine," her mother said curtly. "Only I will not hear complaining about this."

"I won't!" Tulip promised. "Not a single bit of complaining will I do!" When her mother turned, Tulip bent down, deftly scooping Mitten into her hand.

"And you will be putting the kitten down," said her mother. Sighing, Tulip complied.

"Be good, kitty," she said, stroking behind its ears. "Eat lots of mice." When she stood up her shoulders were drooping, and her lower lip trembled. "She was Millie's kitty," she whispered. "Millie gave her to me for safekeeping."

And Jeremy, who hadn't thought he could feel any worse, any more responsible for this entire predicament, found that it wasn't true. He thought about what would happen if he and his family were ever evacuated, or told they had to leave their home, and that they had only an

hour to pack, and that they'd never see their house, their town, their neighborhood, ever again. What would they take? How would it feel? How hard would it be to leave the place where they had built their life together?

"Mreow," said Mitten the kitten. Jeremy looked down to see it twining between his legs, butting its head on his ankle. *It's my fault,* he thought. *My fault that they have to leave. My fault that Tulip and Frederee have to leave the only home they've ever known. All my fault.*

He looked around, making sure that Tulip's mother was busy, then bent down and swiftly scooped the kitten up, tucking it into the pouch of his hooded sweatshirt. He could feel the kitten's claws pricking at the fabric as she settled herself against him while he hurried after Tulip.

Outside, in the twilight, the Yare were assembling by the fire. Jeremy could sense the same kind of impatience and regret he would sometimes feel at the end of a long vacation, as his parents scrambled around, checking and rechecking the rented house or hotel rooms to make sure they'd packed up everything and were not leaving anything important behind.

He saw that Frederee was carrying a baseball bat and a blue wool blanket. He also had a worn, one-eyed teddy bear tucked firmly under his arm. Frederee looked at Jeremy defiantly when he saw Jeremy stare. Old Aunt Yetta held a wooden box with iron bands, about twice the size of a shoebox. A stout leather strap ran around its sides, and let her carry it over her shoulder. All of the adults, men and women, had heavy-looking packs on their backs. All of them looked sad, except Ricardan and his wife, who looked both angry and smug.

Jeremy found Benjamin Burton having a conference with Old Aunt Yetta and Maximus. He touched Benjamin's sleeve. "Before we go, I have an idea," he said.

"Oh, you're not going with them," said Benjamin.

"But I thought—" Jeremy said.

Benjamin shook his head. "We have other work to do."

Jeremy nodded. He was following Benjamin down a path when another idea came to him. "Wait!" he called, and ran to catch up, to tell Benjamin what he'd thought of, and how it could work.

Benjamin listened, nodding, as Jeremy explained. "You're sure that this woman would trust you?" he asked.

Jeremy wasn't sure about that at all. "I think it's worth trying. I think that we'll need a way to tell the story to the world. And this will give us a shot."

Benjamin nodded. "We can try." He turned to Maximus and gripped the other Yare's arm, his big hand wrapping

around just beneath Maximus's elbow, so that the length of their arms were pressed together. Maximus settled his own hand on Benjamin's wrist.

"Brother," he said.

"Brother," Benjamin repeated. They gave each other a single nod, making Jeremy think about the conversation he'd seen. He guessed the men had forgiven each other, or—more likely, from what he'd seen of both men—decided to put their differences aside until the Tribe was safe.

Benjamin nodded once more, then stepped back. Jeremy stood beside him and watched as the Yare began to move, slipping silently off into the forest until they'd vanished into the darkness, leaving not a trace of themselves behind, not a single footprint or a wisp of smoke. None of them, not even the children, looked back.

"Where will they go?" Jeremy whispered.

"North," said Benjamin. His eyes were on the horizon, his expression sober. "To Vermont."

Jeremy felt like he could barely breathe. "And then what? What happens when they get there?"

Benjamin gave him a remote smile. "I guess we'll have to wait and see."

"Oh no," said Donnetta Dale an hour later. She held her hand, with its long, manicured fingers, up in front of her face, as if she couldn't even stand the sight of Jeremy Bigelow. Her face was as lovely as ever, with her dark-brown skin, high cheekbones, and big brown eyes, but her lipsticked lips were pursed, and her expression was skeptical. "Absolutely not. Fool me once, shame on you; fool me twice . . ."

Jeremy stepped aside and watched Donnetta's eyes widen as Benjamin Burton came striding into the news-room. Benjamin's legs were very long in his black jeans, and his face—his famous face—was almost entirely covered by his trademark beard and the mirrored sunglasses he was never without. Donnetta looked him over, from the tips of his cowboy boots to the top of his head. In a very small, very un-newscaster-ly voice, she said, "Oh."

"The boy was telling the truth," Benjamin said. His familiar, deep voice seemed to have gotten even deeper since their time among the Yare.

"About B-Bigfoots?" Donnetta stammered.

"They call themselves the Yare," Jeremy interjected. Benjamin gave him a look. Jeremy clamped his lips shut.

"We want to trade," said Benjamin Burton. "We'll give

you the story, as soon as it's safe, but we need to borrow a camera to shoot with."

Donnetta narrowed her eyes. "I didn't hear a date or a time in there. You'll give me this story when?"

"As soon as it's safe," Benjamin repeated. "Lives are at risk."

"And this is real?" asked Donnetta, still looking at him skeptically. "Like, really real?"

Benjamin held out his hand. Like a surgical nurse who'd been asked for a crucial piece of equipment, Jeremy slapped his phone against Benjamin's palm. Benjamin thumbed the screen to life and turned it so that Donnetta could see the picture of Maximus and Septima he'd taken, just before the Yare had walked into the forest. She leaned forward, eyes enormous, her breath misting the screen (Jeremy promised himself he'd never wipe it off again). But when she looked up, she was frowning, her expression even more skeptical.

"Costumes," she said. "Makeup. Fake fur. Hair extensions."

All Benjamin Burton said, in his quiet rumble, was, "No."

Donnetta looked back at the picture, then up at Benjamin again. "There have been rumors," she finally said. "I grew up in Standish, and for as long as I've been alive, I've heard them." She cut her eyes toward Jeremy. "Which is why I didn't laugh you out of the newsroom the first time you showed up here talking about Bigfoots."

Yare, Jeremy almost said, but this time he managed to keep his mouth shut.

"Hunters who've seen things," Donnetta said. "Campers who've woken up in the morning to find their coolers gone. Families who've lost sweatshirts and sheets off their clotheslines."

Jeremy, who'd read some of those stories on blogs and in the Community News section of the Standish newspaper, nodded, hoping that the rumors would be enough for Donnetta to trust them, and give them what they'd asked her for.

Donnetta cocked her head and narrowed her eyes at Benjamin. "How'd you get these shots? Who are you to them? How'd they let you get close enough to take a picture?"

"We'll explain all of that when the time is right," Benjamin said smoothly. "I promise. Do we have a deal?"

Donnetta blew out an exasperated breath. "Let me make sure I understand the terms first. I let you walk out

of here with an expensive piece of equipment that's only supposed to be used by our camera operators. In return, you promise to give me the exclusive on a story about the existence of Bigfoots at some unspecified date in the near future. Right?"

"Within two weeks," said Benjamin. "Three at the outside."

"Three weeks?" Donnetta widened her dark-brown eyes and flickered her lashes. "And what do I get if you don't deliver?"

"You have my promise," Benjamin said steadily. "You have my word."

She gave him a long, hard look. Then, sighing, muttering to herself about how this was dumb and she'd probably regret it, she bent down under her desk and removed a handled box the size of a carry-on suitcase made of sturdy, scuffed plastic. "You break it, you buy it," she murmured, and handed the case to Benjamin.

"We won't break it. And you won't be sorry."

"I hope not," Donnetta said. "I sincerely do."

CHAPTER 11

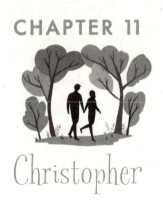

Christopher

By THE TIME HE'D TURNED THIRTY-FIVE, Christopher Jarvis understood the shape that the rest of his life would take. He would work long hours, his mind happily occupied with his research. He would drive the car he'd gotten just out of college, which still ran fine, and he would live in the same one-bedroom apartment that he'd leased when he'd gotten his first job. The place was small, and it had everything he needed: a sink and a shower for washing, a bed for sleeping, a refrigerator to store food and a microwave to heat it, and a table where he could sit as he ate. Once a week, he paid a woman to come and clean his place and do his laundry, and he'd arranged for a weekly delivery of groceries. His life ran smoothly, and if it also ran joylessly, Christopher had trained himself not to notice.

With the money his patents had earned him, he'd bought his parents a house in Cape Cod. His mother had cried, and his father had pumped his hand extra-hard, clapped him twice on the back, and said, "Proud of you, son," in a suspiciously gravelly voice, but Christopher himself had never liked spending time at the beach, or in the mountains. He'd never learned how to ski or to surf; he thought that hang gliding and skiing and snow-boarding were all unnecessarily risky and that hiking and mountain biking were both wastes of time that left you sore, sunburned, and bug-bitten. He'd never taken a trip he'd enjoyed. He had no hobbies, and no taste for fancy cars or clothes or expensive works of art. He did not attend concerts, or dine at fine restaurants, or spend time in museums or at movies or plays, because he'd never found a diversion he preferred to his research.

He would see his family four times a year: once on his mother's birthday, once on his father's, once to celebrate their anniversary, and once on Christmas. He never took vacations. The one time he'd tried to force himself to relax and enjoy a week on the beach in Hawaii, he'd stared out at the waves and the sunset and found his mind returning to experiments he'd been running on nematode worms. After three days, he'd changed his ticket and flown back home, back to his lab and his worms and his one-room apartment.

He'd realized, early on, that he would probably not have a spouse or a family. The family part didn't strike him as a terrible loss. Children were distractions. Worse, they were draining. They sucked up your energy, both physical and emotional. They exhausted your resources, your money, and your time. And unlike a project or an experiment, you never got to be completely done with a child; never reached the point where you could publish your findings, cash your check, and consider your work complete. Children never stopped needing you . . . and they'd keep coming back—after college, between jobs, after breakups or divorces, or in the wake of a layoff—to lie on your couch and lick their wounds and empty your refrigerator and your bank account. Sometimes, they'd even bring *their* children along, and you'd have to deal with two generations' worth of distractions.

Life without children didn't dismay him. But when he was in his twenties and thirties, during the silences of his drives home through the darkness, or in the early morning hours, when he'd eat his microwaved oatmeal sitting at his table, in the kitchen's single chair, Christopher could admit that he was lonely, that he would have liked to have found someone to share his life, and his successes, with. Someone who understood advanced math and science and, thus, could understand him; someone who didn't mind that he sometimes forgot about meals and, occasionally, showers, too, when he found himself in the grip of a big idea. Someone who could enjoy the five meals he'd taught himself to cook, or even teach him how to make a few more. Someone who liked to play Scrabble and chess, someone with whom he could exclaim over a sunset, or a thunderstorm, or the particular pale-blue, orange-tinted softness of the sky at twilight as it stretched over the unbroken surface of the water at his parents' place on the Cape. Maybe even someone who smelled nice, and whose skin felt soft when he touched it.

By the time he'd turned thirty-six, he was running his own research facility. He'd invented a number of other medications, including one for heartburn that was so successful that he could have retired after he'd patented the formula, and been obscenely, ridiculously rich for the rest of his life, even if he never worked another day of it. Of course, Christopher never even considered retiring. What would he do, if not work?

When candidates came to Jarvis Laboratories, the researcher in charge of whatever project the applicant was applying for would spend the day with them, asking them questions and seeing how they handled assignments and how they worked with the rest of the team. The human resources director would have them take tests and fill out forms. Finally, at the end of the interview day, one of the lab's senior scientists would take the candidate to dinner. Christopher's colleagues had referred to a new candidate as Dr. Gold when they'd set up the interview. Christopher hadn't thought to ask about a first name or a gender. Then, at seven o'clock on a Tuesday, a young woman with freckles and an impudent chin and wide-set brown eyes was knocking on the door of his lab.

He'd pushed up his goggles. "Yes?" he'd asked, in a tone that was just on the right side of rudeness.

"Christopher Jarvis?" He'd nodded, and she'd stuck out her hand, which was as small and freckled and capable-looking as the rest of her. "I'm Dr. Eleanor Gold, and I believe we're having dinner together tonight."

He'd looked down at her. When her hand had touched his, he'd felt the thing he'd read about, and heard sung about, but had never quite believed in—the lightning bolt, Cupid's arrow, love at first sight. It was, he would think

later, an instantaneous feeling of recognition, of knowing the person you were meant to spend the rest of your life with. Christopher Jarvis was a man of science, the farthest thing from a romantic . . . and yet. When Ellie had looked up at him with her brown eyes, when she'd touched him, he'd known.

He'd stammered an apology for losing track of time, and he'd looked around, frantically, for his car keys, managing to knock over a rack of test tubes in the process. He'd been apologizing for that when she'd touched his hand. "It's fine," she said. "No rush."

"Thank you," he'd said. Her single, gentle touch was echoing all the way through him. He was trying to remember if he'd been told anything about this plan, if a reservation had been made, if the restaurant was a place he'd be able to find. He hardly ever ate out, and when he did, it was always fast food, unless he was entertaining his parents.

Ellie must have sensed his confusion, because she took him by the arm and turned him toward the door. "Do you like Mexican?" she asked.

Knowing that he wouldn't be able to form words, Christopher had just nodded.

She led him to her car, a newer, nicer one than the car he had. She drove them to a restaurant. Soon, they were ensconced in a booth, with a candle in the center of the table, and they had a basket of chips and two kinds of salsa in front of them and margaritas on the way. Christopher remembered that this was what dates felt like. It had been years, but he could remember sitting in the dark, with a woman who could make your whole body tingle with just a look or a touch.

Except this wasn't meant to be a date. It was a job interview, and he was, potentially, going to be this young woman's boss. He tried to pull himself together, worried that he'd scare her off. He could already tell that he liked her, a lot. The last thing he wanted to do was make her think he was a weirdo with no social skills (even though he was a weirdo with no social skills). So he sat, munching chips and sipping his drink, struggling through the small talk, reminding himself to chew with his mouth closed, trying not to stare. Christopher had no idea whether Ellie was beautiful by objective standards, with her freckles and her wide-set eyes and the enthusiastic way she gestured when she spoke, but he thought she was beautiful, and enchanting, the most desirable woman he'd ever seen.

He was grateful when she took charge of the conversation. He learned that Ellie had grown up outside of

Washington, DC, and that she was the daughter of two English professors. Her older twin sisters were named Lyric and Sonnet, and by the time Eleanor surprised her parents twelve years later with her arrival, her parents had exhausted their entire store of creative names, along with most of their energy. "They were happy to just let me be, and I was happy to be left alone," she said, and Christopher nodded, understanding perfectly. She told him about the science camp her parents had found for her, and when he'd asked if she'd always been interested in science, she'd laughed and said, "Only after my first summer at camp. I think they choose it because it started the day after regular school got out, and went all the way through Labor Day, and they took overnight campers who were only seven years old."

"Were you lonely?" Christopher asked. He was thinking how much he would have liked it if his parents had sent him to a place like that, and he'd nodded when Ellie said, "Oh, no! I loved it! I think I knew from the first time I saw an amoeba under a microscope's lens that I was going to be a scientist."

"Me too," he said. "That's just the way it was for me, too."

She raised an eyebrow. "You have twin sisters with

ridiculous names and parents who sent you away for two months when you were seven?"

"No, no. Not that. The science—the way you knew. I knew too. Only it was frogs, not amoebas, for me." He could remember sixth-grade biology class, the nose-crinkling smell of the formaldehyde, the way some of the girls had squealed and pulled their collars up over their noses, and how even Keith Mulkeen, the classroom bully, had looked a little pale at the sight of the frogs, their limbs pinned down on the black wax trays. Christopher had bent over the frog, scalpel in hand, and he'd forgotten the girls, and Keith, and the smell, and the teacher. The classroom had faded away, until there was nothing but the glide of the blade through the frog's thin-skinned abdomen; his first sight of its tiny heart and, with it, the understanding that every living creature was like that—a series of tiny, perfect machines, all working beneath their skins. It had left him breathless.

"I thought about being a surgeon . . ." Ellie was saying.

"Me too!" he exclaimed. "Neurosurgery!"

"Pediatric cardiology for me," she said, smiling. "But then I realized that I liked research better than treating patients."

"Me too," Christopher said again. He'd arrived at the

same conclusion after several professors had pointed out that even a neurosurgeon had to have a little bit of a bedside manner and could not, for example, tell a mother with trembling lips and teary eyes that the chances of her newborn son surviving were "minimal at best," or announce to a grieving husband that his wife would be "profoundly altered" after her surgery, assuming she survived.

When the waitress came, order pad in hand, Christopher and Ellie blinked at each other, realizing that they hadn't even opened their menus. "What's your favorite thing?" Ellie asked the waitress, who recommended the enchilada sampler platter.

"What do you think?" Ellie asked, eyebrows lifted. Christopher blurted that it sounded fine, and Ellie turned back to the waitress, ordering two enchilada sampler platters and another round of drinks.

Ellie told him that she'd gone to Harvard, then MIT; that she'd studied medical genetics, working with professors to extract and analyze DNA from skeletons more than forty-thousand years old. When Christopher asked her what her thesis was about, though, she'd gotten vague.

"I researched genetic mutations," she said.

"What kind of mutations?" he asked.

She picked a corn chip out of the basket and nibbled away one of its corners, her expression suddenly serious, her eyebrows—a few shades darker than her hair—angled down like a bird's wings. He saw that she was trying to make up her mind, trying to decide how complete of an answer to give him, and he understood her caution—after all, he'd be one of the people deciding whether or not she got the job. Although he knew by then that he was going to hire her, even if it turned out her dissertation was about butterscotch pudding recipes, or Shakespeare's tragedies, or if it turned out that she didn't know any science at all. He was enchanted. Him, Christopher Wayne Jarvis, a man of science, utterly ensorcelled, as completely in her power as if she'd cast a spell on him.

"Okay," she'd finally said. She wriggled around in her seat, squaring her shoulders. "Kingdom, phylum, class, order, family, genus, species," she rattled off, lifting a finger for each category. "Where do human beings split off from apes?"

"Genus," he said promptly.

She picked up another corn chip and broke it into four pieces, lining them up in a row, separating them as she gave each one a label.

"Four species. *Homo neanderthalensis. Homo erectus.*

Homo habilis. And, finally, *Homo sapiens.*" She tapped the last corn chip. "We're the only ones left. The end of the line; the final product of millions of years of evolution. All the others are extinct. Right?" Christopher nodded. Ellie sat back, eyes shining in the candlelight.

"That's what we've all been taught. That's what science has proved. But who's to say that there aren't more?"

"More species?" He stared at her. She stared right back, her gaze direct and challenging, that pugnacious chin lifted, like she was ready for a fight.

"Species that evolved alongside us," she said. "Species that mutated to adapt to their environment, the way *homo sapiens* did."

"You . . . believe this?" he said. He hadn't meant to sound incredulous, but as soon as he'd spoken, he realized that he did.

Her eyes narrowed. Then she smiled at him. "Let's just say I don't *not* believe it. Listen," she said, and reached across the table. When she touched his hand, Christopher felt the world go swimmy, as something warm and sparkling wrapped around his heart and cupped it gently. "Scientists are discovering and reclassifying new species all the time. As recently as 2012, they found chimpanzees living in caves, using spears, the way humans do. The researchers that discovered them are in the process of deciding if they're really chimpanzees, or if they're part of some completely new species."

"Okay," Christopher countered. "But that's reclassifying the offshoot of species that scientists already knew existed. You're talking about discovering something that no one else believes is real."

"Yet," Ellie said softly. When he stared, she said, "Something that no one else believes is real *yet*."

She sat back, smiling. Christopher could feel that his face was flushed and that his mouth was dry. He realized that he'd forgotten to be nervous, forgotten about his awkwardness, forgotten that he was odd and lonely and hadn't been on a date since high school; forgotten all of it in the pleasure of being in Ellie Gold's company, of listening to her and arguing with her and talking about science to someone who understood, and who loved it the same way that he did. He hypothesized that her freckled skin would be soft if he touched it, and that she'd smell like lavender honey, and that her body would fit neatly against him if he were to wrap his arm around her shoulder and pull her close.

"Okay," she said cheerfully. "Here's where the woo-woo comes in." She sat up very straight, moving one of

the corn chip pieces off to the side of the table. "People on every continent except Antarctica have reported seeing creatures whose descriptions more or less match what we call Bigfoots. Just like almost every culture has some kind of story about creatures that are part human, part fish. Now, maybe that's all just a coincidence . . ."

"Or manatees," he interjected. "Didn't researchers eventually decide that the creatures sailors had been calling mermaids were actually manatees?"

She gave him a nod. The smile on her face looked good-natured, but her eyes still had that narrowed intensity that made her look like a hunter stalking her prey.

"I don't know if I believe in Bigfoots or mermaids. But I don't *not* believe. I'm keeping an open mind. I'm looking for evidence. I'm bringing scientific rigor to the question. I'm treating it like any other hypothesis."

Christopher Jarvis put the pieces of what she'd said together. "You're looking for Bigfoot," he said.

"I'm . . . well. Put it this way. I wouldn't be disappointed if someone were to find one somewhere. Oh, hooray!" she exclaimed, clapping her hands as the waitress set two steaming platters in front of them. "I love enchiladas!" She picked up her fork and dove enthusiastically into her dinner.

Christopher lifted his own fork. He was starting to feel like he'd been hit on the head, or like he was having a very strange dream. Maybe this was a joke. Maybe his friends—well, not friends, he didn't really have friends, exactly, but he did have colleagues, and so maybe his colleagues at the lab had set this up, had found this willing woman and gotten her to pretend that she was a scientist, and spin him some story about Bigfoots and Yetis and mermaids and leprechauns, frolicking around a pot of gold. He might be the boss, but the other researchers at the lab laughed at him, Christopher knew that they did. They talked about his awkwardness and probably speculated as to whether he'd ever been kissed (the answer to that was yes, but it had been years ago, when he was thirteen, playing Seven Minutes in Heaven at Logan Zinberg's bar mitzvah, and the girl he'd been kissing thought that she was in the closet with Brad Philips). Christopher knew that he was gawky and odd, he knew that he forgot to get regular haircuts or buy new clothes; he knew that the only reason he remembered to do things like shower and brush his teeth was that, back in college, his roommates had held an intervention and had put a checklist on their suite's door that read CHRIS, DID YOU SHOWER? BRUSH YOUR TEETH? ARE

YOU WEARING DEODORANT? IF THE ANSWER TO ANY OF THESE QUESTIONS IS "NO" THEN TURN AROUND AND FIX IT.

He was weird and odd and awkward, and he'd long ago accepted that it was unlikely that he would ever fall in love and get married. Mostly, it didn't bother him. He could appreciate women the same way he could appreciate a work of art, a painting that hung in a museum, knowing that it wouldn't be coming home with him, that night or any night.

But this—this was like sitting in a restaurant across from a work of art that he'd stolen or spirited off the walls. A beautiful, magical, engaging, funny, sweet, eminently lovable piece of art, that rarest of things: a woman who seemed to like him. A woman who also, he reminded himself, believed in mythological creatures and fairy tales.

"So why, uh, mutations?" he asked, as Ellie made short work of her bean enchilada and started in on her chicken one. "I mean, how'd you get interested in it?"

She bent her head, running her finger around the rim of her drink, gathering salt. He studied the set of her shoulders, the way the part in her hair was slightly zigzaggy, and how her nose turned up, very slightly, at the tip.

"Because I saw one." Her chin jutted out, like she expected him to argue with her.

He couldn't help himself from sounding a little incredulous. "What, a Bigfoot?"

She ducked her head and spoke quietly. "A mermaid. When I was a little girl." When she looked up, her eyes were flashing. "And I know you probably think I'm crazy . . ."

He didn't think that she was crazy. A scientist with her mind and her training and education wouldn't have latched onto a fantasy and pursued it with such diligence for so long. Probably there was something there. But most of him was not thinking about science at all. Most of him was thinking that she was beautiful and brilliant and that he wanted to spend the rest of his life right here, with her, in their private little corner of the restaurant, or on an island near the sea. They could buy a little sailboat and go looking for mermaids together.

"But it isn't just me. That's the important piece." She'd set down her silverware and was moving her hands, gesturing for emphasis. "The scientific piece. It's story after story after story, in culture after culture, all over the world, for thousands of years, describing the same creatures, sometimes in the same language. And I don't care if people think I'm crazy . . ."

Christopher startled himself by reaching across the table and taking Ellie's hands. He rarely touched other people intentionally, and other people hardly touched him. In fact, he couldn't remember being this close to another human being since his last trip to Cape Cod, when his father had given him a handshake and his mother had kissed him goodbye. "I don't think you're crazy," he said. "I believe you."

Ellie's mouth had gone a little slack. Her gaze locked on his, and he felt it again, that pleasant, shivery feeling, like every cell of his body was quivering. Like he was completely awake for the first time in his life.

"I believe you," he said again, and squeezed her hands.

"Really?" she asked, looking incredulous, stunned and happy. "You do?"

"I promise. I do. And if you come work for me, I'd be honored to set you up with a lab . . . and assistants . . . we can apply for grants . . ." He was halfway through promising her something else—probably an unlimited budget, or her own private jet—when she got to her feet, learned across the table, took his face in her hands, and kissed him, right on the mouth. A few patrons at the nearby tables started clapping. "Get it, girl!" one of them called. Christopher could feel himself blushing, shame spiking his blood.

They're laughing at me, he thought. Then he realized that they weren't. They were laughing with him, sharing in his joy. They were cheering him on. They were happy for him.

So he cupped the back of Ellie's head in one of his hands, leaned so far across the table that his tie was practically dangling in the lit candle, and kissed her back, thinking, *I will never let you go.*

Forty years later, Christopher Jarvis stared out into the darkness, the absolute black of a moonless winter night in Vermont. It was starting, he thought. Or, rather, it had started, had already begun. The trap he'd been building for years was starting to close, with his targets squeezed between its jaws, soon to be impaled upon its teeth. Run through and bleeding, dying in agony, he thought, and smiled thinly. Which was better than what they deserved.

He stood on the third floor of his Vermont estate, on the narrow railed deck that went around it, the one the architect had told him was called a widow's walk. "They'd build them on houses by the sea. The wives of the sailors would stand and keep watch for their husbands," the woman had explained. Her eyes had gone misty. "Isn't that romantic?"

"Romantic," Christopher echoed, knowing it was what she expected to hear. Later, when they'd been touring the upstairs rooms, Ellie had grabbed his hand and whispered, *If I was a ship captain and I was out at sea during a storm, would you keep watch?*

Oh, at least for a few hours, he'd told her. Which was a lie. He'd wait for her forever. *What about you?*

I'd give it week, she'd said. *Then I'd hook up with Trevor Freeh.* Trevor Freeh ran their security division. He bred champion English bulldogs in his spare time, and with his squat body and jowly, wrinkled face, he sort of looked like one himself, but Ellie said she found him handsome, that she found bald men "distinguished."

Christopher felt his throat tighten at the memory, felt traitorous tears fill his eyes. He'd had such a good time with her. That was what he missed the most, the part that hurt the worst. Ellie had taught him how to tease, and how to be teased, and he'd learned that there was no better feeling than making his wife laugh, or seeing her contented smile. Every morning, he'd get up early, make a pot of coffee, and bring her the first cup in bed, and at night, she'd play pop music in the kitchen and he'd sit at the counter, watching her dance while she cooked.

And then she'd died, and his days had become so quiet

that they practically echoed, and he couldn't remember the last time anyone had teased him, or the last time he'd laughed.

In the darkness, in the empty house, after all those Ellie-less years, he felt his smile become a snarl. He could feel the wind on his teeth. *Soon,* he told himself. Soon.

So far, everything had worked the way he'd intended. The town was a machine he'd engineered and fine-tuned and greased with money and favors until he'd eliminated any possibility of failure. Now they were coming. Coming for him! The thought of it—the very idea that their ragtag band of Bigfoots and humans and children could defeat him—made him smile.

Let them come, he thought. He'd be ready. Everything was happening according to plan; the pieces on the chess-board were positioned just where he wanted them. He would get what he wanted. He would see his wife avenged.

Oh, darling, he heard Ellie mourning, way in the back of his mind. *This isn't what I wanted. Not for me. Not for you.*

He silenced the voice, grimacing savagely, snarling into the darkness. *I love you, Ellie,* he thought . . . and he tried to ignore the whisper that said, over and over, in his dead wife's voice, *You're more of a monster than they are.*

PART TWO

CHAPTER 12

Christopher

CHRISTOPHER JARVIS REMEMBERED WHEN HE and his wife had found their first Bigfoot.

In 1983, a pair of teenagers had been hiking in the Green Mountains. They'd made their way into an unexplored cave, high on a ridge, and had walked all the way to the back of it (probably looking for a secluded make-out spot, had been Ellie's guess). There, they'd found a pile of rocks, almost a pyramid, something that could not have been accidental. The girl was a college freshman who'd taken an anthropology course and had some idea of what she was looking at. Carefully, she and her boyfriend had pulled apart the cairn, stone by stone, removing enough of it to reveal a hand, large and clawed and furred. To their credit, neither kid had touched it. They had backed out of the cave, taking care not to disturb anything. They'd marked the cave's entrance, and raced down the mountain to find a pay phone and call the police.

In the years that followed that fortuitous discovery, Christopher and Ellie would marvel at their good fortune, the way the stars had aligned to give them what they'd been looking for.

If that girl hadn't been a college student who'd taken some anthropology, Ellie would begin. If she'd just been a regular old standard-issue female, the cops would have told her she was being hysterical and imagining things.

If she hadn't stopped digging as soon as she saw the claws.

If your program hadn't worked so well.

If the captain hadn't said *Bigfoot*.

If we'd been any slower, getting to Vermont. Getting a helicopter. Getting to the top of that mountain.

We are so lucky, she'd say, lips curved into that familiar smile, eyes sparkling with the remembered thrill of the hunt.

But Christopher knew that it wasn't luck. The truth was that his wife had been brilliant. Back in the early days of computers, before everyone in the world had a laptop

and a smartphone, Ellie had made a list of keywords—
Bigfoot, Yeti, Sasquatch, nonhuman primate. The same
terms a boy named Jeremy Bigelow would search for on
the Internet, many years later. Ellie wrote a program that
taught a computer how to "listen" to police radio channels
all over the country. If the computer heard one of those
words on the frequencies restricted for law-enforcement
use, it pinged Ellie. For years, mostly what she'd gotten
were false alarms—a dispatcher in Maine ribbing his
partner about looking like a Sasquatch when he forgot
to shave; kids in Alabama making a prank 911 call about a
skull they'd found in the marsh that turned out to belong
to a possum.

That day, the alert she'd received had been real. "Lady
said she didn't know what it was," the chief of police
had said, when Ellie had gotten him on the phone. "Like
human, only bigger," the officer calling the dispatcher
had said.

Ellie had listened, her eyes getting wide and her
cheeks getting pink, and when she finally spoke, she
winked at Christopher, and then started lying to the
man with a fluency her husband had never imagined
she possessed. "We work for the government," Ellie had
said. Which was true only insofar as Jarvis Industries

had gotten a grant from the Centers for Disease Control three years ago to research a possible treatment for Lyme disease. "We are claiming federal jurisdiction over the site," Ellie had said. "It is imperative that you not allow anyone else into the cave. We appreciate your help, and your diligence, but we'll take it from here."

Five minutes after she'd hung up the phone, they were in a car, on their way to Teterboro Airport. Thirty minutes after that, they were in a plane, on their way north. They took a helicopter to the top of the mountain, and, two hours after the program had pinged her, they were standing at the mouth of a cave, with the fresh September wind ruffling their hair. Christopher had a shovel in his hand; Ellie held a kit full of brushes, each one tinier than the next, for whisking dirt off bones. His hand reached for hers as they peered into the darkness, and they clutched each other, and their flashlights, as they stumbled along. Like children, he thought. Children in a fairy tale, lost in the woods.

The cairn was all the way in the back of the cave, beneath a low-hanging ledge of rock. Ellie had crouched down and duckwalked to the end of the cave. She'd knelt at the cairn and photographed it from every angle before starting to pull away the rocks, moving with care and deliberation, taking her time, stopping often to take pictures or to murmur into her little tape recorder. Her hands were deft and gentle as she pulled off the final layer, revealing the corpse of what looked like a man, only larger. He was dressed in a pair of faded denim overalls and a clean plaid shirt, a man with white fur on his face and neck and chest and long, dark, curving claws at the ends of his hands.

He'd been buried with a book called *Best-Loved Classics of Poetry* on his chest and a gold pocket watch on a chain in his hand. The watched had been engraved with the words "AUDEN. Beloved of FAMILY. Beloved of GOD."

For a moment, they'd just stared. Then Ellie had bent down. She'd pressed two fingers against her lips and then brought them down to hover above the Bigfoot's forehead. Christopher saw tears cutting tracks through the dust on her cheeks. He'd wanted to hold her, but he wasn't sure if she wanted congratulations or comfort, if she was feeling triumph or sorrow or something else entirely. They'd been together for years by then, and in that moment, she seemed like a stranger to him, completely unreadable.

"Real," she'd whispered. Then she'd said it again. "Real."

They'd moved the body themselves, donning gloves, working carefully to wrap it in plastic and shift it onto the helicopter, whose pilot was ex-military, sworn to secrecy, and who'd been told that they'd gone to recover evidence from a crime scene. He'd flown them back to the airport, and a plane had brought them back to their lab. They'd stayed up for three days and three nights, running tests on blood and bones, skin and nails and teeth, cells and DNA.

By the end of it, Christopher had been giddy and depleted, practically hallucinating with exhaustion and adrenaline. "It can't be true."

"But it is." From the bones, they had learned that the Bigfoot—Auden, as Ellie always called him—had been over two hundred years old when he died.

"Why did they bury him there?" Christopher asked.

"I don't know," she'd said, and yawned hugely. For three days they'd been subsisting on delivery pizza and soda and bags of chips from the vending machine, taking turns napping on the couch in Christopher's office, with a security guard positioned just outside the lab's door. "I think the tribes are itinerant. Maybe they weren't always, but now, to stay hidden, they'd have to be. Maybe they had to bury him quickly and keep moving, so they wouldn't be discovered." She bit her lip. "I think he had children. Those names on the watch . . ."

The watch had been engraved with more than a dozen names. Celie. Cade. Malleny. Apple. Mollis. Fenn.

"His blood," Christopher said. "If we can figure out how to clone his DNA, how to translate his immune system, and his strength, to human subjects . . ." He'd let his voice trail off, not wanting to risk speaking out loud what he'd hoped for.

As always, Ellie was braver than he was. "We can end diseases." Her eyes were full of tears. Maybe she'd been thinking about her mother, who'd died of heart disease, or her father, who'd had cancer.

"And the practical applications," he'd said. "We could give people endless energy. Reduce their need to eat, or sleep."

At that, Ellie's expression had become less exultant. She'd bitten her lip, her expression troubled, but Christopher had barely noticed. He was on a roll.

"Think of what the government would pay us to have a patent on that. An army of soldiers who never have to stop to rest or eat." He'd grabbed her hands, giddy and thrilled, and cried, "We're going to be so rich! We're going to live forever!"

He remembered how she'd looked at him, the way her eyes crinkled at the corners as she frowned. "You mean our names will live forever. Because of our discoveries. Our research," she'd said, each word precise. Later, he'd realized that she was giving him an escape route, a way out. But he hadn't been smart enough to take it.

"No, I mean literally. Our buddy in there"—he'd cocked his thumb toward the lab, barely noticing the way Ellie had flinched at his casual tone and gesture—"he was, what, two hundred and change when he died? And that was without doctors, or medicine, or dentists. Think, Ellie! Once we figure out how to copy what he had, how to make it safe . . ." He paused to take a breath and pull his wife into his arms. His insides were fizzing, like he was full of popcorn kernels that were exploding, one after another. "We—you and I—we could live forever."

"But why would we want to?" she'd asked. Her face was puzzled, and Christopher had just stared at her in silence. *Because I love you. Because we're happy. Because I'm afraid of what comes after. Because I never want to be without you.*

Instead of saying any of that, he'd asked her, "Aren't you happy? Don't you want this to last forever?"

She'd pulled away from him. Slowly, she'd said, "I am happy. You know I am. I love you, and I love my work. I love our life. I can't imagine being any happier or more

fulfilled." She'd looked at him then, her eyes clear and her gaze steady. "But I don't want it to last forever. I think that what makes it so wonderful is that it won't be forever. It will end, someday. Hopefully not for a long time. But, to me, the idea that there's an end . . . it makes everything sweeter. Do you understand?"

No, he'd thought, but hadn't said.

She'd extricated herself from his embrace, taken him by the hands, and led him back to the couch. Sitting by his side, she'd said, "It would be greedy, to ask for more than what we're given. Eighty years, ninety years, long enough to see your children safely into the world, to have some fun and do some good, to do work that matters . . . that's what I want. That's all I want."

Christopher pulled Ellie against him, stroking her cheek with his thumb. He held her there for a long time, feeling her heart beating against his chest, memorizing the smell of her hair and the feel of her skin. He wished he could pull her inside him and keep her there, forever close, forever safe.

"We're going to do great things," he had said, holding her close, and God, if he could have gone back to that day, to that moment, he would have told her how much he loved her, how proud he was to be married to her. He would have told her that she was brilliant and creative and beautiful, and that she astonished him every day. She hadn't known she was pregnant yet—that wouldn't happen for another six weeks, when she'd come out of the bathroom, with her wet hair tangled around her shoulders and her bathrobe belted around her waist, holding the pregnancy test aloft and crowing with delight. The seeds of the cancer that would eventually kill her might have already been moving around her bloodstream, sending out roots, like malignant flowers. Even in that moment of triumph, she might have already been sick, on her way to dying. *But aren't all of us dying, every minute we're alive?* Christopher could imagine Ellie asking, her eyes full of love and regret.

But in that moment, neither of them had had any idea. Ellie had tilted her head, looking at him, her cheeks pink and eyes sparkling, as beautiful as she'd ever been, just fifty feet and a single doorway from the table where a dead Bigfoot lay, and repeated his words back to him. "We're going to do great things."

CHAPTER 13

Jessica

AFTER A LENGTHY GOOGLE SEARCH, JESSICA was forced to conclude that there were no hotels or motels in Upland. The only place for out-of-towners to stay was the Upland Inn, a bed-and-breakfast in a rambling old farmhouse on a ridge that overlooked the town square. Jessica and her nana had been lucky enough to get the last room available that night. "We redid the kitchen just last year, and all the bathrooms, too," the owner, Mrs. Mary Hughes, said as she led Jessica and Nana through the property. "Now, you'll be staying in the new wing, which was originally constructed in 1923."

Nana murmured something polite, and Jessica swallowed a yawn. They had left New Jersey in their stolen car at about four o'clock that afternoon, and had driven north for five hours, sticking to the back roads, where there were no sensors to read EZ-Passes or automated cameras to take pictures of speeders. Nana drove carefully, sticking to the speed limit, stopping every two hours so that they could stretch and use the facilities, whether they needed them or not (Nana usually needed). While she drove, she'd instructed Jessica to find them somewhere to stay. Jessica had used Nana's phone to find the bed-and-breakfast and reserve the room (she was confident her parents would try every friend she'd ever made before figuring out that Jessica had gone on the run with her grandmother, so she felt fine about using Nana's phone).

While Mrs. Hughes prattled about the antique quilts on all the beds and how the sideboard (whatever that was) in the parlor was a genuine Hepplewhite (whatever that meant), Jessica tried to look politely interested. She could tell from the look on her grandmother's face that all Nana wanted was the key to their room, followed by a hot shower and a good night's sleep, but Nana smiled politely as Mrs. Hughes had chattered her way from the front porch, where she'd met them, through the dining room ("Breakfast is served from seven to eight thirty, but if you're an early bird, I usually have coffee on by six,") and the living room and a room she called the parlor ("The board games and the DVDs are available to any guest who wants to use them, as are the books."). Finally, she'd led them up a steep flight of stairs to the second floor. "Your bedroom is the last door on the right." The only thing that slowed Mrs. Hughes's twittering was Nana's question about the big house, high on the hill, the one they could see through the round window at the end of the bed-and-breakfast's hallway. "My granddaughter and I couldn't help but notice it on our way to town. Quite an impressive-looking place."

"That's the Jarvis mansion," said Mrs. Hughes. Her voice had lost a few degrees of warmth. "Do you know Jarvis Industries? The founder lives there."

"Jarvis Industries," Nana said. Her voice was thoughtful. "They're the pharmaceutical company, right?"

"Among other things," said Mrs. Hughes, who seemed eager to change the subject.

"So Dr. Jarvis lives here in Upland. Have you met him?" Nana asked.

Mrs. Hughes's mouth had gone from a smile to a

thin, straight line. She shook her head briefly. "I haven't had the honor."

"It's surprising, isn't it, that a scientist like him would choose a place like this," Nana said.

Mrs. Hughes attempted to reboot her smile. She did not quite succeed. "Well, I don't know if you've ever been in Vermont in the fall, but our foliage is lovely!" she said, her voice aggressively cheery. "And there's the mountains, of course, for skiing and snowboarding. And it's peaceful here. Quiet. Away from the hustle and bustle of the city. Maybe he was ready for a change."

When they'd checked in, Mrs. Hughes had plucked a key from a pegboard by the front door. Now she pulled it out of her pocket and used it to unlock the bedroom door. "Here is the Green Room, which gets lovely southern exposure in the morning. I'm sure you and your granddaughter will be very comfortable." Her tone was still friendly, but her shoulders were stiff as she led them into a pretty room with pale-green walls, a fire crackling in the fireplace, hardwood floors, and a pair of high, canopied beds. A girl with brown hair pulled back in a ponytail, who seemed to be a few years older than Jessica, came hurrying out of the bathroom.

"I was just checking the towels," she said in a low

voice. Mrs. Hughes gave the girl a hard look, then smiled at Jessica and her nana.

"This is my granddaughter Charlotte. She helps out around the inn. If you need anything—towels, toothbrushes, anything at all—just let her know."

Charlotte bobbed her head quickly and hurried out of the room. Mrs. Hughes peered into the bathroom. Jessica wondered if she was checking her granddaughter's work.

"Now, we've left enough firewood to see you through the night, but if you need any help—"

Before she could finish her sentence, one of the doors along the long hallway swung open and a head popped out. Jessica felt her mouth drop open when she saw Alice Mayfair, who seemed to have gotten taller, more adult-looking, than she'd been when Jessica had seen her in New York City just that morning.

"Alice!" Jessica squealed, and ran toward the other girl, arms outstretched, as if Alice was her long-lost, very best friend. In a way, she thought, Alice was her very best friend, even though she hadn't been lost for that long. They'd been through something traumatic together . . . and, Jessica suspected, there were worse things looming.

She barely had time to think all of that before Alice came barreling toward her, and the two of them collided in a hug. "You're here!" Jessica said, with her arms around Alice's shoulders. "You're okay! I can't believe it! Oh my God, I am SO GLAD to see you!"

Alice made a noise somewhere between a laugh and a sob. "I'm glad to see you, too," she said. "My mom's here. And Millie. And a—a friend of ours named Miss Merriweather." She lowered her voice. "They were the ones in the car. The ones who got me away from those guys."

"Wow," said Jessica, as she tried to take it in. "So that was your mom? The one who, like, tackled that guy?"

Alice looked shyly proud. "That was her."

"And Miss Merriweather—she's not an educational consultant, is she?" Jessica asked.

"She's a little more than that," said Alice, looking startled. "Do you know her?"

"She's the one who told my parents to send me to the Experimental Center."

Alice nodded, like she wasn't surprised.

"You two young ladies know each other?" Mrs. Hughes asked. The girls pulled apart and turned to find the proprietress giving them an indulgent smile.

"We go to school together," Alice said.

"We're friends," Jessica said firmly.

The woman's eyes narrowed. "And you didn't plan on being here in Upland at the same time?"

"No. Crazy coincidence, right?" Jessica said. Even as she spoke, she realized how unlikely that sounded. She wondered how Alice knew to come here, whether Alice had figured out Jessica's grandfather's connection to the abduction attempt. If she had, it meant that Alice, too, knew something about Jessica's grandfather, and that, maybe, Alice was here to do the same thing Jessica intended. To stop Christopher Jarvis. To stop him, and to save the people he was hunting.

"And Millie's here too?" Jessica asked.

"In the room," Alice murmured. "She's not feeling well."

Jessica could only imagine. Millie had a skin condition, and was homeschooled. She was unsophisticated and shy. She used odd turns of phrase when she spoke. The modern world seemed to bewilder her, and big cities left her terrified. Whatever Millie had imagined for the day, it couldn't have included a kidnapping attempt, a high-speed chase, and a road trip hundreds of miles north to a place she'd never been. Jessica imagined that Millie was curled up in a closet somewhere, holding her knees to her chest and rocking with her eyes squeezed tight.

"How did you get here?" Alice was asking. "How did you know to come?"

"Long story." Jessica took Alice's hand and squeezed it. Alice looked startled—she and Jessica were no longer enemies, but they hadn't ever been friends. After a brief hesitation, she squeezed back.

"Well, this is an amazing coincidence!" Mrs. Hughes's voice was loud, her tone was hearty and somehow false, but Jessica couldn't be bothered to think about it. She wanted to hear Alice's story, to learn what had happened to the two of them and find out everything Alice knew. "I'm sure it's way past everyone's bedtime, so I'll let you all get some sleep."

"Thank you," said Jessica, remembering her manners. "Nana, this is Alice. She's a friend from the Experimental Center for Love and Learning."

Nana cocked her head. "Is that what they call your school?"

Jessica nodded.

"It's lovely to meet you, Alice," Nana said, and yawned widely. "I think it's my bedtime."

"Good night!" Jessica said, and followed Alice down the hall.

CHAPTER 14

Charlotte

NONE OF THE VISITORS SAW CHARLOTTE
Hughes when she stepped into the shadowed alcove at
the end of the hallway, her arms full of dirty towels and
her face watchful and wary. None of them noticed her
turn and walk quickly up the back staircase, the one that
had been built for servants to use, so they could move
between floors while staying out of sight of the home's
wealthy owners. Charlotte slipped into her bedroom, a
tiny room in the attic. She pulled a key out from inside
a ceramic bunny that sat on her dresser, and used it to
unlock a drawer in her desk. The drawer was empty
except for a brand-new cell phone. On the first day of

school, every year since she'd made the deal with the Jarvis people, Charlotte would find a brand-new phone, still in its case, in her locker. Charlotte plugged it in, turned it on, and watched as the screen bloomed into life. She'd never used the phone. She'd never had to use it. Not until today.

Charlotte bit her lip and pressed the button to dial the only number saved in the phone's memory. When the phone rang, she tucked it under her chin, leaning against the wall with her eyes squeezed shut. She pulled the elastic band out from her hair and twisted it around and around her index finger, so tightly that her fingertip went first red, then white.

After four rings, a man's voice answered. "Hello?"

Charlotte stood up very straight. "Yes," she said. "This is—"

"I know who you are," said the voice, which sounded bored, and rude, almost like whoever owned it was sneering. Charlotte ignored the unpleasant feeling that gave her.

"Three girls and three women just checked in. One of the girls I couldn't really see—she had a sweatshirt with the hood pulled up over her face." Charlotte paused and made herself take a breath. "The other two were white girls, maybe twelve or thirteen. One with bushy red hair, the other with brown hair. Two of the women were older,

and they were both white. The third was a white woman with red hair in her thirties. I don't know their names." The women had all paid cash for their rooms. They'd given their names as Jane Smith, Mary Johnson, and Carol Hathaway, and had declined an invitation to sign the guest register. When Charlotte's grandmother said, "We usually do a five-hundred-dollar hold on a credit card," "Jane Smith," the red-haired woman, had pulled five crisp hundred-dollar bills and slid them across the desk.

"We'll be in touch," the voice on the other end of the line said, and ended the call. No *Thank you for your help*, no *Good job.* Charlotte sank down on her bed, remembering that her grandma always said that a job well done was its own reward. Charlotte had done what she'd promised. She could just hope that her duty was completed. The sinking, unsettled feeling in her belly, the watery sensation in her knees, and the quivering in her thigh muscles suggested otherwise, that her work wasn't over, that they'd be asking for more. *You aren't going to get off that easy,* said a voice in her head.

Almost everyone in Upland loved Jarvis Industries, and how the company had brought the town back to life. The First Methodist Church had gotten a fresh coat of paint, the roads downtown received a fresh layer of asphalt, the playground's rusty equipment had been replaced by a new playscape, with a climbing structure, swings and slides, and rubberized mat floors. Sleek new apartment buildings had gone up on the outskirts of town, where ground had been broken for a country club, with a golf course and a swimming complex and eight tennis courts.

Those things—and the new bookstore, and the brewery, and the new Indian restaurant—kept people happy. According to Charlotte's grandmother, they also kept them from asking too many questions about what was really going on beyond the walls and razor wire that circled the Jarvis Industries complex, where you needed two forms of ID just to drive through the gates, and where uniformed men and women with guns guarded the perimeter. The *Upland Crier* said they were researching new drugs—cures for cancer, cures for diabetes—and that the security measures were meant to deter corporate espionage. It made sense. Still, sometimes Charlotte would think about what her grandmother had said, about how the media was bought and paid for and wouldn't ask the hard questions. Jarvis Industries had purchased the town's empty malls and vacant lots and farmland. It had also bought the *Upland Crier*, the town's only newspaper, and was the largest underwriter of the nearest public radio station. How much scrutiny would those reporters give their own employer, or their owner, or the person who ultimately signed their paychecks? Not much, was Charlotte's guess.

For three years, Charlotte had done what she'd promised to do. She'd watched, and waited, and as the time had passed, she'd become more and more convinced that the whole thing was a joke, not a real job. Or maybe it wasn't a joke, but a test . . . and if she passed, maybe she'd go on to bigger things, real things. Maybe she'd even meet Dr. Christopher Jarvis himself. Nobody Charlotte knew had ever seen him in person. Dr. Jarvis, Charlotte sometimes thought, was like God in Upland. Maybe not God himself, the one Charlotte had grown up praying to in church on Sunday mornings, but at least *a* god. You knew he was there, you felt his presence and saw his works, but you never saw him.

He's testing me, Charlotte would think. She told herself that her grandmother was paranoid, a naive and unsophisticated old woman who'd believe whatever conspiracies the *National Examiner* was promoting. Charlotte did her best to ignore the rumors and whispers that circulated about Jarvis Industries and its research facility. About how Upland's woods used to be full of all kinds of wildlife, from deer and mice to squirrels and racoons, and how now the woods were empty, except for the owls and the crows. About how once, during a thunderstorm, hundreds of birds had fallen out of the sky, dead before they hit the ground. About how kids had gone missing.

Charlotte had kept her mind on the money, and the future. She told herself that her job was just a test and that Jarvis Industries wasn't doing anything illegal or immoral or wrong. She had made herself believe it . . . until she'd seen the girl in the sweatshirt. The girl had her hood pulled up and the drawstring pulled tight, but Charlotte had glimpsed dark, frightened eyes. And fur. And she'd understood that the bill had finally come due.

In her attic bedroom, on the edge of her bed, clutching the phone in her sweat-slicked hand, Charlotte could feel the pulse pounding in her throat. She could taste dirty pennies in her mouth, and feel her heart fluttering like a moth trapped underneath a lampshade. She felt angry and ashamed, half-sick with guilt, as she bent her head. *They're just kids,* a voice inside of her cried out. *Just kids! Like me!* And she'd tattled on them, she'd ratted them out, and she strongly suspected that Christopher

Jarvis wasn't looking for them so he could give them a million dollars or a trip to Disney World.

Charlotte clamped down on that thought, pinching it off like she would a spent bloom on one of the geraniums her grandmother made her deadhead. *Maybe they are kids,* she thought, *but not like me. They're spoiled brats, from some big city I'll never get to visit.* She told herself that, and tried not to think about how polite the girls had been, or how the girl with the unruly hair had looked after the smaller one in the sweatshirt. It had given Charlotte a wrenching feeling inside, and it had made her think of her own friends. She pushed those thoughts away as hard as she could, and barely managed to keep from screaming when the phone buzzed in her hands.

She stared down, dully, at the text message that had just arrived. *"Keep watching. Wait for further instructions. We'll be in touch."*

Charlotte buried her face in her hands and groaned out loud, wishing, for the first time in a long time, that her mother and father hadn't died, that they were still alive and still around to tell her what she was supposed to do, and if there was any way that she could possibly make this right.

CHAPTER 15

Jeremy

AFTER HOURS ON THE HIGHWAY, BENJAMIN Burton pulled off at an exit and drove the car along a dirt road, heading west. After a few miles of uncomfortable bouncing, they reached the top of a hill. Benjamin parked the car and sat for a moment, staring through the streaked, dirty windshield into the setting sun.

In the passenger's seat, Jeremy shifted his weight, tugging at his seat belt. He was hungry and antsy after hours of uninterrupted driving, desperate to stand up and stretch his legs and go to the bathroom. Benjamin had barely said a word to him since they'd collected Donnetta Dale's camera and driven out of Standish. Early on the

drive they'd crafted a lie for Jeremy's parents (a school trip to Washington). "Did you tell us about this?" Jeremy's mom had asked, sounding distracted, as usual. Jeremy promised that he had told her, and that she had signed his permission slip, and given him spending money, too. "Okay, then," she'd said. "Have fun!" He felt bad about lying to his mother. Then he felt angry as he realized that his mom would never think to check the school's website to confirm that Jeremy's class was going to Washington, that she wouldn't ask his dad if he'd known about the field trip. One of his brothers had a wrestling meet that weekend, and the other had some kind of Model UN conference, and between those two events Jeremy knew he would have been lucky if his parents had remembered to leave food in the refrigerator, or money for pizza.

"Take lots of pictures!" his mom had said. Jeremy promised that he would. "Good job," Benjamin said after Jeremy ended the call . . . and that had been the last he'd heard from Benjamin for hours. Benjamin had kept them zipping along the highway, his hands tight on the wheel, looking like he was deep in thought. When the gas tank was empty, they'd stopped to refill it. Jeremy had used the restroom, and Benjamin had bought a bag of burgers and fries from Burger King. Jeremy would have preferred a chicken sandwich, but thought it best not to complain.

When they'd gotten back in the car, Jeremy had asked where they were going. "North," Benjamin had said.

Jeremy had asked if they were meeting up with the rest of the Yare. Benjamin had responded with a growl. Jeremy decided to let twenty minutes pass before asking anything else, watching the time click by on the digital clock. When twenty minutes were up, he asked, "So, have you ever met Alice?" That earned him another growl, that one so fierce that Jeremy decided to wait thirty minutes before his next question, which was, "What's the plan?"

For a long moment, there was no reply, no growling, not even a look. Jeremy saw Benjamin Burton's long fingers gripping the wheel, his jaw bulging as he ground his teeth. When Benjamin finally spoke, his voice was rusty from disuse. "To tell you the truth," he'd said slowly, and then sighed. "I don't know."

Jeremy frowned. This wasn't good news. "Do you want to talk about it? Or, you know, bounce some ideas off me? I'm a good listener!"

A ghost of a smile visited Benjamin's face. He shook his head. "Just let me think," he instructed, and Jeremy had agreed.

That had been the last conversation they'd had. Jeremy

had watched the odometer, and the signs. Eventually, he'd pulled out his phone and opened the mapping app, following their progress along the highway, then the secondary roads, then, eventually, miles of old, rutted roads badly in need of repaving as they made their way north, drawing closer and closer to a town called Upland, on the edge of the Canadian border. After hours of this slow, careful circling, with frequent stops and switchbacks that Jeremy figured were intended to make sure that they weren't being followed, Benjamin had stopped the car, and they'd been sitting here in silence for the last nineteen minutes.

Finally, without a word, Benjamin opened his door and stepped into the gathering darkness. After a minute, Jeremy scrambled out of his seat and followed Benjamin as he walked into the woods. Benjamin's long legs ate up the distance, and Jeremy hurried along after him.

When Benjamin stopped walking, Jeremy looked down and saw that they were at the very top of a ridge, with a town spread out underneath them. The cars were tiny as toys, and the people were small as bugs as they moved along the sidewalk, beneath the glow of streetlamps. Through the cloud of his cold breath, he could see the spire of a church, and a gigantic Christmas tree, ribboned in twinkling lights, set in a square right in the center of town. A golden star shone from its top, and people holding oversized folders stood in rows in front of it, their breath emerging from their mouths in frosty plumes. When the wind shifted, he heard a snatch of "Silent Night."

"Where are we?" Jeremy asked.

"Vermont. A town called Upland," Benjamin said.

"And what are we doing here?"

Benjamin sighed. "You ask a lot of questions."

Jeremy thought about reminding Benjamin that he'd met a Bigfoot, been shoved in a hole, lived through a Bigfoot fight, watched a Bigfoot exodus, and been driven hundreds of miles away from his home, after telling his parents he'd be off and safe on a school trip . . . and he still didn't know why. Given all that, he didn't think he was asking an unusual number of questions at all. But before he could argue, Benjamin walked to the very edge of the ridge, where the ground gave way to air. He lay flat on his belly on the cold ground. Looking over his shoulder, he said, in a low, carrying voice, "Come here. Come look."

Jeremy felt his heartbeat hitch. He wasn't exactly afraid of heights, but they also weren't his favorite thing. He forced himself to bend down and commando-crawl, creeping over the cold ground until he was right next to Benjamin. Benjamin was holding a pair of binoculars up to his eyes, peering through the darkness at . . .

Jeremy squinted, blinking. At first he couldn't see anything. When Benjamin handed him the binoculars, he got a better view of the town. He saw its Main Street, lined with a church, a library, a white marble town hall, a few businesses with colorful awnings that, Jeremy just bet, spelled "shop" as "shoppe," and a redbrick super-market with a bright black asphalt parking lot. The pretty Victorian houses all looked freshly painted, and the cars he could see appeared shiny and new.

The view past Main Street was more of the same: neat square lawns covered in snow, carefully kept houses, prosperous-looking businesses, and brand-new schools. Beyond the residential part of town he could see red barns and fenced-off fields, and signs offering fresh eggs and hand-sewn quilts and canned goods.

"This way," said Benjamin, turning the binoculars. Jeremy saw a high fence, made of red brick topped with barbed wire. Past the fence was a series of modern-looking buildings made of gray stone and glass. Even though it was after dark, the buildings were all lit up. Jeremy saw people walking on the paths between the buildings, and in their hallways. He saw a gatehouse, and a guard stopping cars and checking what must have been IDs before a mechanical arm swung up to admit them. And he saw guards in fatigues carrying rifles, stationed at regular intervals on top of the wall. "JARVIS INDUSTRIES," read a sign at the front of the compound, right next to the gates. The name tugged at a thread somewhere in his mind. It reminded him of something, but he couldn't think of what.

"What is that place?" he breathed.

Instead of answering, Benjamin reached out and again redirected Jeremy's binoculars, pointing them back toward the center of town. Jeremy saw a mansion, a big three-story Victorian with a wraparound porch. The house was white, the shutters were black, and the front door and the porch trim were bright red. Outbuildings—a garage and what looked like a shed—flanked its east and west sides. It was a pretty place, tidy and well-kept. There wasn't anything overtly scary about it. Still, just looking at the place filled Jeremy with dread, like he'd swallowed something rotten, or the way he'd felt looking at a downed power line, writhing and spitting sparks onto the street.

"Who lives there?" Jeremy asked.

"Christopher Jarvis." Benjamin's voice was low. "He's the man who owns the labs. And the town, even though

he didn't put his name on that. He funds the Department of Official Inquiry."

Jeremy flinched, remembering Mr. Carruthers, and the threatening letters he and his friend had received; how his parents' credit cards had stopped working and his mom's car hadn't started and their TV had stopped receiving its cable signal. *We can hurt you,* was the message, and Jeremy had heard it, loud and clear. *We can touch every single piece of your life, we can get to every single person you love.* Once Jeremy had agreed to go along with them, they'd fixed his grades and bought his family dinner at Standish's fanciest steakhouse and given him a brand-new bike, and he'd gotten that message too: *We can help or we can hurt. So which do you want? The handshake or the slap?* He'd chosen the handshake. It made him burn with shame, to think that he'd been bought off so cheaply, turned into a government agency's pawn for the price of a steak dinner and a new mountain bike.

"What are we going to do?" he asked.

"We're going to watch," Benjamin rumbled. "We're going to watch the house. We're going to watch the lab. We're going to watch the town. We're going to watch cars and people. We're going to look for patterns. We're going to see who comes and who goes. We're going to figure out where Christopher Jarvis is vulnerable."

Jeremy could feel the hair at the nape of his neck prickle. *You need a haircut,* his mother had told him a few days before he'd gone to New York City. Now he wondered whether he'd live long enough to get one . . . and whether a man who owned a huge lab and had enough money to fund an entire government agency had any vulnerabilities at all.

"And then what?"

Benjamin Burton's eyes were intent on the house, and the weathervane on its roof, as it turned slowly in the waning light. "And then all of this ends."

Jeremy hated to step on what he had to admit was an excellent exit line. Still, he had to ask. He cleared his throat. "So are we, um, sleeping in the car?" he asked. He hoped that the answer was no. Really, he hoped that the answer was *No, of course not, there's a very nice hotel nearby, and I've reserved us a suite. You can take the first shower.*

Instead, Benjamin shook his head. He got to his feet and bounded downhill, back to the car. By the time Jeremy arrived he was opening the truck to reveal a pair of backpacks and a long, narrow nylon bag that Jeremy recognized by size and shape. He felt his heart sinking.

"Ever done any camping?" Benjamin asked.

"A little bit," Jeremy muttered, as Benjamin handed him one of the backpacks. Once a year, his dad would take Jeremy and his brothers on a three-day camping excursion. "You boys have fun!" his mother would say, helping them load the car with food and sleeping bags, the camp stove, and the tent. Jeremy never did. His feet would always get wet. He'd always get chafed or blistered somewhere, no matter how carefully he'd dress. He'd end up with a sunburn or bug bites or poison ivy—sometimes all three. And his brothers . . . he sighed, remembering. If one of your brothers was a mathematical genius and the other was a superstar athlete, if the genius could take a single look at the tentpoles and figure out the fastest way to set up the tent and the athlete could execute his directions in under five minutes and gather a night's worth of firewood in ten, that didn't leave much for him to do, or many ways he could be useful. Jeremy's camping experience consisted of mostly standing at the edge of the campsite with his hands in his pockets, watching his dad and his brothers do things, or wandering in the woods with the stated explanation of bird-watching or digging up worms for fishing, when, really, he'd been looking for Bigfoots.

Which reminded him.

He settled his pack on his back and hurried to catch up to Benjamin, whose long strides had put him far ahead. "Hey," he said. "Where's the rest of the Tribe? Are they meeting us here?"

Benjamin gave him a single nod. Jeremy felt his heart lift. At least he'd get to see his new friends again, Tulip and Frederee. And he'd be able to give Tulip back her cat, which had spent half the car ride trying to claw its way out of the pouch of Jeremy's hoodie, and the other half curled up and purring against him. Jeremy reached into the pouch and rubbed the sleeping kitten behind her ears, feeling her meowing against his belly.

Benjamin didn't even ask for Jeremy's help as he set up the tent. "Go get some wood," he said, as he used a stone to drive the tentpoles into the ground. *Here we go again,* Jeremy thought disconsolately. He wandered back into the forest, where he picked up an armful of logs and a few pieces of relatively dry bark. He brought them back to Benjamin. Once the fire was built and the tent was up, Jeremy wandered over to a neighboring ridge, where he did the thing he'd been doing for most of his life: he stood in the dark, by himself, and looked for Bigfoots.

CHAPTER 16

Alice

I CAN'T BELIEVE YOU'RE HERE!" JESSICA JARVIS said, for the sixth time since encountering Alice in the hallway. Jessica was still holding her hand. She hadn't let go of it since she'd grabbed on to it.

Alice put her key in the lock and opened the door to her suite. There was a sitting room, with couches and a round table at the center and heavy silk drapes covering the windows. Alice could smell cinnamon and vanilla-scented potpourri, and feel heavy carpet under her feet . . . and then she saw Millie, right where she'd left her, huddled in an armchair in the corner of the room, swimming in a gigantic hooded sweatshirt, with a blanket wrapped around her shoulders and her arms wrapped around her knees.

"Millie!" Jessica flew across the room to give Millie a hug. Even through the sweatshirt and the blanket, Alice could see that Millie was still trembling. Millie managed a tentative smile and said, "Hello."

"Are you okay?" Jessica asked.

Millie gave a small nod. "Mostly. I think." Her smile was equal parts rueful and proud. "I was involved in a high-speed chasing."

"I saw," said Jessica. "At least the beginning of it."

"We had to get away from the bad guys. We drove very fast. Then Alice went to say goodbye to her father." Alice didn't miss the way Millie seemed to hesitate before she said "father." "And then we came here."

Jessica bent down and squeezed Millie's hands. "Don't worry. You're safe now."

Millie looked like she was trying to believe it, but the expression on her face said she wasn't convinced. Instead of *I'm safe now,* she seemed to be thinking something along the lines of *I'll never be safe again.* Still, she tried to smile. "I am enjoying Vermong."

"Vermont," Alice murmured, taking a seat on a couch, upholstered in slippery gold fabric.

"Vermont," said Millie. "There are good smells here. Maybe I'll be staying."

Behind her, the older woman who'd come in with Jessica cleared her throat, and Jessica introduced them to her nana, who pulled up the chair from the desk and sat down with a sigh. Then Jessica turned to the other older woman. "I remember you," she said to Miss Merriweather. "You're the educational person. The one who sent me to the Experimental Center."

"That's right, dear," Miss Merriweather said, seating herself in the armchair next to Millie's.

"Do you know about my grandfather?" Jessica asked her.

Miss Merriweather nodded. "We do."

"Wait, what?" Alice said, peering at Jessica. "Who's your grandfather?"

"Christopher Wayne Jarvis," said Jessica, looking a little shamefaced. Alice felt her eyes getting big and her heart start beating faster. She pressed her hands flat on the satin fabric of the couch to steady herself.

"Like the Wayne Clinic?"

"I don't know about the Wayne Clinic," Jessica said. "But I know he's a scientist. A researcher. I saw his logo on the van those men were trying to get you into. And I think he's also been doing, um, experiments on children." Jessica's tongue swiped at her lips. "After you, um, left, I went to the library and did some research, and I talked to my nana."

Alice looked at Jessica's nana, frowning. "Other side of the family," the woman said pleasantly. "Christopher Jarvis is Jessica's father's father. I'm her mother's mom."

"Nana used to be a reporter," Jessica said. "She knew that my grandfather has labs up here. That's why we came." Another lip lick. Then she asked, "Alice, how did you know to come here?"

Alice looked at her mother, whose expression was almost dreamy. "Mom?" she prompted.

Faith smiled faintly. "This is the last place I saw Alice's father," her mother said. "It's where Alice was born. There were Yare here, years ago." She sighed. "We had to start somewhere, and this seemed as good a place as any. It's where everything began, for me, and Alice's father." She gave Alice a warm look. "And for Alice. You were born here, you know."

I didn't know, Alice thought, feeling her face get hot. *Or, at least, you didn't tell me.* She'd been told that she'd been born in New York City, and it wasn't until years later that she'd discovered the truth.

"Your father's been looking for you. I'm sure of it. He'd never stop looking," Faith was saying.

"So I'm the bait?" Alice could hear the pain in her voice, but couldn't manage to hide it. She could feel her face flushing, and imagined her hair had gone wild.

Her mother flinched. "Honey, of course not."

Honey, thought Alice. She felt the endearment grating at her, like a chewed fingernail catching on the loops of a silk sweater, or her hairbrush coming to a stop in a stubborn knot. She glared at her mother and found that she was on her feet, and that all the fury that she'd kept tamped down for the years that she'd been sent away and kept in the dark was surging to the surface, an enormous, unstoppable wave of rage. She raked her hands through her hair, sending clumps to stand up in a frizzy corona. "I'm not your honey!" she yelled.

Alice's mother's mouth fell open. Alice saw her shocked expression, saw the hurt on her mother's face, but she couldn't stop talking, now that she'd started. "You never told me the truth about who I was. You sent me away, every year, every summer, and I was always the new kid, always the weirdo, and now, now that you've decided that it's time to tell the world about the Yare, you drag me here, right up to the doorstep of the man who's trying to hunt me down and take my blood and maybe kill me, because you've decided that you've had enough of hiding, and that maybe my father's going to show up, and that maybe he'll bring more Yare with him." Alice glared at her mother. "Is that about right?"

Faith looked pale and shocked, and Millie had started trembling again as Alice advanced on her mother with her hands balled into fists.

"When do I get a say?" Alice asked. "When does any of this get to be my choice?"

Alice's mother gathered herself. "You're right," she said quietly, and bowed her head. "You're absolutely right. We should have told you the truth before this, and I'm sorry we didn't. We shouldn't be using you, or putting you in danger, and I'm sorry that we are." She looked at the ground, her expression rueful, before raising her eyes to meet Alice's furious gaze, and walking slowly toward her. "We wanted to keep you safe." She sighed. "But that isn't much of an excuse. We should have told you the truth a long time ago. You deserved it." She reached for Alice, who jerked away.

"I should leave," Alice said, almost to herself. "I should just go, right now. I can get back to New York by myself." She waited for her mother to argue with her, to try to convince her to stay, but it was Millie who spoke up first.

"And then what?" she asked.

Startled, Alice looked at her friend, who kept her silvery-eyed gaze steady on Alice's face.

"They will keep hunting you," Millie said. "They'll never ever stop."

"Then I'll hide," Alice said, knowing how futile that was almost before she'd said it.

"They will find you again," said Millie. "They'll look and look until they find you. They'll keep trying to take what they want, unless we stop them." She tilted her head. "And you are not made for hiding," she said. "Not like me."

"Because I'm too big?" Alice asked.

Millie shook her head. "Because you're too brave."

Alice sat down on the couch again, feeling glum and exhausted. Jessica was the one to continue the interrogation.

"I still have some questions," she said, and nodded at Miss Merriweather. "How are you part of this?"

Miss Merriweather looked a little regretful. "Most Yare—what you would call Bigfoot," she said, turning to Nana. "They never leave their Tribes."

Alice looked at Jessica's grandmother, to see how she was taking in this talk of Bigfoot and Yare. Instead of looking at them like they were all crazy, Jessica's nana's gaze was sharp, her expression intent as she nodded at Miss Merriweather to continue.

"And the ones who do—like Millie's mother, for example—manage to find homes in other Tribes."

Millie's eyes had gone wide. "You are knowing my mother?" Millie asked. "My Tribe?"

Miss Merriweather nodded and kept talking. "But some of us want to see more of the world than that. Some of us want to go a-venturing."

"Ad-venturing," Millie corrected, in a tiny voice.

"All Yare have jobs. Callings, really. Some are Leaders . . ." Miss Merriweather nodded at Millie, who cringed in response. "Some are Healers. Some are Watchers. And some of us are Protectors. We go into the world of No-Furs—the world of humans—and become almost human ourselves. We get close to the Yare's enemies. We watch. We spy. We keep the Tribe informed. And we help when we can, to keep the rest of the Yare safe." A small smile played around Miss Merriweather's lips. "Sometimes, there are Yare who have other reasons for leaving." Looking at Jessica, Miss Merriweather said, "Dear, are you all right? You look like you've been hit over the head."

"You're one of them?" Jessica asked. "A . . ." Alice

thought that Jessica was about to say Bigfoot, but she stopped herself in time. "A Yare?"

"I am Yare," Miss Merriweather said serenely. "I'm also an accredited educational consultant. But part of my job as a Protector is to keep children safe. Yare and otherwise." She gave Alice a fond smile. "This one, for example. I had to keep her moving, so Dr. Jarvis would never be able to find her."

"And you had to—what?" Alice asked. "Hide me from him?"

Miss Merriweather and Alice's mother both nodded.

"Would he have hurt me?" Alice whispered. Before Miss Merriweather could answer, Jessica interrupted.

"I think you'd better tell me everything about my grandfather. My nana told me some of it . . ."

". . . but that was mostly guesswork," Nana volunteered. "I know what I saw him do, and I saw other things happen, and I could fill in the blanks."

"But I need to know all of it," said Jessica. She nodded at Alice and Millie. "*We* need to know all of it. Who he is. What he's done." She took a deep, quivering breath. "How we stop him."

Alice looked around the room, at one adult female, two old women, and Alice and Millie—just kids, she thought. Not much of an army. But, maybe, better than nothing. "Because that's what we have to do, right? We have to stop him."

For a minute, Alice wondered if the grown-ups would tell her that she was crazy; that she'd made it all up, that she hadn't been dropped into the plot of some big-budget action movie; that Jessica's grandfather was a harmless old eccentric and that Bigfoots, of course, were not real; and that if there was a villain stealing Bigfoots for his experiments and kidnapping and torturing children, it would not be up to old women and children to stop him. It didn't seem fair, Alice thought. They should have had an army. But at least she wasn't alone. At least Millie wasn't alone. At least there were some grown-ups involved. Maybe the grown-ups would tell the girls, "You just stay here, where it's safe. We'll take care of it."

Alice looked at the adults—Miss Merriweather, Jessica's nana, her own mother. And it was Faith who finally spoke.

"That's right," she said. "We have to stop him."

In the end, they agreed to get a good night's sleep and regroup in the morning. Miss Merriweather and Jessica's

nana decided to take the room Jessica's grandmother had booked, and Faith offered to sleep on their couch. "I'm sure we'll do fine," Miss Merriweather said, and Nana smiled wearily before heading down the hall.

Alice's mother gave her daughter a long, tight hug, which Alice accepted without returning.

"I'm still mad at you," she said, when Faith had let her go.

"I know," her mother said, with a small sigh. "I can't make up for what I did. I can't give you back those years." She swiped at her own eyes, and Alice steeled herself, thinking, *She has no right to cry. I'm the one who should be crying.* "I want you to know that every time I said good-bye to you, every time I sent you away, it felt like ripping out a piece of my own heart." When Alice didn't reply, Faith sighed. "All I can do is promise you it'll be better from now on." Faith touched Alice's hair gently. "Well, good night, then," she said, and walked out, closing the door gently behind her.

Then the girls were alone in the big suite, with its king-sized bed. Millie was still huddled in the corner. Alice walked over, took her hand, and pulled her to her feet. "Do you want to share the bed?" Alice asked. She'd already seen that the canopied bed was truly enormous, with room enough for all of them, plus a few more. She was still so confused, anger and sadness and regret tangled inside her, like she'd swallowed a ball of thorns and it was sitting in her chest, prickling and aching.

Jessica was roaming the room, opening the closet, then the dresser drawers. "Do you think there's a minibar in here?" she asked. "I'm starving."

At the mention of food, Millie perked up. "The lady who gave us the key said something about snackles in the Par Lore."

"Parlor," Alice corrected. "It's just one word. I'll go." Alice grabbed her backpack and dumped it on the bed, preparing to fill it with whatever she could find. Millie wrapped her arms around herself again.

"This was not the happy ending of my dreams," she said, half to herself.

"Not mine either," said Jessica. "But when you sang this morning, you were really good," she added.

Millie's eyes widened. Then she looked away. "You are just saying that."

"No," Alice said. "She's right. I bet if you'd gotten to finish—you know, if those guys hadn't tried to grab me, and throw me in a car . . ."

Millie snorted.

"And if Alice's mom hadn't gotten her away, and thrown you both in a different car . . ." said Jessica.

Millie giggled. "And if I'd never gotten you to pretend to be me . . ."

". . . and if I'd never agreed . . ." said Jessica.

Now all of them were laughing.

"I bet I would have won the entire contest!" Millie said. "I would have been the winner of *The Next Stage*! With the balloons and the silver fonfetti and everything!"

"Confetti," said Alice, as she used her hip to open the door. Downstairs in the parlor she found baskets of treats above a humming mini-refrigerator. A sign in fancy script on a small blackboard read "TAKE WHAT YOU LIKE!" Alice helped herself to a brown paper bag of popcorn, a bag of honey-roasted peanuts, a bag of potato chips, a chunk of Vermont cheddar cheese, green Granny Smith apples, and a plate full of warm chocolate-chip cookies. Back in the room, she unloaded the food onto the table, along with the bottles of water and cans of soda she'd taken.

Jessica found a knife and cut the apple into slices and fanned them out along the edge of the plate. She cut the cheese into wedges and found little bowls for the nuts.

"Millie, are you hungry?" Alice asked.

"I could have perhaps a small bite," Millie said. She

joined them at the table, giving Alice a wobbly smile. Alice smiled back at her and poured soda into a glass. Millie sipped, then frowned at the drink, her nose crinkling.

"Why is this beverage angry with me?"

"It's not angry. It's carbonated," Alice said. "It's been . . ." She looked at Jessica for help.

"Fizzed up with gas," Jessica said.

"Carbon Ate It," Alice heard Millie say softly, before she tried the soda again.

Alice raised her glass. "To us," she said. "Here's to good luck. We'll need it."

Jessica lifted her glass and, after a moment, Millie raised hers, too. They clinked glasses, and ate cheese and apples and cookies. Alice pulled on the pajamas she'd picked up at her apartment, and Jessica dug her nightgown out of the bag she'd packed at school. Millie stayed bundled in her sweatshirt and sweatpants, which covered up most of her body and also had a convenient hood that could, in a pinch, be pulled tight enough to disguise everything but her eyes and the tip of her nose, hiding the fur on her face. They took turns in the bathroom, showering and brushing their teeth. Then they slept, all three of them together in the great, big canopy bed.

CHAPTER 17

Jessica

A T SIX O'CLOCK IN THE MORNING, JESSICA Jarvis crept out of bed and into the bathroom, where her phone had been charging through the night. She locked the door, set the lid down on the toilet, made herself comfortable, and dialed her father's cell phone.

Her dad answered after a single ring. "Jess? Is everything okay?"

"Everything's fine," said Jessica. She reminded herself that, as far as her parents knew, she was still safe and sound at the Experimental Center for Love and Learning, and not off on some children's crusade (or, more accurately, some children-and-old-ladies' crusade) in Vermont.

"You haven't heard from your grandmother, have you?" her father asked, sounding upset and distracted. "We got a call from her facility this morning. She took off in one of the nurse's cars."

"Oh, wow," Jessica murmured, trying to sound shocked as her brain churned. Of course they'd have noticed Nana's absence by now. The question was, had anyone remembered, or mentioned, Jessica being there too? She swallowed hard, deciding that she'd have to assume that someone would remember her. "I actually went to see Nana yesterday. We had a class field trip, to the Museum of Natural History, and then one of the teachers drove me to visit her when we were done."

"Did she say anything to you?" her father demanded. "Was she acting normal?"

"She seemed fine," Jessica said, and prayed that her dad was buying this, that he wouldn't think it was weird for a teacher to randomly drive a student to an assisted living facility without asking permission or clearing it with the kid's parents first. "Totally normal. Like herself."

"Because your mom's on her way to The Place right now."

"I'm really sorry," Jessica said. "I'll let you know if I hear from her."

"That would be great." She heard her father take a deep breath, trying to reset. "So what's up? What can I do for you?"

"Well. Speaking of grandparents, I need you to tell me something," Jessica said.

Her father's voice grew wary. "What's that?"

Jessica sat up very straight and briefly wished there was someplace more dignified to conduct this conversation than on the top of a toilet. "I need you to tell me about your father."

There was a pause. And when her father spoke, Jessica could sense his surprise. "Hang on," he said. "I'm going to call you right back." When he did, it was on FaceTime. Jessica prayed he wouldn't ask too many questions, or realize that the bathroom was not part of her school. She could see more gray in her father's hair than she remembered from when she'd left home in September; a weary look around his eyes.

"What's brought this on?" he asked.

"Just wondering," Jessica said, her voice light. "I guess seeing Mom's mother yesterday made me think about your parents."

Her father nodded. When he spoke, his voice was unusually hesitant.

"I don't know a lot," he said. "My father didn't tell me too much, and I didn't want to ask too many questions."

"Because he wouldn't tell you the truth?" Jessica said.

"Because it made him sad," her father answered. "Because I think what happened—losing his wife—it was the worst thing that had ever happened to him. I don't think he ever got over it."

Jessica nodded. And haltingly, her father, whose name was also Christopher, began to tell her. "I know that my mother got sick when she was pregnant with me. I know she put off treatment until after I was born, to give me my best shot at being born healthy." Her father swallowed hard. "I know my father did everything he could to save her. He found every expert and flew them all in, doctors from all over the world." Jessica's father sighed and shook his head. "But there was nothing they could do for her."

Jessica thought of the only picture she'd ever seen of her paternal grandmother: a woman in a hospital bed with too-sharp cheekbones and deep circles under her eyes and a baby in her arms. The woman had been pale, her lips chapped, visibly unwell, but her expression was triumphant; like she'd just run a marathon on broken legs and had somehow willed herself over the finish line. Her body looked like it was dying—which, Jessica knew,

it was—but the exultant look on her face said *I won.*

"I think . . ." Her father's voice trailed off. For a few seconds, he was quiet. Then he sighed and started again. "I think that after she died, my father was very angry."

"At who?" Jessica asked.

Her father shrugged sadly. "At my mother, for not fighting the way he wanted her to. At the doctors who couldn't help her. At the world, or fate, or whatever, for giving her cancer in the first place." His voice was soft. "At me too, I'm sure."

Jessica swallowed hard. She was imagining a man and a baby, alone together. The man furious at his dead wife, furious at the world, furious, too, at his little son, who didn't know anything, who hadn't done anything except be born.

"I think it was hard for him, because he didn't just lose a wife, he lost a research partner, too. They'd been working together . . ." Her father's eyes were far away, his face lost in memory. "They'd found . . . a tribe? Native Americans? That must have been it. I remember my father telling me that. There was this tribe, and the members of the tribe didn't get the same kinds of diseases that most people did. My father and my mother were doing studies . . . trying to get the people in the tribe to be part of their clinical trials, but the people wouldn't consent . . ." Her father shook his head, giving Jessica a thin, unhappy-looking smile. "Wow. I guess I remember more than I thought I did."

A Tribe, thought Jessica. Only not Native Americans. Yare. Bigfoots.

"That's what I remember," her father said. "She died, and he was angry. Angry, and then busy trying to finish their research, and do the work of two people by himself. He sent me away as soon as I was old enough. And that was that." Jessica could see his adult expression back in place, the face of a man who'd grown up and become successful in his own right. Underneath it, though, she could see the face of a kid like her, a boy who'd been sent away, whose mother was dead and whose father was angry and who hadn't understood why, had only known that he'd suffered because of it.

"Are you sure everything's okay?" her father asked hesitantly. "I'd let you talk to your mom, if she was around . . ."

"I'm fine," Jessica said, but her father persisted.

"Because if this is about your . . ." His voice trailed off. His throat worked as he swallowed. "Your tail, then I know your mother thinks my father was involved, somehow . . ."

"It isn't about my tail," Jessica said a little impatiently. "And I'm fine. I promise. Really."

"Okay," said her father.

Jessica felt herself softening. "And I love you," she said.

Her father looked a little startled, but, when he smiled, it was very sweet. "Why, honey, I love you, too."

CHAPTER 18

Christopher

LESS THAN TEN MILES AWAY FROM HIS granddaughter, Christopher Wayne Jarvis had also woken up early, and was also remembering.

He'd spent the night in his big bed, in the big house in Upland, and had woken from a nightmare with his body twitchy and restless, legs shaking and heart pounding hard. He'd been dreaming of Ellie, of the time when she'd first gotten sick, and he'd come up with the plan to save her.

By then they had managed to locate their first Tribe of Bigfoots, deep in the woods up near the border of Maine and Canada. They'd been watching for months, creeping

closer by the tiniest of increments, gathering data, using drones and long-lensed cameras to take pictures and give them body-heat readings, because the Bigfoots, they'd discovered, did most of their living underground. They'd mastered the art of invisibility. Even the littlest kid in the Tribe could fade into the woods so completely, melting into the ground or vanishing up in the trees, that you could be standing six feet away from one of them and not even know it was there.

It had been Ellie's idea to leave them notes. She'd hand-write them on monogrammed stationery and have them laminated, so they wouldn't disintegrate in the rain, then left at the perimeter of the Tribe's land. "Hello, friends! My name is Ellie and my husband, Christopher, and I would like to talk to you. We think you have a great deal to teach and share with us. We understand that humans have hurt you before, but we promise to do our very best to keep you safe." She'd left her phone number, her email address, even instructions as to where they could mail a written note. Christopher had rolled his eyes. "You really think they're going to send you a postcard?" he'd asked.

"No," Ellie had said sadly. "I think they are going to keep hiding. I think they've probably had terrible inter-actions with humans in the past. I think they've been hunted and abused, and I don't blame them at all for wanting nothing to do with us."

Back in the labs, they continued to study the genetic material from that first Bigfoot corpse, splicing and multiplying cells, parsing the DNA, and trying to transfer its properties to humans. They were positive that the Bigfoots' strength and resilience, the way they were immune to so many diseases, could be transferred to human men and women. They just hadn't quite figured out how.

"It's so frustrating," Ellie had said, on one of the rare occasions that she'd actually given voice to her pique.

"I know," Christopher had said. The Bigfoots—or, as he and Ellie had started calling them, *Homo gigantus*—were, indeed, close to humans, on a cellular level, indicating that, as Ellie had suspected, they'd evolved alongside *Homo erectus*. But close was not the same. Nor was extracting data and information from a corpse the same to studying a living thing. Bones and tissue could give you a snapshot, a blueprint, but a living blood cell was the actual landscape, the real building. So far, though, they'd had no luck getting a living Bigfoot into their lab. That failure occasioned the biggest fight of their marriage—really, the only fight of their marriage. Christopher wanted to bring

in the army, to tell the government what they'd found. If the authorities knew they'd found Bigfoots, if they knew what Bigfoots could do, and how long they lived, he was sure the government and the military would extend all of their resources—night-vision drones and heat-seeking missiles and soldiers—to him and his wife. They'd probably have their living specimen within days. But Ellie had absolutely refused.

"This isn't like breeding rabbits or lab rats," she'd said. "These are intelligent beings, just like us. Maybe even better than us. We can't just snatch one up at gunpoint and force it to give us its blood."

"So we'll just wait for one of them to email us?"

"If that's what it takes," Ellie said, with her jaw clenched tight.

They'd had a half-dozen versions of the same fight by the time Ellie got her diagnosis. That night, they had it again. They sat together at their kitchen table, talking it over. Or, rather, Christopher talked, and Ellie listened, her head drooping on the pale stalk of her neck, her face blanched and exhausted, her hair lank, her hands, with their chewed fingernails, splayed out, limp in her lap. That was what affected him the most. Ellie's hands were always moving—typing, writing, waving, gesturing.

Holding Christopher's own hands. Seeing them, limp, motionless—*lifeless,* his brain whispered—drove him to new heights of fury. He argued, and he pleaded, and he shouted, and in the end, he begged, on his knees in front of her, sobbing, with his arms wrapped around her waist and his head pillowed against the bulge of her belly. *I don't want to lose you,* he'd cried. *I can't. I can't live without you, Ellie. Please. It's the only way. We have to try.*

She'd reached down and brushed at his cheeks with her cool hands. *I'll fight,* she'd said. *I'll fight my hardest. But that's all I can promise you.*

He'd told her to go rest, and instead of arguing, she'd simply nodded and plodded off to their bedroom. For the next weeks, he worked feverishly, around the clock, barely eating, rarely sleeping, pushing himself to unlock the secret that he knew was there in the Bigfoot DNA, the secret that could save his Ellie. He no longer cared about curing diseases or creating supersoldiers or allowing people to live forever. It was only about one person, one life. His precious Ellie.

Time slipped by. Ellie rarely left her bed. She slept most of the time, getting paler by the day. She was so happy when she gave birth, and Christopher tried to be happy, too, but the truth was, he resented their child, and he hated himself for feeling that way. He was frustrated with his wife for adamantly refusing to let him get the government involved. But, more than anything, he was furious at the Bigfoots for being so elusive, for resisting their efforts, their importunings, for refusing to be found.

One muggy August night, as gray clouds covered up the moon, Ellie was back in the hospital, and Christopher was dozing in a chair by her bedside. He woke up to the sound of his wife calling his name.

"What?" he asked, and sprang out of bed. Ellie had lifted her head from her pillow and had sent one pale hand scrabbling, crab-like, across her blanket, over to the night table and a folded map. She opened the map, tapping a thickly forested area of northeast New York with her finger, and gestured for her husband to have a look.

Christopher peered at the map. Then he bent down and brought his ears close to her lips.

"Is there a Tribe there?"

Ellie nodded.

"Are you sure?"

". . . seen them."

"What?" Christopher's face was flushed, his brow furrowed as he thought, *Why didn't you tell me? Why didn't you say that there were more of them?* He struggled to keep his voice calm. "When?"

"Last year," she breathed . . . and, with her last bit of strength, she whispered a name. As Christopher stared, Ellie took his hand. "Don't . . . force her. Ask. Tell her I'm dying," Ellie whispered. "Ask if she'll help."

It was a redo of that first desperate trip to Vermont. Another car trip to another helipad, another ride to another middle-of-nowhere town. Two hours after he'd left Ellie's bedside, he was jogging through the woods, clutching the map, repeating the name in his mind. *Yetta.*

"Yetta!" he shouted into the darkness, when he reached the place where Ellie had told him to go. "My name is Christopher Jarvis. I'm Ellie Gold's husband. She's sick. She needs your help. Yetta!"

He called the name as he trotted through the woods, literally beating the bushes, calling and calling until his voice was a rasping croak. Finally, he had to exercise all his self-control to keep from shouting at her: "Please!"

No one answered. For hours and hours, no one answered. Finally, Christopher sat down on a half-rotted log and put his head in his hands. This was the end. He

was utterly defeated. His wife was dying, and he had no way to save her, and instead of being home, at her side, holding her hand and telling her he loved her, he was out in the woods, running around like an idiot, looking for Bigfoots.

"Please," he whispered, one more time, as his tears dripped over his wrists and fell onto the pine-needle-covered floor. That was when he felt it. He hadn't heard a single sound, not a twig cracking, not a pine needle brushing against the forest floor, but still, he could feel it: the sense that he was no longer alone in the forest, that someone else was there.

He held his breath and stayed very still, keeping his eyes closed, like he was a kid, playing hide-and-seek. Somehow, he knew that if he opened his eyes, whoever was there, watching him, would run.

"You're Ellie's husband?" asked a voice. It was a female voice, low-pitched and quavery. He imagined an old woman, white hair and filmy eyes, but he didn't look up to see. "Yes," he whispered. He was trembling all over, hardly able to breathe. He thought of the honors and the accolades he'd get if he were to go public and tell the world that Bigfoots were real . . . and he thought of his wife, so pale and still in her bed.

"My wife," he said. "You know my wife. Ellie. She's sick. She's dying. She sent me here to ask if you can help."

The silence unspooled. He heard a bird chirp—tooWHIT, tooWHOO, tooWHIT, tooWHOO—and some small woodland creature rustling through the leaves.

"No-Fur man," said the voice. It was slow and thoughtful. He pictured a little old lady again, eyeing her hand of cards at the bridge table, scrutinizing a bingo card, or carefully counting the dollars in her wallet at the grocery store, deliberating before she decided how much to bet or what to buy. "Give me your hands."

Christopher stretched his hands out and felt a strip of cloth float through the air to land on his palms. A blindfold.

"Promise to keep your eyes hidden. Promise you'll keep our secret. If you do, we can parlay."

"I promise," he said, knowing that if she'd asked him to rip his own heart out of his chest and hand it over, he would have done that, too. Ellie. Ellie was his heart.

"Promise solemn," said the voice.

"I do, I do! I promise solemn." He wrapped the blindfold around his eyes and sat very still. A moment later, he felt the weight of the log shift. When the voice came again, it was right beside him.

Silence. And then: "I am sorry for your wife. But what she wanted—what you want—it isn't yours to take."

And just like that, Christopher's sorrow was replaced with rage. "You could save her," he said. His voice shook. "You could help so many people. All I need is a blood sample . . . just a few drops."

The woman's voice was clear, and very firm. "No."

"Why?" he asked, in his hoarse voice. "If you could help people—so many people—why won't you do it?"

For a moment, there was only the sound of the crickets, and the wind sighing through the branches. Christopher could smell the balsam of the pine trees, the sweetness of the grass and the leaves that had fluttered to the forest floor, and a scent a little like nutmeg and cinnamon—the smell of the Bigfoot, sitting beside him.

"Maybe it is true that we could help," she said, speaking slowly, as if she was thinking out loud. "But your people do harm wherever they go. To the land. To the water. To every living thing that isn't them. Why should we help you live longer? So you can do more damage? Hurt more things? Hurt them even worse?"

Christopher's voice was shaking. "Ellie isn't like that."

"No," the voice agreed. "Your wife is a dear heart. But you wouldn't stop with her. Would you?" The Bigfoot answered her own question. "No-Furs never stop," she said. Her voice was sad and also matter-of-fact. "First you'd save your wife. Then you'd want to save all who were sick. Then you wouldn't want anyone to get sick at all, or die, not ever. Every one of you, wanting all of you to live for long-and-long. Maybe forever. To be stronger than you are, to never get the snifflies. Am I wrong?"

Christopher felt like he'd swallowed a stone. He knew the Bigfoot wasn't wrong. First, he would cure Ellie . . . and then what? Even if he swore to stop there, he wouldn't be able to. There'd be other people who would have worked with him to perfect the cure. Some of them would be sick. Or they'd have wives, or husbands, or parents, or children. Word would get out. People would find him. They would come to him like pilgrims, an endless, engulfing tide of them. *Please, my wife . . . my husband's very sick . . . please, my son, he's just five, just four, only a baby, please, you have to help, you have to, you have to, you have to.* And how would he be able to say no? He loved Ellie, but everyone loved someone. He knew that every parent whose child was dying, every man or woman whose husband or wife or parent or best friend was sick would want whatever magic potion he came up with. They'd hunt him to the ends of the earth. And would he be able to deny them?

And then there was the government. They'd find out what he'd done, they'd take away the medicine he'd created, and do all the things that Ellie had worried they would do. They would make an army of soldiers who didn't need sleep or feel pain, who could march for days and brush off bullet wounds like they were paper cuts.

The Bigfoot beside him seemed to know what he was thinking. Her voice was gentle when she spoke. "We all have our time," she said. "I am sorry for your loss."

"No," he said, shaking his head, like a stubborn child refusing to eat his peas or go to bed at the end of the day. His throat was tear-clogged, his eyes were burning. "No, I don't accept that. I *can't* accept that."

"Go back to your wife, No-Fur man. Be a comfort to her. Be a father to your son."

"No. No, you have to help her!" he shouted, and, without any thought or intent, he broke his promise. He yanked off the blindfold and opened his eyes.

At first, he saw nothing. As his eyes adjusted, he caught a flash of red and blue. A red sweater. A blue skirt. Bare legs, covered in gray fur, moving fast as they hurried away.

"Wait!" he shouted, and threw himself after the departing figure of the Bigfoot. "WAIT!" He ran as fast as he could, but the figure was gone. Yetta had vanished completely, as if she had never been there at all.

Christopher spent the day searching the woods. As the sun set, he stood at the edge of the forest. His face was bleeding where a branch had scratched it, and his hair was full of brambles. He'd twisted his ankle, and his clothes were damp. He'd fallen into a stream at one point, and for a while, he'd just stayed there, flat on his belly in the trickling water, feeling stones bruising his elbows and knees, thinking, *If she dies, I might as well die, too.* He hadn't been really alive until he'd met Ellie, and with her gone, he'd sink back to his empty half-life, a colorless existence without laughter or joy.

Trudging toward the helicopter, which he'd paid to wait, he thought, *They could help her, but they won't. They could save her, but they won't.* He made his journey back to New York City, taking the elevator up to Ellie's hospital room, where Ellie's doctor met him at the door.

"I'm so sorry," she said.

"What?" he husked, in his broken voice.

"We tried to call you. I'm so sorry, Dr. Jarvis. Your wife passed at six o'clock this morning."

Pushing the doctor aside, he ran to her bedroom . . . but Ellie was already gone. The bed had been stripped, all the machinery and medications removed.

Christopher Jarvis fell to his knees. *Their fault,* he thought. Their fault. They could have helped her. They could have, and they didn't. And at that moment, with the echoes of his dead wife's last breath still reverberating through the air, he had sworn to dedicate the rest of his life to two things. He would find the Bigfoots. He would steal every secret; take everything he could from their blood and their bodies. And then he would eradicate them. He would eliminate them completely, killing every last one, wiping them off the face of the earth as surely as they'd killed his beloved, his Ellie, his darling, his heart.

PART THREE

CHAPTER 19

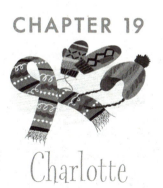

Charlotte

WHEN THE INN HAD GUESTS—GRANDMA Hughes never called them tenants or clients or, God forbid, *customers*, just guests—Charlotte would wake up at six, sometimes even earlier, to collect eggs from the hens and put on the first pot of coffee. Breakfast hours were from seven to eight thirty, but Grandma never wanted anyone to come down the stairs without hot, fresh coffee being available.

The day after their unusual guests had arrived, Charlotte was up and dressed before dawn . . . but she hadn't woken up early. She hadn't slept at all. She'd spent the night rolling from side to side, kicking at her sheets, counting to a hundred by twos and to a thousand by fives, trying to will herself into unconsciousness. At four in the morning, she'd realized it was futile and decided that she might as well make herself useful. She'd put the Jarvis phone in her pocket, along with her regular phone, and had gone first to the laundry room, to do the day's ironing, then to the kitchen, to bake a few batches of bacon-cheddar scones. She'd just slid a tray into the oven when she heard feet coming down the stairs. Straightening up, she put a smile on her face and prepared to call out a cheery, "Good morning!" Except her guests bypassed the kitchen completely. She heard low voices in the mudroom. A moment later, the girl with broad shoulders and wild hair peeked into the kitchen. "Excuse me," she said politely, "but is there a chance you've got any coats and hats and mittens we could borrow? We didn't pack very well."

"I'll check," said Charlotte, plastering a smile on her face. There were baskets full of hand-knitted wool mittens, hats with ear flaps, and brightly colored scarves with exuberant fringes, all made with wool from the local alpacas, that her grandmother kept on hand for guests to borrow. Charlotte walked to the closet, trying her hardest not to stare at the smaller girl in the sweatshirt who stood half-hidden behind her friend, as she pulled jackets and picked up boots—some items that she'd outgrown, some that other guests had left behind.

"Thanks," said the red-haired girl. "Are you in high school?"

Charlotte nodded. "Yep." She didn't want to make conversation, didn't want to do anything that would force her to see these girls as people, but she knew her grandmother would get mad if she was rude. "How about you? Are you all on vacation?" She watched a glance move between the girls.

"Sort of," said the one with the shiny brown ponytail.

"It's kind of a field trip," said the girl with the wild hair. Charlotte saw how the two of them angled their bodies to protect the smallest one, the girl in the sweatshirt, who didn't say anything at all.

"Well, have a great day!" Charlotte said. She went back to the kitchen as the guests equipped themselves, listening as one of the girls said, "These are so not my colors," and the other one telling her to get over herself, but not in a mean way. She listened until the front door swung open, then shut. When she looked through the window over the sink she saw the six of them heading across the meadow. The red-haired woman walked at the head of the line. The wild-haired girl walked beside her, then the two old women and the other girl. The tiny, timid girl in the sweatshirt was bringing up the rear. Charlotte watched as they walked off into the snow-covered meadow, disappearing into the sunrise.

Charlotte was still staring out the window when Grandma Hughes came down the stairs and pulled the scones out of the oven, just before they started to burn. "No breakfast?" her grandmother asked. "Maybe they'll be hungry when they get back."

Charlotte nodded. When the Jarvis phone started blaring in her pocket, it startled her so badly that a little scream escaped her lips. Its ringtone had been set to sound like a fire alarm going off.

"What's that?" her grandmother asked sharply.

"New ringtone," said Charlotte through numb lips as she pulled the phone from her pocket. "UNKNOWN CALLER" read the screen. Except Charlotte knew who the caller was. She felt her heart go cold as she carried the phone back up to the attic and locked her bedroom door behind her.

"Hello?"

"We need you to follow them," said the man she'd spoken to the previous evening.

Charlotte found that she could barely breathe. "What? Why?"

"Never mind why. Just follow them."

Charlotte's throat was dry as paper; her hands felt thick and clumsy as she clutched the phone and realized that the Jarvis people had to be watching her somehow. Watching her inn, watching the woods. Were there cameras somewhere that she hadn't noticed? Were there drones flying overhead? Were they watching her right this minute? She wanted to drop the phone, to turn off the lights and hide under her bed. But there was no hiding. They would find her, and demand the service she had promised. She'd taken their money, their dirty money. And now they were going to hurt their guests, and some of those guests were just kids. And if she didn't agree to help them, they would hurt her. Of this, Charlotte Hughes had no doubt.

"Miss Hughes?" The voice was impersonal. The man on the line might as well have been calling to ask if she'd be willing to take a survey, or was she satisfied with the new dishwashing machine.

"This wasn't the deal," Charlotte said. Her voice sounded shaky as she said, "You asked me just to watch for people, and call you if I saw them, and I did that.

I did everything I said I'd do. I never agreed to follow anyone."

The man didn't respond. Charlotte swallowed hard. "I—I'll do my best—but I twisted my ankle last night. I was carrying some tablecloths down the stairs, and I caught my foot on the runner." She was babbling, and she could already tell that it wasn't going to do any good.

"Do your best," said the man. His tone was almost mocking, like he knew Charlotte was lying to him. "Keep your phone with you. We'll be in touch. And we'll know where you are." There was a click, and then silence.

Charlotte's heart was beating very hard. *They are watching. They can see.* She thought of her grandmother, and how busy the inn had been ever since Jarvis Industries came to town. She thought of the money they'd paid her, piling up in her cedar box. She thought about the inn's suppliers, the people who roasted the coffee and collected the honey and tapped the trees for maple syrup; the ones who sold her grandma meat and fish and her firewood. Amy Arlette, who was just eighteen, came and helped with the laundry and the cleaning every weekend; Mike Grogan, who was in his seventies, mowed the lawn in the summer and plowed the driveway in the winter. All of those people whose livelihood depended on the inn on one side of the scale. And on the other?

A bunch of strangers, Charlotte told herself. Rich, spoiled, private-school girls from New York City who probably thought that they were better than she was. If she went downstairs, she'd probably find unmade beds and piles of wet towels on the bathroom floor. After they'd left Upland, this place where Charlotte and her parents and her parents' parents had spent their whole lives, they would never think of it again. As for Charlotte herself, she was probably just as invisible as the wallpaper or the windowpanes—just another part of the background, a piece of furniture that made them breakfast and carried firewood and fresh towels to their bedrooms and answered them pleasantly while they complained about a lack of jogging routes or asked for oat milk for the coffee.

They were strangers. She owed them nothing.

And yet.

Charlotte thought of the girl with the wild hair, the way she'd stood protectively in front of her friend. And how the other girl, the one with the fancy boots and the earrings Charlotte just bet were real diamonds, had held the door for her grandmother, and carried all the suitcases without being asked. They were kids, her heart cried, not much younger than she was. Girls with dreams. Girls with their whole lives ahead of them.

Burn up the day, she thought. *I can do what I promised, but I can take my time about it.* Maybe that would help. She could buy the guests a little time. Maybe a little time would be enough to make a difference.

Slowly, taking care to limp, Charlotte made her way to the coat closet. She bent down as if every muscle in her body hurt, and straightened up slowly, holding her left boot. She limped to the staircase, eased herself onto the bottom step, and worked the boot onto her foot. Once she'd gotten it on, she hobbled back to the closet for the second boot. She dropped it on her way to the staircase, and bent down with a groan to retrieve it. With the boot safely in hand, she went back to the stairs. Sat down with a grunt. Pulled on the boot, then got up and limped back to the closet for her coat. Then her hat. Then her scarf. Then her mittens. She pulled on each piece of gear, taking care with the ties and the zippers. *Burn up the day,* she thought. By the time she made it out the back door, the sun was high in the sky, and the footprints that her guests had left had been erased by the melting snow.

CHAPTER 20

Alice

"WHERE ARE WE GOING?" ALICE ASKED HER mother. She knew that she was staring, but she couldn't figure out a way to make herself stop. She'd gotten so used to seeing her mother teetering around on high heels, dressed in the most stylish clothes, and she was having a hard time reconciling those memories with the woman in front of her, the woman who was wearing giant rubber-soled snow boots and was bundled into an enormous raspberry-colored down puffer coat, a gray knitted hat with a pink pom-pom on her head. The woman whom Alice had known all of her life would never have been caught dead in such a gaudy ensemble. That woman would never have permitted salt-stained snow boots to be in her presence, let alone on her feet, and her winter coats were either expensive fur or chic black wool, not bulky down. But her mom had owned this coat—she'd taken it out of the closet, back in the apartment in New York. Not only that, she seemed perfectly cheerful. Her cheeks were glowing, and her hair, instead of its usual meticulous blowout, was gathered in a haphazard pony-tail. Tendrils had come loose to curl around her cheeks. She wore no makeup, but her eyes were shining, and she looked happy, and excited, and young. *No, not just that,* Alice thought. With her messy hair and her warm, loose-fitting clothes, with her ponytail and her boots . . . *She looks like me.* It gave Alice a strange, unsettled feeling inside: joy mixed with confusion. And anger. That too. Who was this woman, really; and where had she been hiding, while that skinny, high-heeled lady in New York had made Alice feel so inadequate, so ugly and unworthy and ashamed? Why had she kept her true self hidden for so long?

Alice herself wore her winter coat and her boots, and her backpack, which still contained a few of her assigned reading books from English class, was on her back.

"Do you know where we are?" Alice asked.

"I know this place," her mother said . . . which was not exactly an answer to Alice's question. "This is where I grew up," her mother continued. "When we get to the top of the ridge, we'll be able to see my family's old farm."

Alice still couldn't quite believe it—her mother, the fanciest person she knew, had grown up on a farm. Had worn gum boots and overalls instead of high heels and ballgowns; had milked cows and mucked out their stables; had chopped wood and driven spiles into trees to collect their sap and boil it down for syrup. That woman would have been someone Alice could have gotten along with, whose company she might have enjoyed. But her mother had disguised herself, and had lost herself in that disguise, playing the part of a skinny, brittle, empty-headed society lady who only cared about charity galas and Pilates class so completely that she'd become the character, and had sent Alice away, again and again and again.

As if she were reading Alice's mind, her mother reached for her hand. "Are you all right?"

Alice pulled away without answering. She glared at her mother and made a noise in her throat that was first cousin to a growl. Faith sighed.

"I could spend the rest of my life apologizing and it still wouldn't be enough," she said quietly. Alice could hear the rasp of her voice. "I will never be able to make up for the time that we lost, and I am so sorry—" Her mother's voice broke.

Alice thought her mother meant it—that she'd hated having to pretend, that it had torn at her heart, every time she'd had to send her daughter away. She wanted to believe that this woman was the truth; that the woman from New York City was the lie. And she was still furious. Maybe it had hurt her, but her mother had been able to do it, to send Alice off to school after school, private schools and boarding schools, places where she'd always been an outcast, where, until Millie, she'd never made a single friend.

"I need to tell you . . ." Her mother took a deep breath. "You need to understand that there was a reason for it."

"I know." Alice could hear how sullen she sounded. "You had to keep me safe." On the drive up, her mother and Miss Merriweather had explained that the people who were looking for the Bigfoots knew that Faith had been in love with one of the Yare, and had had a baby with him. With Miss Merriweather's help, Faith had been able to sneak baby Alice out of the hospital where

Alice had been born, and she made her way, on foot, over hundreds of miles, to leave Alice with the Yare in upstate New York, so she could go back to New York City and reinvent herself, disguising herself so thoroughly that she'd be unrecognizable to the people who were searching for her. Alice knew all of that. But she was learning that knowing a thing and accepting it were not the same.

"Yes. Keeping you safe was part of it. But there was more. There were other Yare. Lots of them."

"My parents," said Millie, in her piping voice. "And Old Aunt Yetta. And Aelia and Marten, and Tulip and Frederee."

"All of them." Alice's mother sounded wistful. "And more." The gentle slope was getting steeper, the dirt path narrowing as it wound up the mountain's side. Jessica's nana was leaning on Jessica's arm, taking her time over the fallen trees and patches of ice. Miss Merriweather, meanwhile, was as nimble as a mountain goat, bounding over boulders and deadfalls, lifting branches out of the way. Soon, she was in the lead, with Millie close behind her.

Alice looked at her friend. Millie had pushed back the hood of her sweatshirt, and the fur around her face seemed to be trembling in the breeze. Her silvery eyes were wide, her nostrils were flared, and her mouth was open slightly, as if she was sampling the wintry wind. Alice wondered how the wind tasted, if Millie could detect snow, or notes of fallen leaves and maple syrup. All Alice could feel was the cold. *It figures,* she thought miserably, and shoved her hands in her pockets. *I'm a failure as a human, and I'm a failure as a Yare.*

"Where are we going?" Alice asked again as they reached the top of the ridge. She'd barely finished speaking when she heard Millie's joyful squeal.

"The Tribe!" Millie stage-whispered. "Alice! The Tribe is here!" Millie started to run, half-sliding down the hill, waving her arms in the air.

"How do you know?" Alice asked, as she ran to catch up.

"I can smell them!" said Millie.

Instead of asking about that, Alice just ran, with her boots scrabbling for purchase in the snow. Millie's silvery hair was flying, and Alice had a stitch in her side, which she ignored. For as long as Alice had known Millie, she'd been desperate for her friend to take her to the Yare village, but Millie had never agreed to it. *Too dangerous,* she'd said, leaving Alice with the strong sense that she wouldn't be welcome among the Yare. Now, the prospect of meeting Millie's entire Tribe displaced the anger at her mother, and left Alice feeling giddy and breathless.

"How?" she asked. "How did they get here?"

"Probably the bus!" Millie shouted back. "The one we use for Halloweening. Remember?"

Alice did. Millie wouldn't let Alice see her village, but she'd described how the Yare had an old school bus, and how once a year on October 31, Maximus, Millie's father, drove all the Yare littlies to some distant town, so they could go door to door, filling their buckets and pillow-cases full of candy, while the No-Fur grown-ups stared at them and scratched their heads and wondered why so many of the kids were dressed up in fur suits, and if there was some Paddington cartoon or Ewok spin-off movie that they'd missed.

Millie put on a final burst of speed that brought her to the crest of a ridge, where a boy was standing in front of a fancy-looking tent made of some water-repellent technical fabric. She stopped so abruptly that Alice almost ran into her back, and gave a low whine of dismay. Alice looked over her friend's shoulder and saw the boy who Millie had recognized. Immediately, Alice's hands clenched into fists, and this time, there was no doubt that the noise she was making was a growl.

"Don't hurt me," said Jeremy Bigelow, raising his own hands, palms out and fingers spread. "I come in peace!"

"You!" Millie said, her voice loud and shrill. "Bad, bad, no-good No-Fur boy! What are you doing here?"

"You followed us," Alice said, stalking toward Jeremy. "You led those guys from the government right to us. You lied to me." Her voice was loud and indignant, a furious shout. "I thought you were my friend!"

"I was!" Jeremy spluttered. "I am! I just—well, there was this guy, this guy from the Department of Official Inquiry, and he was threatening me, threatening my family, and I had to tell him something, so I did, but it wasn't everything, and maybe I shouldn't have, probably I shouldn't have, but I did, except I didn't tell him . . ."

"Didn't tell him what?" Alice demanded. She was standing so close that she could see the freckles spattered across Jeremy's cheeks. "Because you sure told him enough for a bunch of goons to try and kidnap me!"

Jeremy shut his mouth. His shoulders sagged as he nodded. "I told them enough. Enough so that they could find you and Millie. I'm really sorry about that."

Alice glared at him. Jeremy cringed.

"Go ahead and hit me," he said in a low voice. He looked at Millie. "You too. I screwed up, and I lied to you. I put you in danger. I deserve it."

Alice might have taken him up on it. And Millie, she

knew, wouldn't have stopped her. She glared at Jeremy, hesitating. Then she let her fists unclench. "I'm not going to hit you," she said.

Jeremy's eyes were wide with relief. "Really?"

"Really," said Alice.

Just then, Jeremy's midsection bulged and twisted, issuing a distinct meowing sound. The end of a tail, gray fur with a dab of white at the tip, emerged from the pocket to wave in the air. Millie's eyes got big.

"Georgina?" she whispered. "Is that my Georgina?"

"Uh, I think so," Jeremy said, digging into his sweatshirt's pouch and producing a small gray kitten with white paws. "Surprise!" Millie snuggled her pet against her cheek, looking happy for the first time since they'd left Standish, on their way to New York City.

Meanwhile, Alice's mother, Jessica and her grandmother, and Miss Merriweather had reached the top of the hill. Miss Merriweather's cheeks were flushed, and Jessica's grandmother was leaning heavily on Jessica's shoulder. Jessica herself wore a gigantic parka in a camouflage print, oversized boots with nubbly soles, and a knitted wool hat in a muddy shade of brown, all borrowed from the inn.

"Are we there yet?" Jessica panted.

Before anyone could answer, the tent flap unzipped, and a man stepped out onto the snow. Millie gasped. So did Jessica. Alice saw her mother stiffen.

"Is that . . ." Jessica whispered.

"Benjamin Burton," Millie breathed, sounding awed as she spoke the name of the head judge on *The Next Stage*.

Benjamin ignored them. He looked only at Alice's mother, and as he did, his entire face changed. Instead of looking stern and remote, he was grinning, almost glowing with joy.

"Nice hat," said Benjamin Burton, in his low, rumbling voice.

Faith Nolan made a noise that was half laugh, half sob. With one hand, she pulled the pom-pom hat off her head, and then she ran to him, crying as she threw herself into his arms, puffy down coat and all. "I never thought I'd see you again!" she cried.

Benjamin Burton held her. He cradled her head in his big hands and, with one thumb, brushed the tears off her cheeks before they could freeze. Then Benjamin looked at Alice. "Little one," he said, and opened his arms wide, and before she knew what she was doing, Alice found that her feet had carried her over the snow, until Benjamin Burton could sweep her into his arms and pull her, and her mother, against him, and all of them were tangled together, laughing and crying.

"Alice," said Faith Nolan, confirming what Alice's body already knew. "This is your father."

Alice would have stayed there forever, tucked up tight in her father's embrace, feeling the warmth and solidity of his arms, feeling like she'd finally come home. *Little one,* he'd called her. She'd never been called "little" in her life. She'd never felt little, or cherished, or as protected or loved, as much as she did in that very moment. Tears spilled down her cheeks as she held on tight, and the man—her father—held her just as tightly. Alice thought that he might be crying too.

"I missed you," she heard her mother whisper. "I missed you so much."

She looked up to see Benjamin stroke her mother's cheek. "You kept her safe," he said. His voice was grave, his eyes dark. "I could thank you my whole life, and it wouldn't be enough."

He turned to Alice. "I'm so glad to meet you. I've missed you for as long as you've been alive. I've spent so long trying to find you."

"Well, here I am," said Alice. She knew she should have felt a little shy, a little conflicted about this man, her real father. She had a father, a man who'd raised her and loved her all her life, and he was back in New York City. But this . . . being wrapped in his arms, smelling the wool of his coat and the faint scent of woodsmoke that it carried . . . it felt good. Better than good. It felt like coming home. *This is what she gave up,* Alice thought, looking at her mother. *This is what she sacrificed to keep me safe.* And, in that moment, she felt the smallest bit of forgiveness toward her mother, glowing inside her like an ember or a tiny firefly.

"Um, guys?" said Jeremy Bigelow.

Alice turned around and saw Millie was standing on the very edge of the ridge, waving her arms.

At first Alice couldn't tell what Millie was looking at. After a moment she caught a glint of yellow paint from deep in the forest below them. She watched closely, and saw what looked like a shadow emerging from the forest's depths. A stream of hooded figures, moving silently over the snow. Millie's Tribe. Alice's Tribe.

Millie gave a yelp and went racing down the ridge. Miss Merriweather followed, at a more sedate pace. Alice stood, frozen, unsure of what to do. She felt her father's hand settle on her shoulder. "Come meet your people, princess," he said. Then he scooped her into his arms

and lifted her onto his shoulders as if she were tiny, as if she weighed no more than a feather. *My people,* thought Alice, and, *Princess.* She laughed out loud, smiling as her father set off down the path, with Faith at his side and Alice on his shoulders.

Two hours later, Alice and her mother and her father and her friends were back, gathered at the dining room table at the bed-and-breakfast. Alice had been surprised at the Yares' willingness to be so public; to accompany them to the inn, an outpost of the No-Fur world in a town more or less owned by Christopher Jarvis. It's the end, she realized, a thought that filled her with equal parts excitement and terror. If the plan was for the Yare to finally come out of the shadows, and let the whole world see them, they had to start somewhere, even in the heart of enemy territory.

In the meantime, Alice wasn't sure how her mother had explained the presence of half a dozen Yare, in their varying degrees of Yare-ness, to Mrs. Hughes. Maybe her mother had told the proprietress some story about skin conditions and genetic disorders, which was how Alice had once tried to explain Millie's appearance. Maybe her mom had just said *My friends are a little odd-looking. Please don't stare,* with enough of her New York City fancy-lady attitude to get Mrs. Hughes to do as she was told. So far, Mrs. Hughes hadn't said anything. Her granddaughter had kept her eyes on the floor as she'd brought in platters of food from the kitchen, piling the sideboard with scones and muffins, doughnuts and cookies, an urn of hot coffee, a pitcher of hot chocolate, and a bowl full of fresh whipped cream.

Benjamin Burton sat at one end of the table, with Faith on his left side and Alice on his right. Maximus, Millie's father, sat at the other end of the table, with Millie on his right side and his wife, Septima, on his left. Between them were Jessica and her nana and Old Aunt Yetta and Jeremy Bigelow.

Between the fire in the big fieldstone fireplace and the late-morning sunlight that came slanting through the windows, the room was pleasantly warm. Millie had piled her plate with baked goods and was blissfully eating her way through a scone the size of a catcher's mitt.

"You have crumbs in your face-fur," Alice said, and used a napkin to brush them away. Millie's silvery eyes were wide, and she was smiling.

"I am not even caring! This is so good!" She winked at

Alice, then plucked two more scones off the platter, wrapped them in a napkin, and tucked them into the pouch of her sweatshirt. From the way it bulged, Alice thought it wasn't the first treat she'd squirreled away for later. As she watched, the pouch shifted and made a low purring noise.

Alice blinked. "Is that your cat?"

Millie reached into the pouch and produced a small gray ball of fuzz. "Her name was Georgina. But it is now Mitten," she said. "Tulip had the care of her, when I was away." Millie seemed saddened by the notion that her pet had been renamed.

"Maybe it's like an alias," Alice told her. "A secret name for a secret mission."

Millie smiled. "I like that!" She fed the kitten a bit of scone. Alice sprinkled nutmeg on top of the whipped cream she'd spooned into her mug of hot chocolate, and sat up straight when Miss Merriweather rapped on the table with her spoon. "Shall we begin?"

The room went quiet.

"I think our first job is to make sure everyone knows who's who and what's what." Miss Merriweather raised an eyebrow in Benjamin Burton's direction, and Alice watched, startled, as the large, bearded man seemed to shrink in his seat, before he gathered himself and stood.

251

"My name—my name now—is Benjamin. I left my Tribe when I was a little older than Millie. I was supposed to be the Leader, but I didn't want that. I wanted to see the world. The No-Fur world. So I came here, to Vermont. And I met Faith." He took Faith's hand, and Alice watched as her mother looked at him adoringly. "Faith and I were married," he said. "And then I was captured. She had a baby—our baby—and then escaped."

"With a little help from some friends," said Faith, and raised her coffee mug to toast Miss Merriweather. "I left Alice with the Tribe in Standish. Jamie—" She looked at Benjamin fondly. "That was his name then. Jamie had told me about it—not anything specific," she added, as Maximus growled softly at his brother, his fur bristling. "I was able to find Maximus and Septima. They took Alice, and kept her safe until I could find a way to bring her to New York."

"So we knew each other when we were babies," Millie said, just as Alice had realized the same thing.

"Yes," Faith said. "But Millie got to grow up in her Tribe. Alice . . ." Alice saw her mother's throat work as she swallowed. "We had to keep her hidden. Which meant I had to keep sending her away. It was . . ." Another swallow. Alice could hear Faith's voice shake. "It was very hard for her."

Maximus looked at Alice, and bowed his head. "We

owe you a great debt, Alice. Your sacrifice kept all the Yare safe. We are thankful to you."

"Thankful," repeated Septima and Maximus, Old Aunt Yetta, Miss Merriweather, and Millie, each of them pressing a fisted hand to his or her heart.

All morning, Alice had felt like she'd been picked up by a strong wave, like she was being turned and tumbled, flipped upside down and right side up and upside down again in a stinging whirl of water and sand. It had been enough of a shock to learn that she was half-human, half-Bigfoot, and that her mother was not who she'd pretended to be and that she'd never wanted to send Alice away. Meeting her biological father and learning that she might have to be the Leader of her Tribe was more than she could take in.

Millie must have seen what Alice was thinking, because she took Alice's hand and gave it a squeeze. "Not to worry," she whispered. "I will be your teacher of all things Yare."

Smiling, Alice squeezed back. She was imagining a life in the woods, a quiet, peaceful life lived mostly outdoors, in glades of trees with quiet ponds and forests dappled with sunlight. A cozy cottage or an underground house, like Millie had described, with a garden in the back. A fire burning in the fireplace, something fragrant baking in the oven. A few pets, a few good friends. It sounded like heaven to her, as much as it had been torture to Millie.

"You should know," Benjamin said, "that I never stopped looking for you. I never gave up." He nodded at Miss Merriweather, his expression a complicated mix of gratitude and frustration as he said, "You hid them well."

Miss Merriweather bent her head. "It was necessary. As you know. The enemy never stopped hunting us."

"And he's here." Jessica's voice was quiet, and her face was troubled. "The enemy. My grandfather. That's who you're talking about, right? Christopher Wayne Jarvis."

Alice remembered a voice on the phone, thin and old and greedy. *Of course, my dear,* it had said when she'd called a place named the Wayne Clinic. She remembered the man's voice sounding like a scaly snake as he'd hissed her name—*Al-issss*—and how, when he'd told her to take care of herself once she'd schedule the appointment, it had sounded more like an order than a pleasantry.

"Tell us what you know," said Miss Merriweather.

Jessica squirmed in her seat. "We think that he was working with the government. That whatever he could figure out how to get from the Bigfoots, he was going to give to the army. I think he did . . . something . . . to my father. I'm not sure. I overheard my parents having a fight,

after I told my mother about . . . after I told her that . . ." Another big gulp. She looked at Millie beseechingly.

"That you are having a tail," Millie said.

Jessica gave a miserable nod. She looked down, then up, quickly, her glance darting from face to face, her shoulders hunched in a way that looked familiar to Alice. Jessica was waiting for someone to laugh at her, Alice realized, or make her feel like she didn't belong. But no one did. The Yare, who all had fur, probably wouldn't see a tail as a big deal. Her nana and maybe even Miss Merriweather already knew. So did Millie, and Jeremy. Jessica's nana gave Jessica's hand a squeeze as Millie's mother, Septima, spoke in a faint, quavering voice.

"My grand-uncle Helman had a tail. It is not such a terrible thing."

Jessica smiled weakly and whispered, "Thanks."

"A man who'd experiment on his own family," said Alice's mother. "So we know he's ruthless."

"And angry," said Miss Merriweather.

"What else do we know about him? Have you met him?" asked Alice. She knew it was possible. Miss Merriweather had infiltrated the Department of Official Inquiry, pretending to be one of their agents while secretly telling the Yare what the real Department agents were doing.

Miss Merriweather shook her head.

"Has anyone met him?" asked Alice. "Besides Jessica?"

"I have," said Old Aunt Yetta.

Everyone at the table turned to stare at her. Old Aunt Yetta turned her coffee cup around and around in her gray-furred hand. "I met him just once. Long-and-long ago, this was. In the forest. When his wife was dying. She'd found us—" Alice heard Millie and her mother gasp. "Her husband knew where to look. He thought if he had some of our blood, that he would be able to save her."

Alice could barely breathe. "Was it true?"

Old Aunt Yetta muttered, "Nyebbeh!"

Alice looked at Millie for a translation. Millie gave her a helpless shrug, as Old Aunt Yetta said, "I told him that what he wanted was not his to take. I told him that we couldn't help her." Old Aunt Yetta sounded sad. "I knew it wouldn't stop with her. He would cure her, and then he'd want to cure everyone, and the No-Furs have done enough harm already." The Yare at the table were nodding. Jeremy looked skeptical. Jessica looked upset, and Jessica's nana was frowning, looking troubled. Alice wondered if Jessica's nana was thinking about herself, or a lost loved one, or maybe a friend who was old and frail and failing, someone who could be saved by Bigfoot blood.

Old Aunt Yetta passed a shaking, furred hand across her face. "I tried to do what was right. What I thought best. I only wanted him to leave—to leave the Yare alone, to stop looking, to give up, and I thought . . ." She gave a deep sigh. "I thought that if his wife died, then he would." She gave another deep sigh. "And now, I see I was mistaken."

"Could you have helped her?" Jessica asked. The room had gone very quiet.

"I don't know," Old Aunt Yetta said. She looked frustrated, tired, upset with herself. "I was angry at him for looking, for presuming that anything he wanted was his for the taking. I just wanted him to go."

"But we are here now." Alice's voice was clear and steady. She could feel everyone looking at her, but, for once, she didn't cringe or shy away from attention. She felt her mind working, very clearly, each thought sharp and precise. Maybe she'd never be able to stand on a stage and sing, like Millie, or be beautiful and stylish, like Jessica. There were a thousand things she could never do, could never be, but maybe she could do this: Keep the Tribe safe. Be Leader of the Yare. Maybe this was what she'd been born for.

Alice took a deep breath and said, "I think I know what to do."

Millie stared at her, wide-eyed. So did her mother and

her father. Her father! Alice only hoped she'd be able to make him proud.

"Christopher Jarvis wants me, right? He wants me for his experiments. He wants to figure out how to mix human and Yare blood, and use it so that he can live forever, and my blood's already mixed. I'm the proof of his hypothesis. That's why he's been trying so hard to get me. So I think I should go to him."

Alice heard her mother gasp. She knew she should have felt afraid, but in that moment, she felt as brave as a knight on a battle horse, a knight dressed in armor and carrying a magic lance. She could do this. She was sure of it.

"You cannot mean to go all by yourself," whispered Millie.

"I'll go with you," said Jeremy. "If anyone should take a risk, it's me."

"I can come," Jessica offered. "I mean, he's my grandfather. He's not going to do anything awful to me, or while I'm there." Her voice sounded a little hesitant as she looked at her nana. "Right?"

Alice shook her head. "Just me," she said. She looked around the table, at Miss Merriweather and Jessica and her nana, at Millie, at her mother and her father. "All of you can watch and make sure that I'm safe." Alice felt fear

creeping in through the cracks in her armor. Her knees had gone watery and her stomach fluttered, but she knew that it had to be done, that this had to end, one way or another, once and for all. "But I have to be the one to go inside. It has to be me."

"I don't like this," Faith Nolan said, her forehead creased with a frown.

"I should go with her. I've already left her on her own too much. I want to be there."

"I agree with Alice. She's got a better shot of getting in on her own," said Miss Merriweather.

"No!" Faith's voice was as loud as Jessica's had been. She lowered it a little. "Maybe she has the best chance, but she's a child. I'm not leaving Alice on her own. Not for this. Not ever again."

Silence around the table, until Alice got to her feet, walked around the table, and took her mother's hands. "Mom." She looked at her mother's face, her trembling lips and tear-filled eyes. "It's the only way."

Faith's voice was hoarse as she asked, "How did you get so brave?"

"I had to be brave," Alice said . . . and, as she spoke, she realized it was true. "Every time you sent me to a new school or a new camp where I didn't know anyone, I had to figure it out for myself. You made me brave." Faith's lips were trembling, her eyes filling with tears, and Alice thought that if she couldn't quite feel entirely grateful for what her mother had done—at least, not yet—she could see how it had worked, how it had shaped her. Being lonely, being ostracized, being the new girl with no friends, over and over and over again, had been hard, and sad . . . but it had made her strong and self-reliant. Brave.

"Please, Mom," Alice said quietly. "It's the only way."

Faith looked reluctant and unhappy, but finally, she nodded. "I'll be here," she said. "I'll be right there. If you need me, Alice, I'll be there for you."

Alice swallowed hard and nodded, knowing the truth of it—she'd be going in by herself. Facing Christopher Jarvis alone.

In twenty minutes, they'd hammered out a plan, and decided who would be watching from cars and who would be watching from the woods and who would stay at the inn, as a backup.

"Tomorrow?" asked Maximus. "First thing in the morning?"

Alice shook her head. She was remembering how, once, Millie had told her that the first thing a Yare baby learned to do was speak in a whisper and hide if they

heard someone coming, that singing was forbidden, and that most of the Yare lived their lives underground. Alice thought about what it would be like to only be able to go out in the world without a disguise on one night of the year, how it would feel to have to always be quiet; to hide, all the time. In a way, she'd spent her life underground, too, only instead of hiding in dark tunnels and lairs and underground hideaways she'd been moved from place to place and shuffled from school to school, never feeling like she belonged. Hunted, just like the Yare were hunted. It was time for her to lead, to do what was right for herself and her family and her Tribe, to lead them all to freedom. It was time for her—and all of them—to step into the light.

"No," said Alice. "Today. Right now. Before he figures out we're here and gets his people ready." Her voice held a note of command. Her face was solemn and pale, and her wild mane of hair, hanging in curls and ringlets around her face, made her look fierce.

"We shouldn't underestimate him," Jessica's nana said. "He's rich and powerful, and everyone in this town is on his side. He's formidable."

"Formidable," Alice repeated. A smile crept across her face, lifting the corners of her mouth. She squared her shoulders and tossed her hair back. "Well, I'm formidable too."

CHAPTER 21

Charlotte

WHILE THE YARE HELD THEIR COUNCIL OF war, Charlotte Hughes was upstairs, in the Green Room, on the second floor. She'd told her grandmother that she'd gone to clean the bathrooms and make the beds, but she wasn't doing either of those things. Instead, she was lying on the hardwood floor with her ear pressed to a heating vent. Her back ached. Her heart ached even worse, but she was doing her best to ignore her pain, along with a voice in her head that sounded like her grandmother's, telling her *Peep not at a keyhole, lest ye be vexed.* The first time Grandma Hughes said that to Charlotte, Charlotte had been a little girl, snooping on her grandmother as she talked on the phone by holding a water glass to the office door. When Charlotte had asked what it meant, her grandmother had said, her voice curt, "It means that if you try to listen to someone else's private conversation, you probably won't like what you hear."

Charlotte hadn't planned on spending her morning in such an undignified pose. When she'd returned from her unplanned trip through the woods, all she wanted was to take a long, hot shower, drink about a gallon of hot chocolate, and try to make some sense of what she'd seen. A flood of silent figures coming out of the forest to gather on a field, maybe two dozen in all. They'd been wearing human clothing, but they were barefoot, their hands and feet and faces covered in fur. Charlotte had stared at them numbly, her mouth hanging wide open, before she'd done the only sensible thing: she'd turned on her heel and blundered back home, half-walking, half-sliding down the hills, trembling with the shock of it. The girl with the hood pulled up over her head, the one with the odd-looking hands. She must be one of them, Charlotte thought . . . and she remembered the *National Examiner* story her grandmother had read her, the whispers and gossip she'd heard, all related to Jarvis Industries, and the lab. Was that where those creatures had come from? Were they dangerous? How had the inn's guests known that they would be there, and how were they connected to those things in the forest?

It was too much to think about, too much for her to figure out. She was just fifteen, still mostly a kid herself. Let the powerful people, Dr. Jarvis and the mayor and the chief of police, deal with the possibility of Bigfoots in the woods. She wanted her part in this to be over, and she wished, with all her heart, that when the man in the black car had offered her the phone, and the job, and the money, she'd said, "No."

As soon as she'd walked through the door, she'd found her grandmother waiting. "Where have you been?" Grandma demanded from her spot in front of the sink, where she was working through a pile of dirty dishes. "We've got to get that table set, and the coffee going . . ." Her voice broke off as she looked at her granddaughter. "What happened to you?" she asked. "Charlotte? Are you all right?"

"I'm fine," Charlotte managed. The front door opened, and Charlotte and her grandmother heard the sound of voices, the low murmur of conversation, high voices and low ones. A moment later, the pretty young woman was knocking on the kitchen door.

"Can I help you?" Charlotte asked, and hoped her voice sounded pleasant, that she looked normal, not terrified. Not like she'd just seen what looked like, for all the world, a pack of Bigfoots coming out of the woods less than a mile from her back door.

"Yes," said the lady. "Some friends of ours are unexpectedly in town. We'd like a place where we can sit down together and talk privately. Would the dining room work?"

"Of course," Grandma Hughes answered. "You're welcome to use the dining room. Charlotte will bring some pastries, and we'll get the fireplace lit."

"It's important that we not be interrupted," the woman said. "We're going to be discussing some confidential matters."

Confidential matters, Charlotte thought. She could feel wild laughter bubbling in her chest, and she clamped her lips together tightly.

"Of course," her grandmother repeated.

"Thank you," the woman said with a grateful smile. She went back to the dining room. Grandma nodded toward the oven. Charlotte pulled out the trays, loaded a platter, and was carrying in scones and muffins as the visitors filed into the room, some human, some not-quite-humans. The little girl in the hooded sweatshirt was sticking close to a woman who had a red scarf wrapped around her head and neck and most of her face. A tall man kept his back to Charlotte, and appeared to be glaring at the very human man beside him. There were the two little old ladies who'd checked in the night before, and a new old lady, with curly white hair on her head, her face mostly hidden by a ski cap with an exuberant red pom-pom on top, and white fur visible on her cheeks.

Back in the kitchen, Charlotte could barely breathe. She'd finally managed to slow her racing heart when her phone had started vibrating in her pocket. She froze, her hands on the counter as the phone buzzed and buzzed. She wanted to throw it out the window or, better yet, into the oven; to turn on the heat and blast it until it was a lump of melted glass and plastic. But that was no good. If she hung up, Christopher Jarvis's minions would just keep trying. If she didn't talk to him on the phone, the man with the pitiless voice would come for her in person. That was the last thing Charlotte wanted.

She pulled out her phone and saw a text from an unknown number. "Listen to them," it said. "Listen to everything they say. Then call us."

Charlotte swallowed hard, holding the phone pinched

between two fingers like a poisonous snake. Then she'd put it back in her pocket and gone trudging up the stairs, to the Green Room, which was right above the dining room. She was thinking back to that day years ago when the man in the car had given her that first hundred dollars, how she'd half-danced down the street, dreaming about everything she'd buy. It had been so easy to give her word back then because the money was real, and the job felt like a joke she'd agreed to go along with. And now, here she was, sprawled flat on the floor, just above a room full of monsters, and she was eavesdropping on the inn's guests, spying on children.

Charlotte did not like what she'd heard so far. The young girl going to Christopher Jarvis's house all by herself, like Gretel from the fairy tale strolling blithely into the witch's candy cottage. *It won't end well,* she thought to herself. Charlotte knew that she should warn the girl. But instead, as the cell phone buzzing insistently in her pocket reminded her, soon she'd be warning the witch.

So she kept listening, crouched over the vent with her hands and feet still numb from the cold, feeling like an animal waiting to spring; taking only the occasional break to stretch her aching back. She'd made a promise,

Charlotte thought bleakly. She'd given her word. She'd taken their money. And it wasn't like she'd be betraying anyone she was friends with, anyone she really knew. These girls were from a big city, far away. Charlotte told herself, over and over, that she didn't owe them a thing.

Except the more she thought it, the less convinced she'd become.

Except the tall girl with the wild hair reminded Charlotte of herself. When she'd been younger, she'd been taller than every other kid in her class, out of step with the rest of them because she didn't like the same kind of music or the same kinds of books. Charlotte knew what it was to not fit in, and to want a life different from what you'd been given.

You promised, Charlotte told herself, and punched the button that would call the number without giving herself the chance to hesitate. This time, the phone didn't ring at all before a man answered . . . and this time, it was not the smooth-voiced, anonymous-looking man who answered her call.

"This is Christopher Jarvis," said a high, cracked voice. Charlotte gasped. She felt like she'd been punched, hard, right in the heart. She could imagine him, the man no one in Upland had ever seen, snatching at his phone with one clawed, age-spotted hand. She pictured thin lips drawn back from yellowed teeth; sly, rheumy eyes; narrow, hunched shoulders; and long-nailed fingers.

"Charlotte Hughes?" he asked, in a voice that made her think of witches, of dying birds and the jagged screech of metal on metal.

Her own voice trembled a little. "Yes?"

"What are they planning?" he asked. "How many of them are there, and what are they intending? Tell me everything. Every single thing you heard. Every detail. Nothing is too small."

Charlotte Hughes cleared her throat, gripping the phone more tightly. She wondered why he cared; why this man who was rich enough to buy an entire town, maybe even an entire state, was so fixated on these . . . these whatever-they-were. Why did it matter? What did he want? What was he hoping to get from them, or do to them?

She shuddered. In her head, she was thinking of lab rats with no eyes, or with extra ones; ribbons of greasy smoke, spiraling up into the darkness; the sound of screaming in the night.

"Miss Hughes?" came the voice of the God of Upland. She heard the threat that hid inside that voice, curled like a snail inside of its shell—*do what you promised, or your lovely life goes away.*

She cleared her throat. And told him what she'd heard. Almost, but not all of what she'd heard. Christopher Jarvis hung up without a word of thanks, and Charlotte stood there, clutching the phone with frozen hands, praying, with all her heart, that this man, with his agents and his all-seeing eyes, wouldn't find out what she'd kept from him, and that it would maybe be enough to keep those girls safe, those girls who reminded her, so painfully, of the girl she herself had been not so long ago.

CHAPTER 22

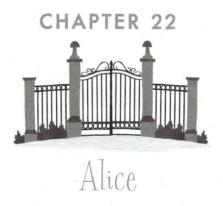

Alice

A HEAVY IRON FENCE SURROUNDED Christopher Jarvis's property, its stanchions nine feet high, with spiked points on top. The gates had swung open as soon as Alice had approached them, without her needing to touch as much as a finger to the key plate. *Come in, come on!* she imagined a voice urging her in a whisper. *We've been waiting for you! We've set the table, and you're our main course. So come in!*

Security cameras, Alice saw, looking up toward the top of the fence. Or maybe motion detectors. Whoever was in the house was watching. She could barely breathe, could hardly believe that her feet were still moving, propelling her forward, instead of racing away.

Jeremy gave a startled bark of laughter. Alice looked over her shoulder, reassuring herself that the grown-ups were still there. She could see the street, and Miss Merriweather's little white car, driving in slow loops up and down the block. Her mother would be in the car, keeping watch. Millie and Jessica were in another car, with Jessica's nana, driving through the neighborhood, staying close. Benjamin Burton, her father, would be watching, and Maximus and Septima and Old Aunt Yetta would all be hidden in the woods, each of them with a lifetime of experience in making themselves undetectable. With all of those eyes on her, nothing could go wrong. At least, that's what Alice told herself as she climbed the steps up to the entryway. She reached in her coat pocket and touched her phone. She'd called her mother before she'd gotten close to the house, and in range of its cameras. The plan was for her to stay connected after she went inside.

The house's front door was painted black, and there was a curious brass knocker hung in its center. As Alice got closer, she could see that it was in the shape of a claw, with long, curved nails extending from each digit. It looked like the paw of a Bigfoot, cast in brass and hung as a warning.

"I'm going in now," Alice said, trying not to tilt her head toward her pocket, knowing that there were cameras watching.

No answer came. But Alice hadn't been expecting an answer. She lifted the knocker, and let it thump against the door, which opened immediately.

"Hello," said the thing that was waiting there.

Alice felt her jaw drop open, felt herself instinctively moving backward, away from the man who stood in the doorjamb.

When she was a little girl, she'd had an illustrated collection of fairy tales. She'd loved to hear the stories of Snow White and Sleeping Beauty, Cinderella and the Little Mermaid, but there was one story she never asked for—the story of Rumpelstiltskin. It wasn't so much what happened in the story, the way a little magical man gave the poor miller's daughter the ability to spin straw into gold. The king had fallen in love with the miller's daughter, and married her, and then, when she was pregnant, the little man had come back to demand their baby in payment, unless she could tell him his name. The fairy tale, at least in the book her parents had gotten, had a happy ending. The miller's daughter had overheard the little man's name. She'd gotten to keep her baby and her husband and the castle where she lived.

The story hadn't bothered Alice. It was the pictures that had given her nightmares. Somehow, the illustration of a tiny, cavorting man, his ugly face screwed up in laughter, lit by flames as he capered in front of his fire, chortling about how the miller's daughter would never, ever guess his name, had haunted her for years. The first thought that Alice had, looking at the man behind the door, was that Rumpelstiltskin had finally found her, that he'd caught up with her at last.

She heard herself inhale, and struggled to keep her face still.

There was a sour smell around him, the smell of unwashed flesh and dirty, decaying clothing, a smell of mushrooms that grew in dark, moldy places, of rotting paper and ancient dust.

In a cracked and wheedling voice, the greedy voice that Alice remembered from their phone call, he said, "Alice?"

Alice nodded. She squared her shoulders and gave her thick mane of hair a shake.

The man eyed her up and down, like he was examining a steak that a waiter had just set on his table, trying to decide where to cut first.

274

"So you've come," he said. Alice heard the voice of Rumpelstiltskin, from her fairy-tale book, echo in her head; Rumpelstiltskin as he tormented the miller's daughter. *Now give me what you promised!*

"Yes," said Alice. "I'm here to give you what you want."

"Well then, come along."

Alice stepped inside and followed the little man into the fetid darkness of the house. She had a sense of soaring ceilings, an impression of windows across which drapes had been drawn, to block out the light. Piles of books were everywhere, stacked on chairs and leaning against walls. Flies buzzed around plates of rotting food, and the smell was indescribable: the scent of decaying flesh and mildewed walls, of every diseased and dying thing. It was probably, Alice thought, the smell of Christopher Wayne Jarvis himself.

"I apologize for the state of the place." The old man's giggle made Alice's skin crawl. "It's so hard to get good help. And I don't get too many visitors these days. You understand."

I understand that you're dangerous, Alice thought. *I understand that you hurt your own family. I understand you'll hurt me, if I let you.* The man led her up a flight of stairs, down a shadowed hallway, and through a doorway into a little room.

He closed the door behind them and hit a switch on the wall. Bright, buzzing fluorescents lit up a room that looked like every doctor's office Alice had ever been in. There was the tiled floor, the examination table, with blood-pressure cuffs and thermometers in hooks beside it. There was a long counter with bins of wipes and bins for the disposal of biohazardous waste and sharp things. And in the center of the room, there was what looked like an electric chair. It was made of wood, with vinyl-covered padding. Thick leather cuffs on the armrests, and cuffs at the base. At the top, above the headrest, there was what looked like a metal pie plate, bristling with wires.

"Have a seat." The man giggled, and gestured toward the chair. "Oh, and I should apologize in advance. Your phone won't work in here."

Alice swallowed hard. Had he known her phone was connected to people outside, or just guessed?

Christopher Jarvis giggled again. "You know the story of the Three Little Pigs? The house of straw, the house of wood, the house of bricks?" His grin was wide and malignant, his teeth jagged, a few of them oddly shaped, as if he'd tried to file them into points. "Well"—he tittered—"I built my house out of gold."

Alice stared at him. "What?"

"Gold, my dear. Have you taken chemistry yet? Have you learned about the properties of the elements?" He stood up straight, or tried to, and took on the air of a professor lecturing students.

"You see, this house isn't just a house. It's a secure research facility. In order to make it that way, I needed to protect it from electromagnetic waves, from interference, from light, from sound, from earthquakes. I needed to make sure I could control any transmissions, in or out." Christopher Jarvis waved one misshapen hand. "You're welcome to record to your heart's content, my brave young visitor! You won't be able to share your photographs, or video, with anyone outside these walls."

"Yeah, but as soon as I leave . . ." Alice started to say. Then she shut her mouth, as she realized that, if Christopher Jarvis had his way, she wouldn't be leaving at all.

Christopher Jarvis leaned forward to deftly pluck the phone out of Alice's pocket. Holding it up to the light, he turned it from side to side to examine it. "Nice piece of tech," he said. "For civilians." He handed it back to Alice, who glanced at the screen and saw no bars' worth of Internet service. "CALL FAILED," read the screen.

Christopher Jarvis opened the examination room door. Two gigantic men in blue suits, with mirrored glasses and blank expressions, were standing in the hallway. One of them had patches of fur on his face; the other had a six-fingered claw where his right hand should have been and only empty space at the end of his left arm.

"Two of my failed attempts," he announced, and nodded at Alice. "Get her into the chair."

The men, or whatever they were, moved swiftly across the room. One grabbed Alice's shoulders, one-handed, and the other lifted her ankles.

Alice fought valiantly. She wriggled and kicked, she screamed and squirmed, and still the bodyguards held her like she was a sack of feathers, like she weighed nothing. They strapped her into the chair, and left her alone with Christopher Jarvis, who was staring at her like she was an insect pinned to a board. His eyes were avid and bright in his face, and he seemed to be drinking her pain, like a gourmet sipping some rare wine, tasting it and finding it delicious.

Alice straightened up. "There are people watching

me," she said. "If they don't hear from me, they'll come."

"They won't." Christopher Jarvis waved one hand at a flat-screen mounted to the wall, and showed Alice what had unfolded since she'd walked through his door.

The screen showed Miss Merriweather's car, with a police car pulled up behind it. As Alice watched, an enormously tall police officer unfolded himself from the car and ambled over. He wore mirrored sunglasses and a wide-brimmed hat, and kept his left hand on the butt of the gun on his belt as he approached them. He knocked on the window. Miss Merriweather unrolled it.

"Ma'am, do you know why I stopped you?" Alice could hear him clearly, and realized that Christopher Jarvis must have set up cameras and microphones everywhere, on every lamppost and light pole, maybe even in the sewers.

"No, sir, I don't." Miss Merriweather's voice was calm.

"Step out of the car, please. Both of you."

Alice could see how his hand had tightened on the gun. She saw, too, that the hand had six—no, seven—fingers, that seemed to be missing a few important joints. She watched Miss Merriweather and her mother step into the street.

"Hands on the roof. Both of you." A second officer had pulled up, lights flashing, siren blaring. That car was followed by a third and a fourth, and soon there were eight police officers surrounding the car. One of them bent down, reached inside the car, and removed the keys, along with Miss Merriweather's sensible leather purse and the backpack that Faith had brought.

"Identification?" the first officer asked.

"My license is in my backpack," said Faith.

Miss Merriweather said, "I'm an employee of the Department of Official Inquiry. My identification is in my wallet. May I reach into my purse to get it?"

Instead of answering, one of the officers turned the purse over, dumping its contents out onto the road. An officer clicked handcuffs around Miss Merriweather's wrists; another one handcuffed Faith Nolan. The women exchanged a helpless glance. Alice saw her mother twist her head over her shoulder to take one last, desperate look at the house on the hill. The police officer shoved her, and she stumbled, almost falling. Instead of apologizing, the man pushed her again, so that she half-walked, half-fell into the van that was idling against the curb. "Not so tough this time, are you?" Alice heard him growl. Before she could answer, he'd pushed Miss Merriweather into the van beside her, and slammed the door shut.

In the examination room, Christopher Jarvis giggled. He waved his remote at the screen, and the scene changed. Alice saw Maximus and Benjamin Burton moving almost soundlessly through the woods. Or, rather, Maximus was moving soundlessly, while Benjamin's motions betrayed his years among the No-Furs. Every time he stepped on a branch or his boot crunched through the snow, his brother would turn and glare at him.

Finally, after rejecting three different hiding spots that all seemed fine to Benjamin, Maximus located a stand of pine trees in the center of the ridge, and arranged himself against a trunk, his brown jacket and pants fading into the bark until he was almost invisible. Dressed in his usual black, Benjamin did his best, leaning beside his brother, and only bumping into one snow-covered bough and sending its freight of snow thudding noisily to the ground.

"You're looking well, brother," Alice heard him say.

Maximus grunted.

"Your wife is lovely," Benjamin said.

"Keep quiet," Maximus grunted.

"Did you miss me?" Benjamin asked.

Maximus turned to glare at him. "Did you miss us?"

he asked. "Did you think of us, even once? Did you think of me? I wasn't raised to be the Leader. It was never what I wanted."

"It wasn't what I wanted either."

"So you got to be free, and I had to stay behind."

Benjamin's shoulder drooped. "I am sorry," he said.

"It's too late for sorry." But Alice's uncle sounded marginally less angry.

"Alice will be a good Leader," Benjamin said.

Maximus grunted again. Benjamin sighed. And then Alice saw three helicopters come blasting through the sky to hover above their heads. They were painted black, with black rotors, and their blades were chopping at the air, making a sound like the end of the world.

Benjamin looked at his brother, shouting, "Run!" But as he spoke, a voice came booming out of the sky, from one of the helicopters, amplified to a level that could have shattered glass, and was probably making the nearby houses shudder in their foundations.

"BENJAMIN BURTON AND ACCOMPLICE, YOU ARE UNDER ARREST FOR TRESPASSING."

Alice watched as the choppers descended. She saw Benjamin Burton and her uncle, frozen in place. She saw the soldiers in fatigues who came pouring out of the

choppers, once they'd landed, each one carrying a semi-automatic weapon with a powerful scope.

Alice saw that the soldiers were more imperfect combinations of human and Yare. One of the soldiers had patchy fur on his face and a lumpy, misshapen torso underneath his uniform. The one beside him had a mouth full of sharp, yellowed teeth, teeth that were far too large for his mouth and were sticking out every which way. Another one looked almost normal—which was to say, almost entirely Yare—but he was laughing, a progression of high-pitched yips that grated on Alice's ears with their wrongness.

"PUT YOUR HANDS IN THE AIR," came the amplified voice. Benjamin and his brother exchanged a glance, and then complied. As Alice watched, Benjamin looked at the helicopters, where Christopher Jarvis's camera must have been hidden, and mouthed the word *Sorry*. Alice felt her heart sinking, realizing how much it would hurt to lose her biological father so soon after she'd found him.

"Keep watching," said Christopher Jarvis, as that bit of film ended and a new one began. This one showed a view of the road, and the car that Jessica's nana was driving. Alice braced herself for the sound of sirens, and the sight of police cars, roaring to a stop right behind the car.

"Step out of the car," came a booming voice. Alice watched, feeling like she could barely breathe, as Jessica's nana got out of the front seat, and Jessica emerged from the back. She didn't see Millie, who should have been with them. At least, that had been the plan. Where was Millie? Alice kept her face very still, as Christopher Jarvis said, "No one's coming to help you, my dear."

You're wrong, she thought . . . and then she hoped that Millie was on her way, that Millie had a plan, that Millie wouldn't get hurt.

CHAPTER 23

Millie

WHEN THE POLICE'S VOICE CAME OVER THE speaker, Millie pressed herself against the floor of the car, making herself as small as she could. She wanted to close her eyes and put her hands over her ears and just give up, to hide with her eyes shut until whatever was happening had happened. But she couldn't do that. Alice needed her.

"Stay there," Jessica whispered to her as the No-Furs in uniforms started yelling, saying, *Keep your hands where we can see them* and *exit the vehicle.* Jessica pulled her phone out of her pocket and pushed it into Millie's hand. "It's unlocked. Use it to call us if you can, and take pictures or video if you can't."

"But—" Millie started to protest, to explain that she didn't know how to work the phone, that she barely knew how to work a top-lap. Jessica talked right over her.

"Wait till they're busy with us. I'll try to make some kind of distraction," she whispered. "Then run."

"Run where?" Millie whispered, even though she knew.

"Go to the big house. See if you can get in. Try to make sure Alice is okay. Try to find someone who can help. And film everything."

"Miss?" a Police said to Jessica. "Step out of the car."

"I'm coming," said Jessica. She opened up the car door, but instead of slamming it shut, she left it open, just a little. More Police were coming, three men and one woman, all in the same uniforms and hats and glasses. Millie waited until Jessica and Jeremy and the Nana were all in front of the car, and none of the Police were looking at it, or in it. *I don't want to!* her brain was screaming. *Don't make me, please don't make me, I'm the littlest one of all, and I'm not brave!*

But she had to do it. Her Tribe needed her. Her friend needed her.

"Stand, and be true," Millie whispered to herself. She touched her pocket to make sure the phone was there before wriggling through the crack of the open door and

onto the pavement. She wanted to run into the woods and hide there, digging herself a hole, covering herself up with leaves or snow, keeping her eyes shut, waiting until it was over. Instead, she made herself roll under the car. The pavement was cold, a cold that seeped through her blue wool coat, through her fur and her skin and into her body. Her teeth wanted to chatter. Millie clenched them tight, as she heard Jessica's voice.

"I think . . . I think I'm fainting . . ."

Then there was a kerfuffle, bodies moving and shouting sounds and people all talking over each other. Millie rolled out from underneath the car. Moving in a scuttling crouch, she ran from the street, down an incline, and into the forest. Christopher Jarvis's house couldn't be far. She'd find it, and she would be brave. She'd find a way to get inside, and help her friend, and save the day.

CHAPTER 24

Alice

ALICE KEPT HER FACE EXPRESSIONLESS AS Christopher Jarvis turned his back to the screen. "No one's coming to help you, my dear." But by then Alice had seen what Christopher Jarvis had missed: a tiny figure, clad in baggy, dark-colored clothing, that had slipped out of the car, then under it, before running off into the woods.

"Just take what you want," Alice said to him, in a loud, raw voice. "You want my blood? Take it!"

"Ah, if only it were that simple." He sounded sincerely regretful as he said, "Even if I could extract what I require and leave you alive, now that you've been here, now that

you've seen what I've done, and what I am, I can't send you back into the world."

Alice was shuddering, her face gone cold, skin prickling with gooseflesh. *Extract what I require,* he'd said. That sounded like a lot more than just a blood sample.

Christopher Jarvis must have seen this knowledge moving across her face. He gave her a leering grin. "It'll all be over soon," he said. "And it won't hurt." He cocked his head, considering. "Well, at least not too much." He gave a high, tittering giggle, turned, and scuttled out the door, leaving Alice trapped and alone, bound to a chair in a house made of gold, with no one coming to save her. With the possible exception of Millie.

Oh, Millie, please hurry, she thought. *Be careful. And come fast.*

CHAPTER 25

Charlotte

CHARLOTTE HUGHES PACED THE LENGTH OF her tiny bedroom, trying to distract herself; trying not to think about what she'd done. She'd given her grandmother some excuse about homework, and then, as soon as she could, she'd escaped up here. Now she was walking back and forth, back and forth, her feet thumping on the floorboards, for once, not even trying to keep quiet. *Brats,* she thought . . . but no matter how much she tried to tell herself that the girls were rich, spoiled snobs who'd look down on someone like her, part of her didn't believe it. Part of her saw that they were girls, like she was. And that part decided that if she didn't do something—the right thing—she wouldn't be able to live with herself. The money she'd collected would burn her hands if she ever touched it; she'd never know a moment's peace. Every bit of food she ate would come salted with guilt. All her dreams would be bad.

With a groan, Charlotte flung open her bedroom door and hurried downstairs to the kitchen, where her grandmother was standing in front of the sink, her hands still, for once, not scrubbing or washing or wiping or drying. She was looking out the window, her head tilted, her gaze fixed on the sky. Faintly, Charlotte could hear the sound of helicopters and sirens. Her heart sank. *Too late,* she thought. *Oh, what if I'm too late already?*

Her grandmother turned around. "What is it?" she asked.

Charlotte swallowed hard. "I need to tell you something."

Her grandmother looked at her expectantly. Charlotte gulped.

"I did something bad. Something really, really bad." Her voice cracked. "And now . . ."

Her grandmother gave her a hard look. "Does it have something to do with our guests? And the lab?"

"Yes." Charlotte inhaled and then, all in a rush, before

she could lose her nerve, she said, "I've been working for someone who works for Jarvis Industries. He paid me to look for people. Unusual people, like the ones who checked in last night." She gulped. "I called him and told him about the people staying here, but I think Dr. Jarvis—I think he hurts children, or maybe he's going to hurt children." Another gulp. "I was listening when they were talking, and they were saying how Dr. Jarvis hunts—people like them." Yare, they'd called themselves, but Charlotte wasn't going to confuse her grandmother with new terminology. "And the girl with red hair said she was going to his house, to try to stop him, but I don't think she'll be able to. I think he's going to hurt her. Hurt all of them." Charlotte paused, then blurted, "We have to stop him."

Her grandmother stared at her, an unreadable expression on her face. The silence seemed to stretch out forever.

"Get your coat," Charlotte's grandmother finally said, and wiped her hands on the dish towel. "Then wait for me." Her grandmother went clomping down the hall. A minute later she was back, holding a shiny black pistol carefully in her right hand.

Charlotte stared. "I've had it for years," said her grand-

mother. "Sometimes guests pay in cash, you know. And I'm a woman alone." She looked at the gun with distaste. "I've never used it. Never even had to take it out of the safe." She shook her head, then put the gun in her pocket and picked up the keys to her car.

"Come on," she said, giving Charlotte the tiniest smirk. "If these people are as bad as my newspaper says they are, then we don't have any time to waste."

CHAPTER 26

Millie

_I_ T CAN'T BE FAR, MILLIE TOLD HERSELF. SHE raced down a steep slope, into a ditch, where an iced-over stream trickled over slippery rocks. Her foot went crashing through the ice, into the freezing water. Millie gasped and wrenched her foot free, and kept going, up the opposite side of the hill where she prayed she'd see the back of Christopher Jarvis's house.

Millie crept quietly over the snow, moving soundlessly from shadow to shadow, from a clump of bushes to a conveniently fallen log. She could see a barbwire fence running around what must be the perimeter of the property, and she scrambled lightly up a tree, higher and higher, until she could look down and see everything. There were men with guns walking on the inside of the fence. And there were cameras on the roof of the house, on the tree branches, on the high fence posts, cameras that probably covered every inch of the property and would alert anyone who was watching to the presence of unwanted visitors.

"Nyebbeh," Millie muttered, hopping down from the tree. She'd have to try the front yard. Maybe even the front door, if it came to that. But Jessica had told her to try to find help, so that was what she'd do. Even if it meant talking to a No-Fur stranger and risking them snatching her up for a zoo or a museum. Even if it meant she'd be kidnapped, never to see her parents or her Tribe again. Alice was her friend. She had to try.

Millie spun in a circle, wishing there was someone there to tell her what to do, wishing that her father was there to give instructions and her mother there to keep her safe.

Oh, really? a voice mocked inside her head. *You, who would be Leader, asking for help? Needing instruction? Needing someone to keep you safe!*

I don't want to be Leader, Millie told the voice. *I never wanted that. I only wanted to sing!*

You wanted to live in the No-Fur world, the voice informed her coolly. *Well, here you are.*

Millie stood up as straight as she could. She turned toward the house and studied it carefully. There was the tall iron fence topped with razor wire. She could climb as far as the wire, and then maybe she could jump to the drainpipe and climb to the roof. And, running around the third floor, Millie could see a narrow walkway with an ornamental railing. There was a guard walking in circles around it, but if Millie timed it right, she could leap from the pipe to the walkway, and then through a window, while the guard was on the other side of the house.

And right into the arms of the guards, she thought, because surely there were guards indoors as well as out. But it didn't matter. She knew she had to try.

Millie tightened the strings that kept her hood taut around her face. And then, moving in a fast, low scuttle, she started to run.

CHAPTER 27

Alice

ALICE MAYFAIR WANTED TO CRY, BUT SHE knew that Christopher Jarvis probably had cameras in the room. He was probably watching, and she refused to give him the satisfaction of knowing that he'd broken her. He could have (or would take) her blood, her bone marrow, her brains, and her DNA. She would not give him, with all of that, the satisfaction of her tears.

I did my best, she thought. *I tried to learn the truth about myself, and to protect Millie. I did my best. I tried, and I lost, and now I'm going to die if I can't think of a way to get out of here.*

She gave her wrists an experimental wiggle. Neither one budged.

Okay, she thought. *So maybe, if I'm really a Bigfoot—and not just a Bigfoot, but a Leader—maybe I've got some kind of psychic connection to the rest of the Tribe. Maybe there's a way for me to call them and tell them I'm in trouble.*

Alice remembered the meditation techniques she'd learned from Phil and Lori back at the Center, ways to calm one's thoughts and clear one's mind. She made herself take five long, slow breaths, counting to four with each inhalation and exhalation. She pictured the faces of the Yare she'd met: Millie and Miss Merriweather. Shy Septima and Old Aunt Yetta, and big, tall Maximus with his deep voice. Benjamin Burton, who was her real father. She held the image of their faces in her mind, and then she thought, as hard as she could, *I NEED HELP!!!*

She waited, trying to keep her mind blank, hoping for an answer.

None came.

Maybe Millie was on her way, she thought. She imagined her friend, scooting and scurrying across the snow, pounding on the door, demanding admittance . . . and then being captured by Christopher Jarvis's goons. Maybe Jeremy had called for help, she thought. Then she imag-

ined Jeremy trying to convince a bunch of skeptical police officers that his half-Bigfoot friend had been kidnapped by the local beloved billionaire, the savior of Upland.

Her mother wasn't coming. Neither her biological father nor the man she still thought of as her real one was coming. Miss Merriweather wouldn't save her, and neither would Old Aunt Yetta, or Jessica or her nana.

No one was coming to save her. She would die the way she'd lived most of her life—all alone. Unless she could find a way to save herself.

Alice closed her eyes. She breathed in, one, two, three, four; held her breath, one, two, three, four; and blew out, slowly and steadily, one, two, three, four. When she felt a little more calm, she tried to think. What did she know about the Yare? That they lived longer than humans. That they healed faster. And that they were strong.

Alice looked down at the thick leather cuff that kept her right wrist pinned to the arm of the chair. She looked at it for a long, long time, until it stopped being her wrist, and could have been any wrist. She turned that anonymous wrist from side to side, feeling it move against the leather, and thought about strength.

Girls in her world weren't supposed to be strong.

They weren't supposed to enjoy their bodies much, no matter what those bodies looked like, or what feats they could perform, as far as Alice could tell. The point of a woman's body was to be small, first and foremost; to be smooth-skinned and wrinkle-free; to have long, shiny hair on your head and no hair anyplace else; but, most of all, to be small. To not occupy too much space, to not make too much noise, to not demand much of the world.

Back when her mother was still impersonating a fancy New York City lady, Alice had watched Faith restrict her diet until it was mostly just steamed vegetables and lean proteins, and cram herself into clothes and shoes that pinched and squeezed and had to have hurt. She'd watched her mother attach fake lashes to her eyelids with glue and magnets, watched her wax and pluck and shave and paint and powder. A body, Alice had come to understand, was a thing to be tamed, to be disciplined and managed and controlled. And her body was big and unruly and undisciplined . . . and, thus, unacceptable.

It wasn't until Alice had gone away to the Experimental Center that she'd learned to enjoy her physical self. She'd loved the sensation of running, the feeling of her body moving, fast and free, through the cool air of the shadowed paths that ran through the forest surrounding the school. She'd run in sunshine and in rain, on hot days and cold ones, days where the wind gusted and days when the air was hot and thick and still. She would run until her skin tingled, until she could feel her heart pounding and taste blood in her throat. She'd leap over tree stumps and streams and fallen logs, she'd race up steep hills and down steeper ones, splashing through streams, moving rocks and trees and anything that stood in her way, picking them up and moving them aside because she was strong.

Yes, a voice inside her head whispered. Strong. Maybe not brave; at least, not all the time. Not the funniest, not the wittiest, not the smartest or the prettiest. Not sweet and lovable and talented, like Millie; not brilliant like her roommate Taley or athletic like her roommate Riya or pretty and popular and at ease in the world, like Jessica Jarvis, but strong.

You can do this, Alice. You're strong. You always have been. And that voice did not sound like her own voice, not her mother's voice, or Benjamin Burton's. It sounded like Mark Mayfair, the man who had raised her; Mark Mayfair, who hadn't been her biological father but who'd still loved her as much as he could.

I'm proud of you, Alice imagined her father saying. *And I know you're going to do incredible things. Only not if you stay trapped here, so Alice, you've got to be as strong as you can be, stronger than you've ever been.*

Alice turned her wrist back and forth, back and forth. She clenched her fist and pulled her arm toward her, straining as hard as she could. Her face turned red. The cords of her neck stood out. Her breath came in teakettle squeaks between her clenched teeth. The leather cuff didn't give even a millimeter, but Alice thought that she'd heard it creaking, just a little bit.

Okay, she thought, and took some more deep, slow breaths. The voice in her head was her mother's. Her real mother. *Alice, I know you can do it. You're so brave. I'm so proud of you. Try again.*

Again, Alice strained, muscles clenched, pulling as hard as she could. This time, she not only heard the leather creak, she felt it give, just the tiniest bit.

She refused to let herself look. She could see it with her mind's eye—her hand, her wrist, her forearm, the leather. The dark-blue sweater, her jeans, her boots. She inhaled, slowly, and heard—or imagined she heard—a tiny voice, high and sweet and brave. *Alice! Hang on! I am coming!*

Millie, she thought. She pictured her friend's face, and strained, as hard as she could, clenching every muscle

from her calves to her thighs, her abdomen and back, her shoulders, her neck, her jaw, everything, clenched and pulling. She curled her toes and tensed her legs, throwing every ounce of herself into the effort, hearing her bindings creak and groan. *For my friend,* she thought. *For my Tribe. For my family, for everyone who's ever loved me. For every girl who's ever felt different.* She turned her hand so it was facing her, and held her breath and pulled, and the world went red behind her eyes, and she pulled, and the world went black, and just as she knew she was going to pass out, still bound to the chair, just as she thought, *I am going to die in this room,* the cuff snapped.

CHAPTER 28

Millie

MILLIE USED HER ARMS AND THIGHS TO grip the cold metal of the drainpipe, trying to hold very still, trying not to make a sound. She could see the guard making his rounds. When he came to the corner of the house, he'd be close enough to touch her; close enough to see her, if he thought to look just a few inches around the corner. *Please don't look,* Millie thought, and shut her own eyes as if that might keep the man from seeing her. She heard the heavy tread of his boots approaching. Time seemed to stop. Millie hung on, frozen, her muscles quivering, until finally, finally, she heard the man walk by.

Millie waited, taking a deep breath and unclenching her muscles before she leaped lightly from the drainpipe onto the walkway, and collapsed on her hands and knees. She took a few seconds to catch her breath and calm her racing heart before she straightened up, ducking under a window, then standing up to peek through it. She saw four men in a hallway, four guardsmen in suits. Some had patchy fur, and one of them had just one large eye, off-center in his forehead. Millie ducked down again, flattening herself on the walkway, knowing that she had to do something, she had to go somewhere, or the guard would see her.

She crept forward to the next window, then straightened her head enough to see through it. And there was Alice, strapped in a chair, wriggling and straining and trying to get free. She banged on the glass, but it was thick and soundproofed. Alice couldn't hear her.

Alice! she thought, as hard as she could. *Hang on! I am coming!* She pounded at the window again, but it was too thick to break.

She held her breath and told herself not to look down, and she climbed up onto the railing and stood on her tiptoes to grab the edge of the gutter. Once she had it, she gathered herself and pulled herself up. She could hear the gutter creaking, protesting under the burden of her weight.

Pretend you're doing a pull-up, she thought, and she worked herself slowly up, up, up, until her chest was pressed against the slope of the roof. She wriggled forward on her elbows, until her entire body was all the way on the roof, every limb and digit trembling. She inched her way up the slope of the roof toward the bubble of a skylight. Once she'd reached it, Millie looked around for something she could use to break the window, hoping for a convenient rock, or even a hammer. There was nothing . . . but she could see the other side of the house, and the edge of the property, and a road. An old-looking green car was driving toward the Jarvis property. As Millie watched, the car stopped, and the teenage girl and the older lady from the bed-and-breakfast got out. They walked through the gates and up the walkway, and stood at the front door of the big house. Millie could hear the echoes of their knocks on the door, and then a commotion, the sounds of the guards conversing, the sound of feet moving down the stairs. Mrs. Hughes—that was the lady's name—was knocking harder, shouting, "Dr. Jarvis! We know you've got a child inside!"

Now, thought Millie. Now or never. She dragged herself up, along the shingles, until she was lying over the

skylight. Then she wriggled into a squat, shut her eyes so she wouldn't see how far up she was, and how far away the ground had gotten, jumped up, letting her body come down as hard as she could. She felt the glass shudder, and she tried again, then again, until she felt it shatter underneath her feet. She fell through the skylight, feeling the jagged edges of the broken glass scraping at her coat. She landed on the carpet in a shower of glass and lay in the hallway, breathless and bleeding from various cuts and scratches. She scrambled to her feet, shook the glass out of her fur, and ran, almost smacking into Alice, who'd come through a door, with a leather cuff dangling from her wrist.

"Come on!" said Millie, as she heard the inn lady outside saying, "Open the door right now or we'll shoot the lock! We have a gun!"

The guards were yelling at one another, and a screechy old man's voice was hollering orders. "Don't open that door! Get the girl! Get her back in the chair!" Feet were pounding up the stairs. Millie grabbed Alice by the hand and flattened herself against the wall, trying to melt into the shadows . . . but she'd learned all the Yare tricks of invisibility, and Alice had not. Maybe the guards wouldn't see Millie, but they'd see Alice, for sure.

"Open the door, or I'm counting to three, and I'm going to shoot!" Mrs. Hughes was calling as the first guard reached the top of the staircase and came running down the hall toward them, teeth bared, fists clenched. There was the sound of a gunshot. The guard's head turned. Alice and Millie looked at each other. *Downstairs,* Alice mouthed.

Millie nodded. The two of them ran down the hall, slipping past the bewildered guards, down the stairs and into the foyer, where an old No-Fur man, in a move so smooth it might have been rehearsed, snatched Alice out of the air and yanked her against his chest.

Millie shrank against the wall, cringing, staring at the man, who had to be Christopher Jarvis. The No-Furs from the inn were also staring at him in shock. She reached into her pocket, praying that the telephone Jessica had given her had survived her fall. She fumbled for the camera app, set it to video, and aimed the lens at Christopher Jarvis.

"Charlotte Hughes. And Mary Hughes, I believe," he was saying, in a voice that made Millie think of rusty can openers and rat's claws scratching at dirty windows. "What a disappointment. After all I've done for you! After all I've done for this town."

"Do you think we're going to stand here and watch you torture little kids?" Charlotte asked hotly.

"Yes," said Dr. Jarvis. His voice was silky. "That's exactly what I think you're going to do." He stepped forward, dragging Alice along with him. "No genius is ever appreciated in his time. But I am ridding the world of monsters, and I am using their blood and their bodies to cure incurable diseases." He raised his voice until he was almost shouting. "I can make humans strong. I can make us immortal. We can be gods. And if a few monster-children have to die for that to happen . . ." His lip curled, revealing pointed teeth. "I don't think that's an unreasonable sacrifice. Life is all about compromise." His smile was a horror.

"You're killing children." Mary's voice was flat.

"Not human children," Dr. Jarvis replied. "Not real children. They're Bigfoots. They're monsters."

"Alice isn't a monster," said Millie. "Alice is my friend." Dr. Jarvis whirled around. Millie kept the camera focused on his face.

"Would you care to say that again?" she asked sweetly. Dr. Jarvis stared at her as Millie did a slow pan, moving the camera's lens from Dr. Jarvis's face to his body, where he still held Alice against him, to the terrible, wrong-looking guards on the staircase behind him.

"If he doesn't, I will," said Charlotte Hughes. "He said he was going to kill children so he can be immortal.

He said they don't really matter because they aren't human."

"Film all you like," Christopher Jarvis said, in his screeching, gloating voice. "It doesn't matter. You can't transmit anything from inside the house."

"How about from outside?"

Everyone turned. The door that Charlotte's grandmother had shot was still open, with a jagged, splintered hole where the lock had once been. Standing on the other side of it was Jeremy Bigelow, who was holding a camera of his own.

Jeremy grinned. "I should tell you, Dr. Jarvis, that this is being broadcast, right now, on the Internet, and all over the world."

Christopher Jarvis's mouth worked soundlessly. Jeremy, still grinning, pressed a button to turn the camera to selfie mode, so it was his face the viewers would see. "And by the way, for those of you who are just joining the broadcast, this is Jeremy Bigelow of Standish Middle School, reporting live from Upland, Vermont, with this breaking news . . . Bigfoots are real!"

CHAPTER 29

Millie

AFTER THAT, THINGS HAPPENED VERY FAST.

While Jeremy broadcast footage from Christopher Wayne Jarvis's mansion to Donnetta Dale, and Donnetta sent it out to the world, Millie used Jessica's phone to dial 911. "We need some Polices who are not Dr. Jarvis's Polices, please," she said to the befuddled operator.

"What is the nature of your emergency?" the operator asked. In the background, Millie heard someone in the police station shout, "Turn on the TV!" and another voice say, "Oh my God, that's here! That's Dr. Jarvis's place!" and a third voice say, "What are those things?"

"Please hurry!" Millie said to the operator. "He was

trying to hurt my friend!" Dr. Jarvis was slumped against the staircase like he was frozen, maybe because the lady from the inn was pointing a gun at him, maybe because Jeremy was still doing the same with his camera. He looked exhausted, broken, and, somehow, ashamed. Millie suspected his days of hurting anyone—Yare or Human—were over, but you could never be too careful. Her mother always said so.

"Okay," said the operator faintly. "You just . . . hang on, okay? I'm going to call the state troopers. They'll be there soon." Jeremy kept filming, and the No-Fur lady kept her gun steady, and, ten minutes later, three cruisers full of Vermont state troopers came roaring up the driveway.

"Charlotte," said the No-Fur lady with a jerk of her head. "Go tell them what's happened." She nodded at Millie. "Show them what you filmed." Millie did, and found that she wasn't even afraid to talk to the big, uniformed No-Fur men. It seemed that she'd absorbed some of Alice's courage.

A few minutes later, the troopers were in the house, telling Dr. Jarvis that he needed to come with them.

Dr. Jarvis held out his hands for the handcuffs without saying a word. Jeremy filmed it all, and then turned the camera toward Alice.

"Alice, care to comment?"

Alice's eyes were narrowed, and her face was pale. She held up her wrist, displaying the mark that the leather cuff had left. "My name is Alice Mayfair." She breathed deeply. "I'm half-Bigfoot. Half-Yare, which is what the Bigfoots call themselves. Christopher Jarvis has been hunting Bigfoots and trying to capture me. When I came to his house, he strapped me to a chair. He said he was going to torture me. He said he was going to take my blood and my bone marrow and my DNA so that he could live forever." She turned toward Millie with a smile. "And Millie saved me!"

"It was nothing," Millie said modestly. Then Alice's mother and father were running into the house, closely followed by Millie's parents. Alice's father grabbed Alice. Millie's mother grabbed Millie. Someone hugged Jeremy, and someone else picked up Charlotte Hughes, whirled her around, and smacked a noisy kiss on her cheek.

Dr. Jarvis and his goons were led away in handcuffs, and the troopers ushered Alice and Millie and their friends outside. There, on the lawn, Jeremy kept filming, interviewing Millie and Maximus and Benjamin Burton, telling the story for the millions of people watching, first in New York, then in the United States, then all over the world. There were tears, and hugs, and questions and answers, until, finally, Mrs. Hughes said, "Well, is anybody hungry?"

It turned out, everyone was.

News from All Over

IN STANDISH, NEW YORK, NOAH BIGELOW, Jeremy's older brother, was scrolling through TikTok when a bulletin made his phone buzz. It was a push alert from the *New York Times* that read "A teenage boy in Vermont is broadcasting live footage and making the startling claim that Bigfoots are real."

Jeremy, thought Noah. Bad enough that he'd gotten their whole town to go chasing after a little girl with a skin condition. What had that maniac of a little brother done now?

"Noah?" called his mother from the living room. "Ben? You two need to come in here and see this." Noah ran to the living room . . . and there was his brother, on television, and behind him, creatures larger than humans, covered in fur. A scientist was talking from a smaller screen in the right-hand corner, saying, "Of course we need to consider the possibility that this is a hoax, but my best guess is that this young man, Jeremy Bigelow, has, in fact, found an entirely new life-form."

"OMG," said Ben, and let the twenty-pound weight he was holding drop from his hand to the floor.

"Good God," said Noah's father. And as Noah stared in mingled envy and disbelief, his mother, smiling proudly, said, "I always knew he had it in him!"

The Experimental Center for Love and Learning did its best to limit students' screen time. There was only one television set in the entire school, and it was in Lori and Phil's living room. Ten minutes after the first news alert, every student and teacher in the entire school had crammed into their house to watch a boy from Standish announcing that Bigfoots were real, with Alice Mayfair and Alice's friend Millie standing behind him.

"So Alice is . . ." Riya's voice trailed off. Taley was remembering what had happened the time the towns-

people had gone chasing after Alice, who'd led them to the Center's gates, how Alice had stepped forward and said, *Everyone's a freak.* "Well. I guess it explains a lot."

Taley, for once, didn't sound congested. "Everyone's got something," she said . . . and hoped, with all her heart, that Alice, wherever she was, *whatever* she was, would be happy.

At Davina Aimes's town house on the Upper East Side, a few of Felicity's society-lady friends watched the breaking news. Felicity—identified by the boy reporter as Faith—was wearing a bulky down-filled jacket, a knitted wool hat that was decidedly not vintage, and a pair of . . . Davina Aimes squinted at her enormous flat-screen TV.

"She's gained weight," Larissa Carstairs murmured. "And are those"—her lips curled—"Uggs?"

Samantha Cole shuddered. Amity Jones rolled her eyes in mock horror. Davina cringed. Except, she had to admit that, even in her unfashionable clothing, even with her hair in wild curls and her face makeup-free, Felicity looked happy. Happier than she'd ever seen her. Davina felt a pang in her midsection . . . but she was used to ignoring those kinds of pangs. She reached for her hot lemon water, checked the time, and realized that she'd be late for her appointment with her personal shopper . . . and if that ran over, she'd be late for her appointment to get her eyelash extensions replaced. "Bye, girls!" she called, and hurried out the door, trying her hardest to ignore the way her shoes pinched her feet and to put Felicity Mayfair's smiling, happy, makeup-free face out of her mind.

"My goodness," said Lee Washington, who'd been Felicity and Mark Mayfair's driver, and who'd taken Alice to each of her six summer camps and seven private schools. He'd pulled to the curb when the radio cut in with the breaking news, and had watched it on his phone, smiling so widely his face ached a little. Lee had always hated leaving Alice at each new place, had always hoped that one of them would stick and that, the following September, he'd be bringing her to a place that was familiar instead of another one that was brand-new. He suspected, looking at Alice as she stood with her mother, that Alice's wandering days were over. She knew what, and who, she was . . . and, once you knew those things, it was a much simpler matter to find out where you belonged.

CHAPTER 30

Millie

BACK AT THE BED-AND-BREAKFAST, MRS.
Hughes defrosted a few gallons of her famous Sunday
gravy. Jessica's nana boiled water for pasta. Charlotte
Hughes made garlic bread, and Alice and her mother
made a salad, and humans and Bigfoots alike sat around
the table for a feast. Faith held Benjamin Burton's hand,
looking radiantly happy. Miss Merriweather sat next
to Charlotte Hughes and listened as Charlotte told her
story. Jeremy spent most of the meal jumping up to take
phone calls—from his parents, from Donnetta Dale,
from a producer at the *Today* show, who wanted him
on the air first thing the next morning. It wasn't until

Millie had eaten two plates of spaghetti and sauce and four slices of garlic bread and drank two glasses of milk that she made herself ask the question that had been troubling her ever since Jeremy's camera had captured her face.

"The No-Furs know about us now."

Jeremy nodded proudly. The adults, Millie saw, did not seem quite as thrilled, and Alice looked worried as she poked at her pasta.

"Will they hurt us?" Millie asked. She looked around the table, feeling shivery and small, studying each of the adults' faces, watching as they exchanged glances.

Benjamin Burton was the one who finally spoke. "We won't let them."

Millie was trembling, from the tip of her head-fur to the fur that curled over her toes. "But how will we stop them?" she whispered. "They will hunt us. They won't let us live with them. They'll only want to use us. To take from us."

Miss Merriweather smiled thinly. "That doesn't mean we have to let them."

"We can help them," Maximus rumbled. "If they treat us well. It can be our choice."

"And if they don't?" asked Millie. "If they don't treat

us well . . . if they keep hunting us . . . what then?"

A sigh moved through the room like the wind. Septima took her daughter's hand. "We will have to be brave and hope for the best," she told Millie. "We will have to give this new way a chance."

Millie nodded, still feeling rattled and afraid. It was then that she noticed a member of their party was missing. "Where is Old Aunt Yetta?" she asked her parents.

"She's going to the jail to talk with Dr. Jarvis," said Miss Merriweather.

Millie felt her eyes get wide. "But he's dangerous!"

"Not anymore." That was Jeremy, who, ever since the broadcast, had been strutting around with his chest puffed out, as if he'd single-handedly saved the world. Millie had overheard him, on a phone call with his parents and brothers, asking if they'd recorded his appearance on CNN.

Alice turned to Maximus. "What's she going to do?"

"Tribe business," Maximus said.

"What kind of Tribe business?" Alice asked, thinking that if she was to be Leader, this was the kind of thing she'd need to know.

Maximus smiled. "She is the Healer. I expect she'll heal him, if she can."

Alice shook her head. "Even after everything he's done? All the harm he's caused?"

Maximus's face was grave as he nodded at his niece. "Even so."

CHAPTER 31

Christopher

CHRISTOPHER JARVIS SAT ALONE ON THE hard mattress in a cell in the Upland Township jail. At the end of the hallway, two FBI agents stood guard, talking quietly. A pair of state troopers was positioned right outside the cell. Not men Christopher had met, or bought. They were all new.

"Are you sure?" one of the FBI guys was asking someone Christopher couldn't see.

An old woman's quavery voice—a familiar voice—replied, "I'm an old friend."

Christopher sat up straight. He smoothed his tie, then his hair, and tried to compose his face. His looks didn't matter any longer. He would, he knew, be with his Ellie soon. But a man still had his pride.

The agent escorted the elderly Bigfoot to his cell, taking pains not to stare at her. They left her on the other side of the bars. For a moment, she stood there, staring at him. Christopher stared back at her, thinking that, if it wasn't for the fur on her face and her hands, and the fact that her nails were curved and black, more like claws than fingernails, she could have been any little old lady, on a bus or in a supermarket or on her way to a bingo game.

"Christopher Jarvis," she said. That was when he knew for sure.

"You're the one I met. The one from the forest," he said. *The one who wouldn't help my love,* he thought.

She nodded. "I would speak with you, Christopher Jarvis of the No-Furs."

"No-Furs," he repeated. "That's what you call us?"

"That, and worse," she said, raising her chin.

Christopher shook his head. "If you came for an apology, then I'm sorry," he muttered.

"No. I came to give you an apology," she said.

Christopher blinked.

"I understand why you wanted our blood." She gave

a heavy sigh. "I think, sometimes, of all the trouble we could have spared if I'd just given you some. Or if I'd let you keep me in a cage and take me away." She stared past him, at the barred door, her face troubled, her eyes far away. "I'd been in a cage once before. It didn't suit."

"My wife was dying," Christopher said.

"Humans die," said Old Aunt Yetta, not unkindly. "Yare do too. We're not immortal, no matter what you think. Every living thing dies. Usually, too soon for the people who love them."

"Ellie," he said. There was a lump in his throat, and his eyes were burning. "My Ellie. She didn't deserve to suffer the way she did." Tears trickled down his cheeks. Angrily, he swiped them away. "I couldn't stand to see her in pain. I only wanted to help her."

"You wanted help for your love. Once. Then you wanted revenge on those who denied you," said Old Aunt Yetta. "You wanted to live forever. But I tell you now, Christopher Jarvis, that in the end you would have begged for your life to be over. Because a life without love is no life at all." She reached through the bars and took his hand. Her hands were callused and warm. "Are you ready to be with her again? I can send you, if you like."

He stared at her, startled. She looked right back at

him. "I am a Healer," she said. "And, sometimes, a guide."

"A guide through the forest?" Christopher asked. He was trying to sound scornful, but couldn't quite pull it off.

"A guide from this life to the next," Yetta replied.

Her face was wrinkled, and her hair was white, but she had lively golden eyes. Pretty eyes. Eyes like Ellie's. Christopher Jarvis looked into her eyes. He felt like he was drowning, sinking into warm water that bore his weight. His head felt light and somehow sparkly, and he was not afraid.

"Would you be done with this world?" she asked. "Would you cross the passage? Would you be with your beloved?"

Christopher shut his eyes. Tears were running down his face. He swallowed hard and nodded. He wanted to tell the Yare that he was sorry for the harm he'd caused, for the children he'd killed and tortured and hunted; sorry for the town that he'd terrorized and kept in his grip; sorry that he'd been a poor excuse for a father to his son. Instead, he voiced his deepest fear, whispering, "Will she forgive me?"

Old Aunt Yetta touched his face, gently cupping his cheek in her hand. "I think," she said, and her voice was very gentle, "that she will understand."

A few minutes later, Old Aunt Yetta went gliding out of the jail. A few minutes after that, a state trooper checked on the prisoner and found him lying on his bed, on his side, looking peaceful, with a faint smile on his face. Sleeping, the trooper thought. It wasn't until the next morning that the guards tried to wake him, and found that he wasn't sleeping at all; that he'd died at some point in the night. "It was the strangest thing," the trooper told his wife that night as he sat down for his dinner, tucking his napkin into his collar so as not to stain his tie. "As terrible as he was, all the awful things he did, and he still looked peaceful. He had this smile on his face like he'd just won the lottery."

His wife spooned pot roast onto his plate, and bent to kiss the top of her husband's head. "I guess you just never know."

EPILOGUE

THE NEXT SEPTEMBER, ALICE MAYFAIR returned to the Experimental Center for Love and Learning. When classes were over, she would take one of the school's kayaks and paddle across Lake Standish, to where the Yare lived. They'd stayed in their village, after the town of Standish had deeded them the land, but instead of living underground, as they had for so many years, they'd built houses. Alice and her mother and father lived in a handsome colonial in the center of town, a house right by the Lookout Tree that Millie used to climb to spy on the No-Furs across the water and dream of befriending one of them someday.

Jessica Jarvis also went back to the Center. After learning the truth about her family, and surviving her time in Vermont, she was a wiser, kinder girl who cared less about clothes and hair and makeup than she did about being happy and generous with her gifts. She became a mentor to many of the young Yare, who wanted to learn about the human world. Jessica's pretty face and friendly manner made her a shining exemplar of No-Fur confidence and beauty, while her tail, which she no longer kept hidden, made her one of them, and, thus, approachable.

Millie was now their classmate at the Center . . . and, once a week, she would travel to New York City, where she appeared on a TV show, produced by her uncle Benjamin, called *Follow Your Dreams*. Every week, a child—Yare or human—would be selected. They'd share their dream, of skydiving or cooking at a five-star restaurant or singing the national anthem at a baseball game, and Millie and Benjamin would help them make their dream come true. The pair spent some weeknights in New York City at Miss Merriweather's cozy town house, or in the high-rise apartment where Alice had lived, and where the man she'd known as her father kept her bedroom exactly the way it had been when Alice had lived there.

"How's the Bigfoot Queen?" Mark Mayfair would ask

when Alice came home, which she did, at least once a month, and Alice would smile and say, "Yare. We call ourselves the Yare." If Mark felt sad that his wife had gone back to the man she'd always loved, Alice couldn't tell. She thought that Mark was very careful not to show Alice that his heart was, maybe, a little bit broken, and that made her love him even more.

Jeremy Bigelow had also become an entertainer. He'd reunited with his best friend, Jo, and their YouTube show, *Fact or Fiction*, which featured his investigations of legends and rumors, about elves and vampires and whether you could really explode by drinking soda after eating Pop Rocks, had become one of the online platform's biggest hits. His brother Noah, the science genius, made regular appearances; his brother Ben, the athlete, was Jeremy's travel coordinator, and the head of Jeremy's security detail. Best of all, Jeremy's parents finally realized that Jeremy had talents of his own, and that he'd been telling the truth, all those years ago, about seeing a Bigfoot in the woods.

Dr. Jarvis, who'd died in prison before he could stand trial for his crimes, had left his vast fortune to his only son, who used it to make the town of Upland self-sustaining. The lab that his father had founded would continue its work in eradicating diseases, only instead of hunting Bigfoots and trying to take their blood and their DNA by force, the lab welcomed volunteers. Many of the Yare, at Alice's urging, had agreed to give samples of their blood and samples of their DNA. They'd stay at Mary Hughes's bed-and-breakfast when they visited. Frederee had taken a summer internship at the lab. He was planning on going to college, then to medical school, where he'd study epidemiology. He wanted to learn how to keep people from getting sick, and how to help them get better. Alice also thought he had a crush on Jessica Jarvis, but, so far, he hadn't admitted it.

Her parents were happy. Her uncle Maximus and especially her aunt Septima had been uncertain at first about their new, visible, aboveground lives, but they'd settled in, slowly but surely. Now Septima ran the Yare's Etsy store, where the demand for the organic jams and bath scrubs and lotions the Yare made had exploded. Maximus and Old Aunt Yetta served as the Yare's unofficial historians, telling visiting scholars and journalists the story of the Tribe as far back as their memories extended, which turned out, in Old Aunt Yetta's case, to be all the way to the end of the Civil War.

Marcus Johansson, Skip Carruthers, and the half-

Yare goons who'd guarded Christopher Jarvis had slipped back into the shadows and were never seen again. Now they were the ones hiding, the ones living underground, always looking over their shoulders. This suited Alice just fine.

Alice spent time with Old Aunt Yetta and with Maximus, learning history and healing, learning about each member of the Tribe and their extended families, learning how to be a good Leader of the Yare—how to watch out for her Tribe's interests, how to keep them safe without sealing them off from everything the world had to offer.

Of course, not all the Yare were happy to have a half-human girl who'd been raised mostly in the human world in charge . . . but when Ricardan grabbed the Speaking Stick one night and tried to argue that only a true Yare, a pure Yare, should be Leader, Benjamin Burton claimed the stick and said, in his menacing growl, "I'm a pure Yare, and I left the Tribe. Would I make a better Leader than Alice?" Ricardan and his wife had grumbled, but had eventually agreed that the best Leader was the person who was suited for the job, and who wanted to do it well. And that was Alice. She'd never felt so happy, or so comfortable and at ease in her own skin, as she did in the Yare village, where her wild hair went unremarked upon, where her strength and love of running were both normal and accepted, where she had a mother and father who loved her, just as she was, and, in Millie, a true friend.

Christopher Jarvis was laid to rest, per Old Aunt Yetta's request, in the Yare burying ground, at the very edge of what had been their hiding place and was now their village. His grave was marked by a simple, handsome headstone, a flat slab of granite into which had been etched the words "CHRISTOPHER WAYNE JARVIS. BELOVED FATHER OF CHRISTOPHER. BELOVED HUSBAND OF ELLIE." Sometimes, Alice would go sit beside his grave. She'd put her hand flat on the sun-warmed granite and think about all the ways her life had changed, and how those changes were due to a man who had only wanted to harm her and those she loved.

Life is strange, she would think. Then she'd give the stone a final pat and go back to her Tribe, her friends, her family, and all the people who loved her.

Acknowledgments

Once upon a time, my younger daughter, Phoebe, was obsessed with Bigfoots. I started talking with her and her sister about what would happen if Bigfoots were real. Where would they live? How would they avoid detection? What—if anything—would they want from the human world?

There were other questions on my mind. I thought about what it was like for me, to grow up as a girl, and what it's like for my daughters, and their peers, in today's world, with all the pressures that young women continue to face. I thought about how hard and lonely growing up can be, and how at one time or another, almost everyone feels like a monster.

Eventually, Alice and Millie started coming into focus: two girls, one human (or so she believes), one Bigfoot (or so the humans call her), both ill at ease in their worlds, neither feeling like she fits in, both longing for friendship and connection and a place that feels like home.

Alice and Millie began their stories lost and unhappy, and ended up settled and seen, in all of their complicated glory. That is my wish for my daughters, who are teenagers now, and my wish for anyone who reads these books.

I'm grateful to Amy Cloud, who started the journey with *The Littlest Bigfoot*, and Kara Sargent, who helped me cross the finish line with *The Bigfoot Queen*.

Ji-Hyuk Kim helped the characters come to life on the books' beautiful covers, and Sara Mulvanny is responsible for the lovely little illustrations between them.

At Aladdin, I am grateful to Laura Lyn DiSiena, Irene Vandervoort, Chel Morgan, Julie Doebler, Alex Kelleher-Nagorski, Lisa Quach, Valerie Garfield, Anna Jarzab, Kristin Gilson, Christina Pecorale, Michelle Leo, Louisa Solomon, Erica Weintraub, and Ana Chan. Very special thanks to Stephanie Evans, Stacey Sakal, and Kayley Hoffman, who did a meticulous job copyediting and proofreading and making sure everything in Book 3 was consistent with Books 1 and 2. Any mistakes are my own.

Thanks to Keith Nobbs, Emma Galvin, Jen Ponton,

Sophie Amoss, Tara Sands, and Fred Sanders, who gave their voices to the audio versions.

I am grateful to my agent, Celeste Fine, and John Maas, who helps make my work shine. Thanks also to Andrea Mai, Emily Sweet, Elizabeth Pratt, and Mahogany Francis for all of their help and support.

Thanks to my husband, Bill, who shares me with imaginary people in imaginary worlds, and to Lucy and Phoebe, who inspired me, then and now. Thanks to my muses Moochie and Levon, who provided steadfast, silent encouragement by snoozing in the corner while I wrote.

And, finally, my deepest thanks to all the readers who've spent time with Alice and Millie. Every one of you deserves a happy ending—whatever you decide that looks like. Go out and claim your crown!

About the Author

JENNIFER WEINER is the #1 *New York Times* bestselling author of nineteen books, including *That Summer, Big Summer, Mrs. Everything, In Her Shoes, Good in Bed,* and her memoir in essays, *Hungry Heart.* She has appeared on many national television programs, including *Today* and *Good Morning America,* and her work has been published in the *Wall Street Journal* and the *New York Times,* among other newspapers and magazines. Jennifer lives with her family in Philadelphia. Visit her online at JenniferWeiner.com.